Edited Out

Edited Out

A Mysterious Detective Mystery

E. J. Copperman

CROOKED
LANE

NEW YORK

Copyright © 2017 by E. J. Copperman.

Published in the United States by Crooked Lane Books, an imprint of The Quick Brown Fox & Company LLC.

Crooked Lane Books and its logo are trademarks of The Quick Brown Fox & Company LLC.

Library of Congress Catalog-in-Publication data available upon request.

ISBN (paperback): 978-1-68331-846-0
ISBN (hardcover): 978-1-68331-130-0
ISBN (ePub): 978-1-68331-131-7
ISBN (Kindle): 978-1-68331-132-4
ISBN (ePDF): 978-1-68331-133-1

Cover illustration by Robert Crawford
Book design by Jennifer Canzone

Printed in the United States.

www.crookedlanebooks.com

Crooked Lane Books
34 West 27th St., 10th Floor
New York, NY 10001

Hardcover Edition: May 2017
Paperback Edition: August 2018

10 9 8 7 6 5 4 3 2 1

For Roger O. Thornhill, Rufus T. Firefly,
Francis X. Furillo, and Bullwinkle J. Moose

Chapter 1

For Duffy Madison, the period between missing persons cases was never wasted time. Relieved not to be working against an ever-ticking clock to find someone who had been abducted or had simply vanished, Duffy would not let his mind go unoccupied; he'd do research into the latest technologies for evaluating crime scenes or sharpen his observational skills even on short strolls through his own neighborhood.

"That man is lonely and frustrated," he told Angela Mosconi on a walk through Schooley's Mountain Park this Saturday morning. "He looks only at women, but not in a leering fashion. He presses his hands together and flexes his arms whenever he sees a woman he finds attractive, but not to show off any musculature. It's a gesture of anxiety and hopelessness."

"Maybe he's just cold," Angela said. "It can't be more than forty degrees out here today. I should have worn a heavier coat." She hugged herself for warmth, but Duffy, in his intense desire to be more observant, missed the signal that perhaps she would like to have *his* arms around her.

He shook his head. "It is forty-seven degrees today, and the temperature will rise to about sixty later in the morning. That's not weather-related. Look at the way he—"

"Look, we haven't known each other very long," Angela broke in. "But there's something I think you might need to know."

"If this is about your two failed marriages or the childhood bicycle accident that resulted in your left leg being a quarter inch shorter than your right, you have no reason to be concerned," Duffy said, still watching the man he'd deemed lonely as he walked through the park. "I don't believe anyone but I is aware of those things without your knowledge."

Angela stared at him for a moment with a mixture of admiration and annoyance. "I know you well enough not to ask how you know about those things," she said. "But I was getting at something else entirely."

"Interesting," Duffy answered. But his mind was clearly elsewhere. "See that woman in the orange T-shirt? I believe she might once have spent time in county prison."

Angela sighed a little too heavily. Getting through to Duffy Madison when he was trying desperately to focus on something in the absence of an immediate problem to solve was a daunting task she was just beginning to understand.

"Duffy," she began again.

But his face had already frozen in place, and his gait, until now difficult to match, had stopped completely. Duffy looked ahead and stared, so Angela followed his gaze. People were running and gathering at a spot easily two hundred yards ahead.

"Perhaps you'd better stay here," Duffy told her. He began running toward the crowd before she could reply. Angela pursed her lips and followed him.

At the crest of the hill in front of him, Duffy found the crowd gathering. Some women were moaning rather than weeping, and some of the men had to turn away. Duffy shouted, "Morris County Prosecutor's Office," and still had to gently push a couple of people out of the way to get to the edge of the hill and look down.

Off to one side of the hill was a drop of about thirty feet, which had been fenced in to avoid exactly what had happened: A man dressed in bicycle pants and a blue T-shirt was lying faceup, staring blankly at the sky. He was impaled on one of the fence posts that had been poorly maintained and had pierced his chest. The man was dead.

"What a terrible accident," a woman next to Duffy said.

Duffy took in the scene as closely as he could. "This was not an accident," he said, more to himself than to the woman. "That man was murdered."

* * *

I stared at the screen and scowled. I know I scowled because my face was reflected in the screen of my computer, and there was no mistaking the look on my face. It perfectly matched my mood.

Usually, beginning a new Duffy Madison mystery novel was my second favorite part of the writing process. (The favorite part for every writer everywhere is typing the words *The End*, and I also enjoy seeing the name *Rachel Goldman* on the front of the book.) But this one seemed heavy-handed and clumsy. The fact that I just used two terms that mean the same thing might give you an idea of how I felt.

Paula Sessions, my part-time assistant, looked at me from the door to my office, which is in my house in Adamstown, New Jersey, and belongs more to Valley National Bank than to me. "You just started, and you're already unhappy with it?" she asked.

"It's trite and stupid," I said, at least using adjectives that meant separate things. "It's like I'm trying too hard, as if I were writing someone else's character. I used to know Duffy Madison, and now he's a mystery to me."

Paula stifled a chuckle. "Imagine that," she said.

It had been six months since a man had called my house claiming to be the living incarnation of my fictional character. He called himself Duffy Madison, and instead of working for the Morris County Prosecutor's Office as a consultant on missing persons cases, this Duffy had creatively chosen to present himself as a consultant on missing persons cases for the *Bergen* County Prosecutor's Office. See that subtle change there?

The problem was, I'd discovered that he really did work for the Bergen County prosecutor, he really did consult on missing person cases, and everyone he had met knew him as

Duffy Madison. They had no idea I wrote a series of mystery novels with a character by that name, so I had both the utter confusion of the situation and the thrill of knowing that no one working one county over from where I lived had ever heard of my books. It's a writer's dream, truly.

I'm being sarcastic. It's a Jersey thing.

The flesh-and-blood Duffy had told me at the time that he believed I had actually created him four years earlier, because he had no memory of anything before that time. He'd said it with a straight face and seemingly in earnest, so after he was out of earshot, I'd asked Paula to do as much research on the supposed Duffy as possible. She came up with very little; he had records stretching back to high school, but no one she contacted could ever remember seeing or talking to him. He seemed to have no family. He existed only on paper. Which somehow seemed appropriate.

"Maybe you need to see Duffy again," Paula suggested now. "You've been ducking him for months."

"I haven't been ducking him," I protested. "I don't want to go off on a pointless crusade with him, but that's not ducking."

In the course of her research on "Duffy," Paula had discovered the wispy trail of a man named Damien Mosley (note the initials), who was the same age as my Duffy, had grown up in the same town, attended the same college, and then vanished at almost the exact moment flesh-and-blood "Duffy" had arrived at the Bergen County Prosecutor's Office and helped with his first missing person.

After our adventure, which had ended in a harrowing fashion for me, Duffy had decided we needed to find Damien Mosley in an effort to prove to me (!) that he, Duffy, was real and not a literal figment of my imagination. I had resisted that suggestion on the grounds that he was nuts.

I thought that was a pretty strong argument, personally. But Duffy had been calling regularly every three days since then, and now it had been six months. Duffy might be crazy, but you couldn't say he was easily dissuaded.

"It certainly is ducking," Paula said, turning her back as she walked back to her office, across the hall from mine. "If it wasn't ducking, you'd talk to him instead of making me lie every time he calls."

"Duffy knows where I live," I reminded her, loudly now because she was probably behind her desk, which is larger and disturbingly neater than mine. "If he really believed it was necessary, he could come here to persuade me."

"He's been here twelve times," Paula said, not raising her voice at all. She just has an air of confidence that stems from always being right. "You keep pretending you're taking a shower because you know he'll get embarrassed and leave."

"You work for me, you know."

"You don't want to fire me," Paula said, and again, she was correct. "You think your whole life would collapse if I ever left." And it would. Paula thinks it wouldn't, but I barely make it through the days she's not working.

I sat there and stewed for a while. There was obviously no point in trying to debate the point with Paula, especially since she'd continue to insist on being right about everything and taking all the fun out of it. But staring at my computer screen and seeing the fairly turgid prose I'd been turning out, with a deadline pressing in only three months, wasn't helping.

The thing about every writer is that we're sure we're frauds, and sooner or later the world will catch on. Even the midlist types like me—who sell enough books to keep getting published but not enough to live on a tropical island and have young men fetch us drinks in coconut shells—see writing as a gift, and the thing about a gift is that it can be taken back at any moment. Even if you keep the receipt.

What I was seeing in front of me was clear evidence my gift's warranty period had just expired.

This was going to lead to sleepless nights. Clenched stomach. Long hours spent looking at online employment ads. A strong consideration of going back to school to obtain a master's degree in . . . something. And I'd no doubt gain six pounds in the next month, watching my screen stop accumulating words in significant numbers.

I'd watch the calendar and calculate how many words I'd have to write each day to hit my deadline before my editor, Sol Rosterman, started getting impatient. Sol had nurtured me through five Duffy Madison mysteries, the latest of which would be published in four months. He expected number six in three months, and sitting here on the first day I'd begun writing, I saw no clear path to delivering it on time.

The problem was the character. Duffy had always come naturally to me; I'd never really had to think about how he'd react to any situation. I just knew it because the character was part of me.

But now the character could stand in front of me and tell me how he'd react to something, and that was putting a serious damper on my creativity. What if Duffy read the book and thought I'd gotten him wrong? It had already happened once, but I'd had a completed draft then. This was new territory, and it wasn't friendly.

The rational thing to do, of course, was to banish the living Duffy from my thoughts completely, to not care what he'd think because I'd never see him or talk to him again and therefore didn't have to worry about his reaction. After all, he'd told me more than once that he was simply himself and had never read any of my books in his life. He said he didn't even know there were Duffy Madison novels until he'd had to research a case involving a mystery novelist and stumbled across one of my titles.

Imagine the ego boost: Even the character I wrote almost every day for five years hadn't read any of the books about him. And here I was, despairing over what he might think of the mess I was making of *his* character.

My interior life can be very complicated.

I stared at the screen another few minutes, changed three words that were especially egregious, and then sat back in my deluxe lumbar support swivel chair and sighed. The story in my head was okay, but it needed Duffy to show up and be himself. The way I saw it, there was only one possible solution to this problem, and I didn't like it one bit.

I picked up my phone and called Duffy Madison.

Chapter 2

"The way I see it, we should plan on driving to Poughkeepsie, New York, as soon as possible." Duffy Madison, or the deranged soul believing himself to be Duffy Madison, sat opposite me on the futon I used to use as a sofa but which now was covered in papers, books, folders, one pillow, and a large stuffed dog (not the real kind). And of course one tall, thin, odd man squeezed into the near corner. It was the only seating space in my office aside from my work chair, and that chair is my personal domain.

Duffy had answered on the first ring, seeing my name in his caller ID. He'd been so happy to hear from me that he'd suggested driving to my house in the first six seconds we were on the phone, and I figured that was the quickest way to move forward. But my plans and Duffy's were clearly not in sync, since I had no plan to go to Dutchess County. I had writing to do in New Jersey.

"Poughkeepsie?" I said reflexively.

"Yes." Duffy sat with his left leg crossed over his right. "That is the last known residence of Damien Mosley, so that is the most logical place for us to begin searching for him."

I had realized, of course, that Duffy would expect my call was about Damien Mosley. It was the subject occupying his mind, especially if he did not have an active case he needed to consider, so he would assume I'd be equally obsessed. It's how his mind works. I know. I invented his mind.

But being somewhat self-centered myself, I had failed to look past my own motivations in the moment. I hadn't considered actually searching for Mosley, so Duffy's attitude had startled me just a little.

"We're not searching for Damien Mosley," I informed him.

Duffy's eyebrows rose. "But it's important that you understand my existence," he said. "I can't have you assuming I am delusional. Tracking down Damien Mosley, a matter that appears to be a cold case for the authorities involved anyway, is the logical step to alleviate your concerns. I am Duffy Madison. It's necessary for you to understand that. Finding Damien Mosley should achieve the goal. You'll see he is a separate human being and accept who I am."

Perfect: This was the explanation of a man who admitted he had no memory before five years ago—the problem was all in *my* mind. "Duffy," I said in what I hoped was a gentle tone, "I don't see the issue the same way you do. We've talked about this before." It was true; when Duffy had first broached the subject of searching for the man whose existence seemed to lead directly to his, I'd argued— successfully, I'd clearly been wrong in believing—that there was no upside to going to Poughkeepsie and looking for a man who had vanished there five years before. I urged him to seek some therapy, and he'd said that had not had any positive effect on him in his (limited) memory. In other words, Duffy had tried the talking cure, found it wanting, come to terms with what he saw as the only logical solution, and was now attempting to convince me of the same.

"Then why did you ask me to come here today?" Duffy said. The fact that he'd more or less invited himself over when all I'd done was pick up the phone seemed unimportant even to me.

"I'm having difficulty writing the next book," I said. I couldn't face him as I said it; the inability to conjure my Duffy once I'd met his Duffy was embarrassing, although I didn't really have a handle on why that should be the case. "I've been trying to write Duffy the way I always have, and I keep running into difficulty because your interpretation of the character is blocking mine these days. I think of him, and I see you."

Duffy scowled; I was not accepting his logic when it seemed crystal clear to him. "I have no interpretation of your character. I have never read your books. I am Duffy Madison. Do you want me to become someone else?" The question was meant to be a taunt, but the fact was I thought he *was* someone else and he just didn't want to admit it to himself.

"I don't want you to do anything," I said. "I'm flailing here. I'm confused. There's no reason for you to be who you say you are, and no matter which way we interpret your identity, I should be able to write my original Duffy the way I always have. So I've asked you here today because I want to say good-bye so I can go back to the way things were before."

Duffy sat and squinted at me for a moment; it's what he's always done when confronted with behavior he believes to be irrational. I wrote that for him. This guy who claimed never to have cracked the cover on my novels had my character's mannerisms down cold.

"You are asking me not to contact you again?" he said. "You believe if I absent myself from your life that you'll be able to revert to your old style of writing?"

I turned away from him again. I had to like the guy; I'd written him over and over again. It was very painful to hurt his feelings this way because I was one of the few people on the planet who knew he *had* feelings.

"That's basically it," I mumbled.

Duffy stood up; I could see the movement from the corner of my eye. "You realize this behavior is not rational," he said. I figured he was the expert on irrational behavior, so maybe I should consider what he was suggesting. "Banishing me from your sight will not erase me from your mind."

I hate it when he has a point.

"No, it won't," I told him. "You're a good man, and you literally saved my life, so I'm more than grateful to you. But this is my means of making a living, and you're standing in my eyeline when I'm trying to write. You're a distraction."

"I'm not sure I understand the issue," Duffy admitted. "Have I done anything or in any way behaved in a fashion that is inconsistent with your concept of the Duffy character?"

I acknowledged that he hadn't done so without saying aloud that I believed it was because he'd internalized the character from my books so completely that he could do a truly admirable impression. He'd have told me he never read a Duffy Madison book before I gave him my rough draft after we met.

"Then how is the concept of the character at all affected by my presence?" he asked.

It was a good question, and I had been considering it for some time, so I had an answer ready. "The thing is, I like you, Duffy. You're a nice guy, and I don't want to see you come to any harm."

That didn't seem to impact real-life Duffy significantly; he looked puzzled. "Your writing a novel will not cause me any harm," he said.

"No. But in order to make the story work, I have to put Duffy Madison through the wringer. The job of an author is to take the character and create a situation that tests him to his limits. This is the sixth Duffy book, and each one requires me to raise the stakes a little. In my head, I have to come up with more and more trying circumstances for the character to face. And knowing you makes it hard for me to torture the character because I feel like it will be torturing you. Like *I'll* be torturing you."

"I understand there is an artistic process, but I have to say that is not a rational argument," Duffy told me. "Nothing in your books has ever actually happened to me. The cases I've worked with Ben Preston on at the prosecutor's office have never even mildly resembled the ones you've written. You're not going to do me any harm." The nutjob was telling me what was rational. And it was still early in the week.

"Maybe not, but your personal circumstances are almost exactly like the ones I've written for you. Like this: I just started writing Duffy a romantic interest."

The reaction I'd expected and hoped I wouldn't get was exactly what happened. Duffy grimaced a little and stood still. "I have recently started seeing someone," he said quietly.

I pointed at him, acknowledging the coincidence we both noted. "I'm planning on killing Duffy's love interest." (I hadn't actually decided on that yet, but why quibble on the details?) "Do you want me to take that chance?"

"If this magical connection exists as you seem to suggest," Duffy said, "the consequences will occur whether I am a presence in your life or not."

"Maybe, but maybe not. All those times I wrote about Duffy before I met you, I wasn't worried about hurting you, and you were all right as far as we know. Maybe if we're not in contact, that will still be the case. I just don't want to take the chance."

Duffy pursed his lips and nodded slightly; he was thinking. Pretty sure I gave him that move, too.

"I'll make a bargain with you," he said. Duffy's speech tends to lean a little British when he's thinking because I think of Sherlock Holmes when I'm writing those moments. "I think I can help you with your problem."

Well, I hadn't seen that coming.

"You do," I said. It was a placeholder. In a couple of hours, I'd think of what I should have said there and double back in my mind. It's why I'm an author and not, say, a stand-up comedian.

"Yes. As you see it, the impediment to your writing me as a character is that as a three-dimensional man standing in front of you, I change your perspective on the person you're writing; is that correct?"

"More or less, yeah."

"So if you were to prove once and for all that I am *not* Duffy Madison, that I am in fact someone else who perhaps suffered a trauma and took on this personality after reading your novels, despite the fact that you hadn't published them at that time, you could go on writing your fictional Duffy without any further difficulty. Does that make sense to you?" Duffy was pacing in front of me, slightly stooped and with his hands clasped behind his back. If Groucho Marx was a tall, thin, serious man and gave up the greasepaint mustache and eyebrows, he'd be Duffy.

I thought through what he was saying, feeling like it was going in a direction I didn't like but not actually understanding how it was getting there. If we could prove this Duffy wasn't my Duffy, would that help me write him—my Duffy, for those keeping score at home—again?

"Yes, I guess it makes sense," I said.

"So then we have a common purpose, even if we are approaching it from opposite viewpoints." Duffy stopped pacing and looked down at me, as I hadn't moved from my swivel chair. "If we find evidence that I am actually Damien Mosley, I can stop being Duffy Madison in your mind and perhaps heal some hideous memory I have been repressing. You will be relieved of the notion that I am your character and can go back to writing him as you always have."

The trap was springing around me, and there was pretty much nothing I could do about it, but I gave it the old college try. "Suppose we find no evidence of Damien Mosley and you continue to insist I made you up and you sprang to life five years ago? That's what you believe we'll find. How does that help me?" The best defense, I felt, was a good get-Duffy-out-of-here ploy.

He spoke quietly and with serious gravitas. "If that is the case, perhaps we can both find some peace of mind, no?"

My immediate thought was *no*, but somehow three days later, I found myself in a car with Duffy Madison, heading to Poughkeepsie, New York.

Chapter 3

"I still don't understand why we couldn't just make a few phone calls," I told Duffy, who was driving efficiently and lawfully on a highway that saw no other drivers doing the same. "Why do we have to go all the way up to Poughkeepsie for this?"

Duffy never shows his impatience with me even when I'm doing my very best to elicit it. He did not sigh, and he would never, under any circumstances, roll his eyes while driving a car at exactly sixty-five miles per hour in the right lane. Without the benefit of cruise control.

"I have explained this," he said in a mild tone. "I did the background on the phone months ago. I have contacted anyone I could find online who might have a connection to Damien Mosley. I have so far been unable to find his mother, and his father is dead. A few acquaintances from high school remain, as does one coworker from a tavern at which Damien worked as a bartender. Other than that, there is very little with which to begin."

"Clearly, the two-hour drive is well warranted, then," I said. Just because Duffy was taking the high road (in the conversation, not toward Dutchess County) didn't mean I had to.

"It's always best to get a sense of the area and see the people face-to-face," he said without a hint of emotion. Dammit. "I will take video records with my iPhone that will make it possible to reference both places and people once we are back in New Jersey. This is not a major trip, Rachel." In fact, Duffy and I had driven to the Jersey Shore the first day we started to "work together," and that had taken roughly as long as this trip would on paper.

Instead, there was quite a backup at the Tappan Zee Bridge, which was going through major renovations—they were actually building a new Tappan Zee Bridge next to the existing Tappan Zee Bridge, which had been threatening to fall into the river for years—and that meant a wait of about forty minutes during which Duffy and I had nothing to do but talk. Which he did.

He went on about Louise Refsnyder, who waited tables while Damien had tended bar at Rapscallion's, a local watering hole that apparently thought "Rapscallion" was someone's name. She had told Duffy on the phone that Damien was a popular bartender with the customers because he made drinks quickly to avoid long waits and always scanned the bar even while mixing cocktails because he didn't want patrons to feel they had to vie for his attention.

It wasn't that this information wasn't fascinating, you understand, but I didn't have much idea of how that pertained to our finding Damien, assuming that I wasn't actually sitting next to him in the car right now. But that didn't matter because Duffy had more to tell me. I actually sat back and closed my eyes to let it wash over me and distract me from the fact that we *still weren't moving*.

This, and we were waiting to get onto a bridge that had been repeatedly declared unsafe for the amount of traffic it gets in the course of an average day. And Duffy droned on, making me even gladder I had signed on for this goofy trip, which would require us to take this same bridge back again after our scheduled meetings with reported Damien Mosley acquaintances later today. All supposedly so I could purge my mind of the Duffy next to me and write the Duffy I had created and used to know so well.

I don't want you to think that I had stopped writing. I don't stop writing because I am not happy with what's coming out. I don't believe there is such a thing as writer's block. There is the fear of writing something lousy. Writing something lousy means you have something you can improve later. If you don't write anything, you can't improve the nothing you've written. So I had three thousand more words of total and complete crap that would hopefully be improved upon after the Damien Mosley adventure had been concluded, which I sincerely wanted to be only a few hours from now.

Duffy then explained to me that Andrea Vorczek, the girl Damien had taken to the senior prom, who was now the woman Damien had not contacted in years, had nothing of import to say. She'd agreed to the date because she didn't have a boyfriend and still wanted to go to the dance. They'd known each other from theater class in school. Damien hadn't been an actor in high school productions but had worked with makeup.

Again, not exactly the kind of "aha!" moment Sherlock Holmes would relish.

When I could finally cram a spare word in through Duffy's lecture, I brought up a point I'd been thinking about since agreeing to this merry escapade. "Won't you recognize the landscape and the people?" I asked Duffy. "After all, you went to high school here. You grew up in Poughkeepsie." We inched forward another car length. Only fifteen more minutes until we could crawl onto the Death Bridge.

"I have no recollection of that," he said. "I've told you, I do not remember anything before five years ago."

"But you should." If I said it enough times, he'd see the logic, right? "I gave Duffy that backstory. If you're Duffy and I created you on the page, you had that childhood."

"What you write and what I experience do not seem to be connected," he reminded me. "I have the personality and the circumstances of your character, but I do not share his every plot point. You know that." I knew that was what he said; whether I believed it to be true was another question.

No point in saying it again. Instead, I sat back. We'd come this far; we weren't turning around. Trying to argue against it was pointless. Besides, there's part of me that's a hopeless gossip. "So who's this woman you've been dating?" I asked Duffy. I honestly hadn't known about that aspect of his life when I'd written my Duffy a love interest.

I saw Duffy's mouth tense up a little. He doesn't like to talk about personal issues; the only thing he's comfortable with is his work. "Her name is Emily Needleman," he said. "I met her at a photography class I've been taking at William Paterson University."

"Photography?" Odd that was the part I found interesting, but my Duffy had no interests at all outside those that could help him find missing people.

"I have not been consulted by the prosecutor since you and I worked on the case together," he said. I wouldn't have characterized the incident that way, but that's how Duffy's mind works. "I felt that learning more about the composition of a photograph might help me learn more about the pictures taken at crime scenes." Maybe I should have taken notes on our conversations to help me write my version of this guy; again there was nothing but his mission in life, which was to find the missing and see justice done.

"Is that why you have time to look for Damien Mosley now? Because you're not working currently for the prosecutor's office?" After months of not doing so, I was falling back into the pattern I'd noticed the first time I'd spent time with this Duffy Madison—I was interviewing him for character traits I might need when I wrote again. Which I would do sometime tonight when I got home. The book deadline waits for no woman.

"I have been devoting any spare time since you first mentioned Damien Mosley to finding him," Duffy said.

"That doesn't answer my question."

His lip curled a tiny bit. "I have not been consulted for a few months. I consider that a positive because it means there have been no missing person cases reported to the prosecutor's office in that time."

"What are you living on when you're not working for the prosecutor?" I asked. It had never occurred to me, I have to admit. My books always take place when Duffy *is* working.

"I have a modest savings account and some investments," he said. "I do the investigative work because it is what I feel I am best suited to do, not for the money."

"Still, you take the money."

We made it onto the bridge and picked up speed to a mind-blowing twenty-five miles per hour as Duffy smiled a little lopsided smile and said, "I'm not crazy."

"We'll see," I said.

We arrived in Poughkeepsie a little before eleven in the morning. It's both a city and a town, in that there is the City of Poughkeepsie and the Town of Poughkeepsie, right next to each other but separate because being just one municipality wouldn't be confusing enough. Duffy had not stopped for breakfast and had only reluctantly allowed for a quick break at a rest stop so I could, you know, rest. He did not appear to have actual human needs for things like food or restrooms, which actually seemed kind of logical. In my mind, he still wasn't a real person. Which I guessed was what we were here to prove—or not. Luckily, I had thought to fill a thermos with coffee (which had after all necessitated the rest stop), or I would not be a bit useful today.

"What's our first stop?" I asked as I gratefully stretched my legs.

"The obvious place to start." Duffy pointed. He stepped out of the car as if he'd simply forgotten his keys in the drive-way and had been in the car only a few seconds. I decided to write him a leg cramp as soon as possible. We were stand-ing in front of the City of Poughkeepsie civic complex, and I hadn't been paying attention closely enough to notice the sign reading, "Police Department." Okay, so that did make some sense.

*　　*　　*

"As I told you on the phone," said Sgt. Phillip Dougherty, "there just isn't anything to tell you about Damien Mosley."

We sat in Dougherty's office, which could charitably be described as cramped, and he, a tall, solid man in his fifties, sat behind his desk looking very competent and concerned. He had it down to an art.

"The man vanished from his home here in the city," Duffy said, no doubt not for the first time. "It's hard to imagine why there was no investigation. I am not trying to impugn your department or yourself, Sergeant. I'm merely trying to understand."

"Nobody complained," Dougherty answered. "The landlord got in touch just as a formality to evict the guy, who hadn't been in the apartment or paid his rent for three months. The same was true of the utility company. He had no family in the area.

No one reported him as a missing person. There was no crime to investigate."

"A friend didn't call?" I asked. "His mother at least was alive then. Did you get in touch with her?"

Dougherty looked at his computer screen, which no doubt held the case file on Damien Mosley. "The mother was called," he said. "She was living in New Rochelle at the time. She didn't know where her son was and hadn't heard from him, but she said that wasn't unusual. Apparently, they weren't really close."

Duffy had obviously lost any hope the Poughkeepsie police were going to be a fount of information. "You don't mind if we ask around?" he said.

Dougherty shrugged. "Ask all you like, as long as you don't harass people," he said. "But it's been five years. You want to talk about a cold trail."

"We'll manage," Duffy said.

Chapter 4

"What's next?" I asked as Duffy pulled his car up to a spot on a completely nondescript street. Of course, never having been in this city before, none of Poughkeepsie's roadways were especially descript to me.

"The apartment where Damien was living when he vanished," Duffy said. "As you might suspect, there is another tenant there now, but it might help us to see the layout of the rooms. Our other appointments were only available later in the day." It never would have occurred to him to leave later, avoid some traffic, and let me sleep in past six in the morning. Of course not.

"Does the new tenant know anything about Damien?" I asked. Duffy had parked the car in a public lot, an open space with meters, saying Poughkeepsie was too large a city for us to walk to all our destinations and we'd need the car again later.

"Her name is Rosalind Woo," he said. "She is seventy-two years old and moved here from Cooperstown three years ago. She is not even the tenant who lived in the apartment immediately after Damien. I have done a little research and see no connection between the two of them." He pointed at the three-story brick apartment building. "Second floor."

I stopped walking, and Duffy stopped, confused at my action. "Look around," I said. "This is your hometown. Does anything look familiar?"

Duffy's eyebrows rose a bit; the thought hadn't occurred to him. He stood in the middle of the street, which was okay because luckily, no one was driving through at the moment. Duffy took in the scene slowly and turned a complete 360-degree circuit. He looked up and down, out in every direction.

"Nope," he said finally.

* * *

Sure enough, Rosalind Woo seemed a little puzzled about our reasons for looking over her apartment, which seemed natural to me. I had no idea what we were looking for, either.

"None of the things here were this Damien's," she said after ushering us in. She had put out a plate of Oreos and a pot of tea on her dining table, but Duffy had refused the snack. I saw he was in full investigator mode, but Rosalind clearly had never seen that before and was eyeing him warily. In order to appear normal, I took an Oreo. Okay, three Oreos. Did I mention Duffy hadn't let me stop for breakfast?

Duffy stood in the center of the living room, which had a fireplace and built-in bookshelves on one wall. There was no television in the room, as Rosalind said she preferred to read until bedtime, so she had the TV in the bedroom.

"Were these bookshelves here when you moved in?" he asked.

Rosalind nodded. "Far as I know, they're original equipment."

Duffy took in the information and scratched his nose. I hadn't written him that little move, so I assumed it was just itchy. "Did the landlord tell you how old this building might be?"

She looked at him for a while this time, no doubt wondering why this strange man would think she'd know about the history of the building in which she had rented an apartment. "Somehow it didn't come up," she said.

Duffy nodded. He does that and makes you think he's agreeing with you. The fact is he's thinking something, and the nod means he's agreeing with himself. His eyes glanced around the room in a way that would seem casual if, unlike me, you didn't know he was essentially taking pictures with his eyes. He'd probably ask Rosalind in a moment if he could use his phone to take a few shots, and she'd once again give him an expression indicating that he was quite insane.

"May I look in the bedroom?" he asked. That was enough for a strong glance from the current lessee.

But she couldn't think of a reason to keep him out. "If you want," she said without a whit of enthusiasm in her voice. "Did you say you were from the police or something?"

"We are not acting with the authority of any law enforcement agency," Duffy told her with an air that said he'd explained this before. "I do sometimes work as a consultant with the Bergen County Prosecutor's Office, but I am not here in that capacity today."

"Bergen County?" Rosalind sounded like the words were coming at her too fast.

"New Jersey," I said.

"Oh." That explained everything, apparently.

Duffy let her lead us to the bedroom, which was down the hall past a galley kitchen. Rosalind opened the door, and Duffy stepped in first, probably to make sure she didn't change anything in the room. We were, after all, searching for a man who hadn't been here in five years.

The bed was made, thankfully, and there were no clothes strewn about the room. Duffy looked around, particularly at the higher sections of the walls, which to my eye were entirely unremarkable. He did not attempt to open the closet door.

He did, however, drop to the floor and look under the bed. Rosalind gasped, either because she hadn't expected that or because she was considering the idea of a stranger assaying the dust bunnies next to her slippers. Duffy spent a few seconds down there, then got himself back to his feet.

"Very well," he said, heading for the bedroom door. I guess he thought we understood.

He gave the kitchen a closer look on the way back but did not comment on anything. Rosalind was by now watching Duffy the way one would watch a dangerous mental patient and was especially tense when he got near her block of knives, but he didn't touch anything.

Back in the living room, he stopped again and looked up at the ceiling. He pointed at a small section of the wallboard that appeared to be damaged or purposely cut into a rectangular shape. "Is that removable?" he asked.

"What?" Rosalind looked up, and her mouth twitched.

"Is there a step stool?" Duffy said, looking around. He spotted one in a corner not far from the ceiling cutout and started walking toward it. "May I use this?"

"No!" Duffy stopped in his tracks when Rosalind shouted. "Now that's enough. You've come into my house and looked around at all my things. You've looked under my *bed*. I'm not going to let you take my living room apart. I'd appreciate it if you'd leave now, please."

I felt like I was watching a very odd movie. Duffy stared at Rosalind, no doubt trying to determine her motivation and coming up with very little. "I just want to—"

"I said no." Rosalind's tone had less volume but more immovability. "You said yourself that you have no authority to come in here. You're just looking around because I let you in. For all I know, you're casing the place so you can rob me later. I've had enough of this, and I want you to leave." She turned toward me, and her voice softened. "Please."

"Let's go, Duffy," I said without looking at him. I'm sure his face was registering astonishment at my capitulation. He saw a perfectly clear reason to do what he wanted to do, and this irrational woman was recruiting me to frustrate him.

"But—"

"Ms. Woo has been very hospitable, and we've taken up enough of her time. We have other people to talk to, so let's go." I actually took him by the arm and started leading him toward the door.

Duffy did not say anything as we walked out, but his face was absolutely stricken with my lack of understanding. He'd spotted something that probably had no connection to Damien Mosley at all, and here I was insisting he leave. But Rosalind Woo smiled warmly at me as we left.

"Thank you," she said.

And she handed me another Oreo.

Chapter 5

"I don't understand what kind of investigator you believe yourself to be," Duffy Madison said to me.

We were sitting in a booth at Patty's Diner, which was probably not owned by anyone named Patty and was a diner, by Jersey standards, in name only. This was a little café trying desperately to appeal to hipsters. The exposed brick and beams were juxtaposed ironically with neon signs and menus that offered no fewer than seventeen types of coffee. We'd each ordered a regular, visibly disappointing the multipierced server.

It was further evidence of a view I was forming of Poughkeepsie, that it was a city (or town—who knew which we were in at the moment?) that had once fallen on hard times and was now trying to gentrify itself into a haven for students and faculty of Vassar College, which it counted as one of its assets. As with most such efforts, the areas trying to be cool were putting in so much effort, you wanted to sit them down and explain that these things take time and that they had no reason to worry.

"I don't think I'm any kind of investigator," I said. "I think I'm a crime fiction writer. Look, we went into that poor woman's home with no authority whatsoever, and we poked around in places she didn't want us to poke around. She said nothing."

"Exactly. She didn't want me to look under her bed, and yet she did not protest. But when I wanted to check a small irregularity in her living room ceiling, she asked us to leave. Do you not find that suspicious?"

Marlene, our server, came by to ask if we wanted any lunch. I asked for a tuna salad on rye toast, and again Marlene appeared to disapprove of my choice; she clucked her tongue a bit and then looked hopefully at Duffy. He was even more of a letdown—he just asked for a refill on his coffee. Duffy rarely eats when he's working a case because he's so engrossed in the task at hand. Probably I was trying to lose some weight when I first wrote that behavior for him.

As soon as Marlene left the table, I picked up where we had left off. "No, I don't find that suspicious," I said. "I find it a woman who had put up with enough finally drawing the line. Damien Mosley hasn't been in this town in five years. Why do you think a hole in the ceiling of his former apartment is going to make a difference?"

Marlene refreshed Duffy's coffee and walked away. "The problem here," Duffy said, "is that you are approaching the case with a particular solution in mind. You expect us not to find Damien Mosley because you believe that I am Damien Mosley. So you are not treating the situation with an open mind."

"And you are? Do you even acknowledge the possibility that you used to be Damien Mosley?"

Duffy didn't get the chance to answer because a man at a table next to our booth looked over at us. "Excuse me," he said. "Did you just say Damien Mosley?"

We had said it so often, I was starting to think it had become our mantra. But Duffy was already the embodiment of attention; his posture had straightened, and his eyes were wide. No doubt he was taking every possible solution into account. "Yes we did," Duffy told the man. "Do you know him?"

"To tell you the truth, I kind of thought you were Damien," the man said. He reached his hand out to Duffy. "I'm Walt Kendig. I went to high school with him, and I was on Damien's bowling team for a while." He looked carefully at Duffy. "You do look a lot like him."

I gave Duffy a significant look, which he worked valiantly to ignore. "Does he?" I said. "Could you tell the two of them apart?"

Walt looked at me, then back at Duffy. "I haven't seen Damien in years," he said, shaking his head. "It's hard to tell. Why? Is there something I can help with?"

Duffy shook Walt's hand and smiled his ingratiating but professional smile, the one that's supposed to make witnesses more likely to tell him more than they want to say. "It's nice to meet you, Walt. My name is Duffy Madison. I'm here trying to find Damien Mosley."

Walt Kendig laughed, which was sort of unexpected.

"I'm sorry, what did you say your name was?" he asked.

Duffy, eyes narrowing just a touch, regarded him with some bafflement. "I am Duffy Madison."

"Really?" What did that mean?

I decided to break the moment by sticking out my own hand. "Hi, Walt. I'm Rachel Goldman. Duffy and I—"

Walt laughed again. "You're Rachel Goldman?" Did he do this to everybody?

"Yeah. And we're looking for Damien Mosley."

Walt sat back in his chair and looked mightily amused. "Rachel Goldman and Duffy Madison," he said, shaking his head. He turned toward Duffy. "I didn't think you were real."

Duffy has a sense of humor so dry, you'd swear it was from Arizona. "I get that a lot," he said, looking at me.

"I mean, I read all the books." Walt was addressing me now. "And I'm a big fan, but it never occurred to me you were basing them on a real person."

"I'm not," I answered somewhat automatically. "He's basing himself on what I wrote."

Walt, not surprisingly, looked confused.

"What Ms. Goldman is saying is that it is a coincidence that I have the same name and profession as her fictional character," Duffy told him. "But I am wondering about Damien Mosley. We're searching for him, and we have very few leads. Do you know anything about where he might have gone?"

Wait. I'd just met a fan who actually had read my books. I got slightly annoyed that Duffy was stealing my moment in the spotlight. It just doesn't happen all that often.

Walt shook his head again, but he was just absorbing all he'd heard and not responding to Duffy's question. "Rachel Goldman and Duffy Madison," he said to himself. "Go figure that one out."

It's always nice to meet a fan, believe me. There's nothing better than knowing that someone has taken the time to read my work and, even better, that they enjoyed the experience. I would have happily discussed every Duffy Madison novel with Walt for the rest of the day and gone home a satisfied person, but the apparition across the table from me had other plans.

"Damien Mosley," Duffy reminded Walt. "Is there anything you can tell us?"

That seemed to bring Walt back to the present moment. He looked at Duffy again. "Well, like I said, I was on his bowling team, but that's gotta be five years ago. I didn't know him much outside of that, even when we were in school. Different years. He was a bartender at a place near here, Rapscallion's. They've gone out of business now, though, and a new bar called Oakwood opened where it used to be."

"How did you happen to end up on the same team?" I asked, trying to stay relevant to the conversation and not laugh at the very thought of Duffy Madison in a bowling shirt.

"Damien worked at the bar, and one of the waiters there was on the team with me." Walt sat back in his chair, reveling in the ability to help out a fictional detective and the author who made him up. He'd have a story to tell the little woman when he got home, for sure. "I don't even know if they were friends or anything. Barry—that's the waiter—knew we needed a fifth guy, and I guess he talked Damien into it." He looked at Duffy again, studying him carefully. "You do look a lot like him."

That was fueling my argument, so I followed up on it. "Really? How much?"

Duffy gave me his raised-eyebrow look that was supposed to be withering and came up somewhere around mildly irritated.

Walt considered his answer and sucked on his front teeth briefly. "Well, it's not like they'd be identical twins or anything, but again, you're talking about a few years already, and I didn't know the guy that well. What made you come up here to look for him now? Is he gonna be in the next Duffy Madison book?" He sounded so excited; it was adorable.

"No," Duffy said flatly. "Damien Mosley will definitely not be featured in a work of fiction. *Nothing* in those books is real." Duffy rarely lets emotion cloud his judgment, and I wasn't sure he was doing that even now. But he certainly wanted to communicate to Walt that there was a difference between Book Duffy and Living Duffy.

"Too bad," Walt said. "I could say I was there when it all happened." He turned toward me. "Would you mind signing something for me, Ms. Goldman? I'm really a big fan, and if I'd known you were gonna be here, I would have brought a book for you to autograph."

"Of course I will," I told him. I'll pretty much sign your mortgage statement if you show some interest in my books. I mean, it won't do you any good, but I'll sign it. I reached into my purse to see if there was a blank scrap of paper and a pen. But Walt was quicker than I was; he proffered a fairly clean sheet of paper from the pocket of his pants and pulled a marker from his jacket.

I didn't ask Walt if he wanted an inscription. That's something you do if you're signing a book, because some people just want the signature (those are the ones more likely to try and sell it on eBay twenty minutes after you die) and feel the book loses value when personalized. This was simply a piece of paper, and Walt seemed like a legitimate fan. I don't run into those every day, so I wanted to show my sincere gratitude.

Hence I wrote: "To Walt, with sincere gratitude, Rachel Goldman."

I never know what to write to people I just met.

"Wow," he said when I handed him the paper. "I can't believe it."

Duffy, impatient with what he undoubtedly saw as an unnecessary distraction from the matter at hand, cleared his throat to get our attention and said to Walt, "Do you have any idea why Damien Mosley might have left Poughkeepsie, or where he might have gone?"

Walt looked blank and shook his head. "No idea. Like I said, I didn't really know the guy that well. But listen, if there's anything I can do to help you two find out what you need to know, well," he looked at me, "it would be an honor."

There are fans and there are scary fans. I wasn't sure which kind Walt was yet. I mean, I've never had a real Annie Wilkes kind of nut, and hope I never do, but there are a few people out there who know my books better than I do, and that means I keep a file called "Duffy Bible" open whenever I'm writing a book so I'll remember that he never eats meat but isn't a vegan or that his cousin Rafael was once mentioned in passing on page 215 of *Little Boy Lost*. Because if I make a mistake, the e-mails will pour in.

I also have Paula for exactly that reason, and many more.

Duffy, however, was less concerned with my welfare than his goal, which was finding Damien Mosley. Whether or not he remembered the reason he wanted to do that—to prove to me that they were not the same person—was anybody's guess.

"You could be helpful indeed if you knew people who were more intimately acquainted with Damien," he told Walt. "Who should we try to contact? Who might know more than you do?" Duffy doesn't mean to sound insulting at least half the time. He doesn't really hear his own tone and rarely takes into account how his words will affect others because he sees the good and the urgency in finding the missing person.

The fact that Damien Mosley had been missing for five years took some of the immediacy out of the situation, but Duffy was not changing his usual technique.

"Well, Barry, the guy from Rapscallion's, moved out of town about a couple of years ago. He wasn't on the bowling team; we just knew him from the bar. He ended up in

Georgia or West Virginia, something like that. I don't really remember. The rest of the team was . . . let's see . . . me, Damien, and this girl Lou, who I think was Barry's girlfriend at the time. I don't remember her last name."

Duffy, who had taken no notes because he knew for a fact he didn't need them, nodded his head. "That would be helpful indeed, Mr. Kendig. Please see if you can find the name. Would it be possible for us to have your cell phone number in case we have any other questions while we're here in town?"

Walt looked like we'd asked if we could name our first child after him. And let me be clear, Duffy and I are *never* going to have a first child. Walt beamed and gave me—not Duffy—his number, which I dutifully entered into my iPhone. I'd resisted the whole smartphone thing as long as I could, but when I found out I could order pizza with an app, I was lost forever.

"We really appreciate the help, Walt," I told him as we got up to leave.

Duffy had our next appointment planned out, said it was across the city and would require about fifteen minutes in the car, so we had to stick to the schedule. He said.

"Are you kidding?" Walt gushed as we walked to the door. "It's the highlight of my whole week. Make sure you call me. Let me know what you find out, okay?"

I checked Walt's hand for a ring, and there was none. So maybe there was no little woman for him to tell this amazing story to tonight. I felt a little bad for him and made a mental promise to call him later no matter what Duffy and I did or did not discover about Damien Mosley.

We all left the diner together, then Walt waved at us and walked off toward his job at an accounting firm two blocks away. Duffy began striding purposefully (the only way he ever strides; I'm thinking of writing in a limp so I can keep up without gasping for breath) toward the car.

"What's the rush?" I wheezed at him as we speed-walked toward the parking lot.

"No rush. Why? Am I walking too fast?"

He did not slow down, just as a footnote (get it?). "No. It's fine. You seemed like you wanted to get away from our pal Walt as quickly as possible, that's all."

Duffy looked mildly surprised at the suggestion. "He had given us all the information he could offer. I didn't see any reason to continue the conversation. Was there something you thought we should have asked him that I missed?"

"No. I just thought maybe he was lonely and needed the company."

Duffy raised his eyebrows a tiny bit as he opened the car door. "He was going back to work," he said. "And so should we."

Chapter 6

"Where are we going now?" I settled into the passenger seat and considered why it is called "shotgun," which goes back to the days of the stagecoach; the person not holding the reins would carry a shotgun in case things got hairy while traveling through dangerous territory. It was an interesting fact but didn't really have tons of bearing on what we were doing now. I hoped.

"To see Louise Refsnyder," Duffy answered. "It makes sense that she is the 'girl named Lou' Walt remembered from the bowling team. She worked with Damien at what used to be Rapscallion's."

The ride took a little more than ten minutes with the GPS instructing Duffy to make numerous turns along the way. We pulled up in front of a rather tired-looking A-frame house on what could be described as a suburban street. "Louise asked we arrive now because she will not have a shift at her job until five this afternoon. She wanted to sleep late today."

I didn't really care why the day had been scheduled in this particular order but didn't answer him. We walked up the front steps, and Duffy knocked on the door, as there appeared to be no doorbell.

After a moment, the door opened, and a woman of about my age stood in the hallway. She had fairly short hair and was dressed, let's say, casually, meaning she was in cutoff denim shorts and a T-shirt. The shirt bore no logo; Louise apparently did not need to draw attention to her shirt area. A lot of guys would just naturally focus their eyes there.

If you know what I mean.

"You're Duffy?" she asked the one of us who was Duffy. Or at least thought he was. She smiled warmly. Then she looked around him at me and did not seem quite so thrilled that I had arrived as well.

Duffy nodded, mostly because that is who he believes himself to be. "I am. This is my associate, Rachel Goldman."

Louise realized she was supposed to take note of me, so she nodded in my direction and then focused her attention back on Duffy. "Come on in," she said. "I've got coffee." There was a slight Canadian inflection in her "coffee."

We walked inside, and Louise led us to her kitchen, where we were instructed to sit. She'd put out two cups despite Duffy having clearly told her there would be someone with him, and we sat at the table while she deigned to get another mug for me.

"How can I help you, Duffy?" she asked as she sat down and gazed upon him. Having made the man up, I could be proud of the fact that Louise found him attractive, but I had to remind myself that his parents actually made him up, and then my head started to ache. That's been happening more often since I met Duffy.

"We are attempting to find Damien Mosley, as I told you in my e-mail," he answered, probably oblivious to the interest he was somehow attracting. It wouldn't have occurred to him to think about a woman while on a case, and it definitely wouldn't occur to him if he was indeed involved with someone named Emily Needleman. "We're hoping your past association with him might give us some trail to follow. How did you know Damien?"

Duffy already knew the answer to that one. It's a technique when questioning someone to get them talking, and talking about themselves. They think they're having a nice chat while really you're drilling them for information.

Louise took right to the bait, although to look at her, you'd think the bait was catnip, and it was all being stored in Duffy Madison's pupils. "I knew him a little in high school and then worked with Damien at Rapscallion's when it was still Rapscallion's," she said, her gaze never deviating from him. "You look a little like him, you know. Are you related somehow?"

Duffy avoided my glance. "No. We are not related. I have never met Damien Mosley. So he was working as a bartender, and you were waiting tables?"

"That's right," Louise said. "You know, you split tips in a place like that, so you want everybody to get along and help out the cause, right? So we used to spend a lot of time together, that group. It's not that much like that now. The place is called Oakwood, and it's supposed to be classier because they're gentrifying certain areas of the city now. They're getting college students and professors, people like that. And it's more upscale, so the money's a little better, but the people aren't that much fun anymore." She stopped after all the words had flown out of her mouth. "What did you want to know, again?"

Duffy hadn't actually asked her a question yet, so this was his opportunity to jump in before Louise began rambling again. "Can you tell us what kind of person Damien Mosley is? We really don't have very much information about him other than his education and the time he vanished."

Louise, clearly pleased she could help the handsome (if you liked that sort of thing) investigator, smiled and thought very outwardly and seriously. She wanted her face to communicate that process, so her eyes looked down a little, and her lips stuck out just a bit.

"He was a complex guy," she said. "He'd have different moods, and you never knew when it was gonna change. Like, you'd bring a drink order to him, and he'd be all funny and smiling, but when you came back to pick it up, he'd barely look at you. Very odd."

Duffy must have believed this to be significant information, because his eyes were boring into Louise's as she spoke. It was not the same kind of attention she was giving him; she was flirting, and he was trying to see into her brain, but her face kept getting in the way.

Louise clearly took this as encouragement, so she kept talking. That was probably what Duffy wanted, but it was starting to make my temples ache just a little; her voice was not soothing. Unless you find fingernails on slate soothing. To each his own.

"Damien told me he'd had a rough childhood, you know," she went on. "His mom raised him pretty much alone, and she wasn't the easiest person in the world to get along with, he said. It was funny, because he said she'd change moods real fast and with no warning. And that was exactly what *he* did!" She wanted to make sure we had gotten the point, and given that we were cognizant adults, I believe Duffy and I had made the connection.

"Interesting," Duffy said. Everyone's entitled to an opinion. "Did he still have a relationship with his mother when you knew him?"

She shrugged while I sipped at the coffee, which was fairly awful and might have been instant. Who makes instant coffee in the twenty-first century? "I didn't ask him," Louise said.

"We're told that you were on a bowling team with Damien before his disappearance," Duffy said, not wondering aloud what kind of friend doesn't ask the question after being told his mother was a source of pain and a possible key to some emotional problems. But hey. "Is that correct?"

"Wow, you're good," Louise gushed. "Who told you that?"

"We do substantial research," Duffy noted, not adding that we'd happened to have run into a guy in a diner. "But you saw Damien outside work."

Again, that wasn't a question. But that was calculated on Duffy's part, I knew. Say it as a statement, and there will be unspoken implications, as if you are simply reciting a fact. If Louise had no reaction, it could be inferred that she and Damien were more than work acquaintances; if she did react, the style of her response could give Duffy insight into whether she was being honest. He'd tell me that I'd decided I didn't like Louise—which was only partially true—and therefore had colored my judgment by making assumptions.

It was a big pain having both our minds inside the same brain.

"Oh, don't think there was anything going on between me and Damien!" Louise exploded (she didn't really explode; it's an expression—don't get me started on the whole "said" argument in writing). "If that's what you're thinking, forget it. I didn't really know the guy all that well." Since she'd discussed his mommy issues with Damien, that seemed a hollow claim, but I'd wait for Duffy's view before I made up my mind.

"No, I didn't think that was the case," he said smoothly. "In fact, I was told you were seeing a man named Barry at the time. Is that still true?"

Louise, no doubt thinking Duffy had motives other than professional ones in asking about her love life, immediately took her indignation down about four notches and smiled at him. She was an attractive woman, I had to admit. But her coffee was terrible.

"Nah," she said. Noel Coward would have gnashed his teeth with envy. "I broke up with Barry maybe three years ago. He lives in Phoenix now, I think. Or Peoria. Someplace that begins with a *P*."

"Like Poughkeepsie," I pointed out.

It was as if Louise had just noticed I was in the room. Her head swiveled toward me, and her face went from enthralled to irritated in a microsecond. "Yeah, like that," she sneered.

"Do you have Barry's current address?" Duffy asked. Duffy's not much for confrontation when it's not in the service of an investigation, and he was trying to head off whatever it was Louise was aiming at me. "We'd like to talk to him about Damien, too."

"I don't have it," Louise answered. "After we broke up, I didn't bother keeping in touch. What's the point?"

Duffy leaned forward to communicate he was getting to the heart of the matter. "Do you have any idea why Damien Mosley suddenly left town?" he asked.

Louise looked disappointed; she'd doubtless thought he was going to ask about her. "He didn't say anything to me," she answered after a second. "Do you want more coffee?" Duffy's cup wasn't even half empty yet. Or half full, depending on one's level of pessimism. I couldn't say as I blamed him. Mine was emptier, but Louise hadn't asked me, which was good.

"No, thank you. I'm wondering if you had any sense at all that something might be bothering Damien in the last few weeks he lived here in Poughkeepsie."

I saw where Duffy was going, and it was unlike him. He was a real advocate of having an open mind in an investigation;

I've written him as someone who never makes assumptions and never brings a theory he then would try to prove. He's all about facts.

But like I said, I saw where he was going, and so did Louise. "Wait. You think maybe he killed himself?"

"I am not saying that at all," Duffy answered, possibly noticing the look I was giving him. "I don't have enough facts to reach that conclusion. It is a possibility among many possibilities. I am simply trying to determine what state of mind Damien Mosley was in that might—or might not—have led to his sudden departure from his home."

Louise stared at him for a long moment. "What?"

"He's trying to figure out why Damien left," I translated. I speak fluent Duffy Madison, having made up the language.

"Oh." Louise stood up and walked to the refrigerator, which she opened. She peered inside as if trying to find the proper trajectory through a black hole. "You want a bagel or something?"

"No, thank you. I would like you to stop avoiding my questions and simply tell me what you know so that I might be able to find Damien Mosley." Duffy has little patience for people who lie, especially when they do it badly.

Louise spun around, startled by Duffy's change in tone. She left the refrigerator door open. "I told you, I don't know anything. Listen, I have to get ready for work, so maybe it's time for you to go."

I had stood and was halfway to the door in the blink of an eye, but Duffy stayed put in his chair, immobile and serene.

He was gentleman enough not to lace his fingers behind his head and lean back to indicate he could wait all day if necessary.

"Your shift does not begin for another four hours and twenty-five minutes," he reminded Louise. "I think you can spare a little more time."

"Yeah, but I don't want to talk to you anymore." Louise, having given up her momentary infatuation with Duffy, had dropped her voice about a tone and a half. "So why don't you leave?" She pointed to the door as if the problem here was that Duffy didn't know where to find it.

"We will, but first you will have to tell us what you've been trying, very poorly, to conceal." Duffy's was in full Holmesian mode now; there was no moving him, and I was certain there would be no Americanisms until we were back in the car. "Is there something about Damien Mosley's disappearance that would affect you? Are you concerned about being found out about something that happened at that time?"

"I'm not afraid of anything," Louise said in as unconvincing a tone as could possibly be imagined. "I just don't like talking about things like this to suspicious cops when I have to get to work soon." No doubt Duffy would note the exact number of minutes before she had to go wait tables again.

But no, he decided to bypass the last part of her silly statement and clarify the beginning for her. Again. "We are not here representing any law enforcement agency," he said.

"I do sometimes consult for the Bergen County prosecutor, but I am not here in that capacity, and Rachel is a mystery author who has no ties to any police force. What you tell us will remain confidential." Unless of course a crime had been committed, in which case you could count on Duffy to rat Louise out in a heartbeat. He has this thing about justice.

Louise closed the fridge, which made me feel better. Then she flopped down into the chair opposite Duffy, defeated. She was still overplaying her role, but at least she was quieter about it now.

"I'm not holding anything back," she sighed. "I promise." Wow. She expected that to work. She clearly didn't know Duffy like I do.

Nobody knows Duffy like I do. Not even Duffy.

"You are," he said. It was a fact, not an opinion. "If you had nothing to say, you wouldn't have put on such a show about having nothing to say. Now please. What happened that might have prompted Damien Mosley to suddenly leave town?"

Louise looked around the room and made a sort of clicking noise with her tongue, like she was a cheetah about to bite down on the fresh antelope it had brought down. (Do cheetahs and antelopes live in the same territories?) "I broke up with him," she said.

I walked back toward the kitchen table, my hands up near the sides of my head in exasperation. "You said you didn't have a thing with Damien," I told her, as if she didn't actually know that. "You said you barely knew him and you just worked together."

"I didn't want you to think I just slept with everybody I know," Louise said, looking straight at Duffy. "I didn't want you to think that I dumped Damien, so he just packed up and left—do you really think he killed himself?"

"Again, there is no evidence to suggest that," Duffy said, which wasn't an answer to Louise's question. "How long did you and Damien have a romantic relationship?"

Louise blinked, apparently absorbing what he'd asked. "Romantic? We just went to bed a couple of times. It was *never* romantic."

Duffy didn't respond. That sort of thing makes him nervous.

I filled the void. "It was never romantic, but you think your breaking up with him might have prompted him to leave town?" I said. There's the slightest possibility my voice had a tinge of challenge in it.

"No! I'm saying I don't think that had anything to do with it at all!" Everyone spent a long moment avoiding eye contact.

I decided I'd end the awkward silence. "We've been to Damien's old apartment," I said. "There didn't seem to be much there. Any other places you think we should look?"

Louise looked over to me slowly, as if waking up and realizing she had been asked to do something. "His apartment here in town or the other one?" she asked.

Duffy perked up.

"There was another one?" I said.

"Oh, yeah. Damien had a place his mother gave him in West New York."

I glared at Duffy. We'd driven for two hours. "West New York," I repeated.

"Yeah," Louise said, misunderstanding. "Over in Jersey."

Chapter 7

"We can see that apartment tomorrow," Duffy Madison said. "I don't see why you are so upset about this."

"I'm not upset!" I shouted. Luckily, Duffy had the car windows closed, or my not being upset would have been heard three blocks away. "I'm just wondering why I'm here in Poughkeepsie, New York, today not writing when I could be home in Adamstown, New Jersey, not writing."

Duffy wasn't clutching the wheel especially tightly; his ability to remain calm in heated situations was infuriating. "There is still more value in being here than in the West New York apartment," Duffy said. "The fact that Damien spent more time here and just used the New Jersey home on weekends is particularly important. He knew people here, and they knew him. We would have had to come here anyway."

I sat back and closed my eyes, which I do sometimes in an attempt to lower my blood pressure. I don't have blood pressure problems, but it's never too soon to start being healthy.

"I think what bothers me is that you didn't know about the West New York place," I said when I could breathe normally again. "You know everything. That seems like something you would have had filed away weeks ago."

"Obviously, I don't know everything, or we wouldn't need to investigate at all," he answered, voice as unemotional as if he were informing Captain Kirk that logic dictated turning the ship around. "That is an area I had not investigated because Damien's salary at Rapscallion's seemed incapable of supporting two residences. It had not occurred to me that he might have been given one by his mother."

"Louise said his mother gave it to him," I reminded him. "Does that mean the mother is wealthy, or did she die and leave it to him?"

"Louise didn't know," Duffy reminded *me*. "But I could find no obituary or death notice for Damien's mother, which would be very unusual if she had died even in the past twenty years. I think it unlikely."

Opening my eyes, even after the coffee at the diner and the single sip I'd taken at Louise's, wasn't an attractive prospect. It felt nice to have them closed, so I kept them that way. It was an advantage to having my fictional creation drive the car.

"Where are we heading now?" I asked him.

"There is a high school friend of Damien's for us to question," he answered. "Rod Wilkerson had stayed in touch with him until Damien disappeared. He might be able to provide a trail even if he doesn't know it yet."

A thought occurred to me that caused me to open my eyes and look at Duffy. "Shouldn't we be looking for people who knew you?" I asked. "People you went to high school with, someone who could confirm that you were here back in the day?"

His mouth twitched just a bit; he had come to hate my suggesting he actually had a past before I'd started writing him, or whatever it was I had started writing. "That will not help us find Damien Mosley," Duffy said.

"No, but it could get us to an answer to the bigger question. You want me to believe you sprung full-blown from my iMac? Fine. At least make the effort to prove your point."

It was dirty pool, no doubt, to challenge Duffy using his own thought process, but if I couldn't do that, who could? He took the time to consider it, which Duffy would do, and nodded slightly.

"Perhaps that is something we should do on a later trip," he conceded. "But right now I can't provide a list of people who might have been here at the same time you believe I was growing up. There is no one to interview."

"I can provide that," I said. "It's not like I want to make it a regular practice to hike up here so we can ask people if you exist." I reached for my phone and texted to Paula:

Can you send a list of people who went to high school with Duffy?

I knew she'd done that basic research when living Duffy had first surfaced months before, so she would have the information available. Sure enough, she answered my text moments later. Paula is the most efficient person on Earth.

How many do you want?

It was a good question. No doubt Paula had a list of the entire graduating class for Duffy's assumed senior year and the ones immediately before and after it in case he'd been held back or skipped a grade. But time limitations for a one-day visit to Poughkeepsie meant we should be as efficient as possible.

Send up to four, if any were in the same clubs or anything. What does Duffy look like at 18?

Paula must have been anticipating that question because the answer came back quickly, even for her.

No pic of Duffy. Damien could grow up to be Duffy based on his pic but can't really tell.

And she sent the picture of Damien to my phone, which did not help much. It was tiny to begin with and worse on a phone screen. When I tried to enlarge it, the photo became grainy and almost impossible to see.

"There is a Duffy Madison entry in the yearbook, but no photo where a picture should be," I reported to my traveling companion.

"Well, that proves my point," he answered.

"I really don't think so."

The list of classmates arrived two minutes later, and I read the names to Duffy, whose face showed no reaction at all. But two names caught both of our attention.

Rod Wilkerson and Walt Kendig.

"Well, that's convenient," I said. It's possible there was just a hint of satisfaction in my voice.

Duffy said nothing for the rest of the drive.

We arrived at Rod's house a few minutes later. It was a well-appointed but small brick-faced building with an attached garage and a well-tended lawn. As we got out of the car, Duffy photographed it for his files.

"Let me do the talking, please," Duffy said as we approached the door. The news that Rod might have been a classmate of his as well as Damien's seemed to have shaken him.

"Not a chance," I said.

"That's what I thought."

He rang the doorbell, and we waited a bit until Rod Wilkerson opened the door and asked us in.

He was a large, jovial sort of man who seemed to find it awfully entertaining that a county investigator (sort of) and a famous (not even close) crime fiction writer had asked to talk to him. He led us into a room he called his office, where he worked as a real estate agent and financial advisor from home.

He started by offering to grease the wheels with the local authorities as a way to show what an important guy he was. "I have some friends in the police department," he said.

"I don't believe that will be necessary," Duffy told him. Duffy has little patience for people who try to curry favor with influence. Or anything else.

Rod shook his head a bit in wonder. "When I first saw you at the door," he said to Duffy, "I thought you were Damien. You look like him."

"But then you realized I am not Damien Mosley," Duffy told him, just in case Rod had any doubts as to what he had realized.

"Yeah. But then I haven't seen Damien in five years, and it's not like I keep pictures of him around the house." Rod's home was fairly neat. He told us he was divorced and had kept the house because his ex-wife had moved back to her family's home in Missouri. He had considered selling the place—he did work in real estate, after all—but he'd inherited it from his parents and did not have to pay a mortgage, so he'd held onto the house.

I considered showing Rod the yearbook picture of Damien that Paula had sent to my phone, but naturally, he would have a copy of his own and could probably look at it whenever he wanted. The picture was clearly at least fifteen years old by now anyway.

"Were you good friends with Damien?" Duffy asked. "When we e-mailed, you indicated you'd kept in touch with him after high school and were very upset when he suddenly vanished."

"Yeah, depending on when," Rod told us. "Before I got married, he and I would have dinner once a week or so, and

Damien was at my wedding. But you know, you get married, and your life tends to be eaten up with that. My wife Brenda wasn't that crazy about Damien, and even though she never said she didn't want him around or didn't want me to hang with him much, the message got across."

"Why didn't she like Damien?" I asked. I was building up to my own question and had to establish myself in the conversation.

Rod considered and sort of flattened out his mouth in a *who knows* expression. "Some people are oil and water. That was Brenda and Damien. He didn't like her either and warned me not to marry her the night before the wedding. I guess he was right, considering how things ended up."

Duffy was eager to get the interview back on the track he'd decided it should be on, so he didn't give me time to follow up. "Damien was working as a bartender before he disappeared," he said. "Did you ever go into Rapscallion's and talk to him over a drink? Without your wife there? Anything like that?"

Rod nodded, then reconsidered and shook his head. "Well, I did see him, but not at his work," he said. "It wasn't like Brenda, you know, forbade me from seeing an old friend. It was more like I sensed how she felt and over time just saw Damien less and less. I really couldn't figure it out when suddenly he was gone like that." He took a breath. "I mean, I hope nothing happened to the guy, you know?"

"Why didn't you go to Rapscallion's?" Duffy asked. I thought it was a redundant question, but he seemed to think it was important. "You seemed to say it as if that wasn't a possibility."

"Well, I didn't go in there much," Rod told him, "even before I was married. It's just not my thing."

"Not your thing?" Now I wanted to know what that meant.

"Yeah, you know. A strip club. I always thought those are the saddest places on Earth. All those guys watching this girl and thinking they had a chance with her. Sad."

"Rapscallion's was a strip club?" Duffy said. Obviously, his research had not unearthed that piece of information.

"Yeah, you didn't know that? Damien didn't seem to mind—I guess he got used to the place because he needed the money. But I never really took to it. So when he and I would get together, it was at the diner or another bar called The Look Inn on nights he wasn't working."

Duffy blinked a couple of times. I seriously doubted he'd ever been inside a strip club in his life, and now he was trying to absorb what he was being told. I *have* been inside one, doing research on a book, so I wasn't nearly as scandalized. It's a way some people make a living; whatever.

Duffy's reaction did give me an opening, though, and I was definitely going to use it. "Do you remember another classmate?" I said. Duffy's eyes focused sharply, and he turned toward me but too late. "Duffy Madison?"

Rod blinked and looked confused. He turned toward my odd companion. "I thought you were Duffy Madison."

"I am," Duffy said.

"Did we go to high school together?"

"No."

"If you look through your yearbook, you'll find a space for a classmate named Duffy Madison with no photograph next to it," I told Rod, ignoring Duffy's glare. "I just wanted to see if you remembered anything about him."

Rod looked at me, then at Duffy, then back at me with consternation in his eyes. "I can't say as I do." He turned toward Duffy. "I'm sorry."

"Don't be," the impostor said. "You and I were not classmates. Now, we came here from the home of Louise Refsnyder. Do you know her?"

Rod's face changed just for a microsecond, but I saw it, and I'd bet that Duffy, having successfully changed the subject back to his topic, did too. Rod looked just a little panicked, like he'd been caught doing something he shouldn't.

"I don't think so," he said, his voice still in an ingratiating and confident tone. "Should I?"

"She was a . . . friend of Damien's and worked at Rapscallion's with him," Duffy informed him. "We were wondering if you had ever met her."

Rod shook his head, and if I hadn't seen that flash on his face a moment earlier, I'd have believed him. "I don't think so. Was she one of the dancers?"

Actually, that was a very good question. "We were told she waited tables," I said.

He shrugged. "As I understand it, some of the dancers work the tables when they were not onstage to pick up extra tips. Personally, I don't know that much about the place, but that is what Damien told me."

Uh-huh. I was getting the impression that good ol' Rod knew the strip club better than he wanted us to think. Why he'd care about our opinion of him—and why he'd think it would be unfavorable if we knew he went to a strip club now and again—was beyond me at that moment.

"So you couldn't tell us if Damien Mosley and Louise Refsnyder were lovers who broke up just before he vanished," Duffy said. I noticed him watching Rod's face closely.

Again the reaction was brief but telling. Rod's eyes widened in surprise, then he self-consciously wiped them as if they'd been tearing, which they hadn't.

"Damien never said anything like that," he said after a quick recovery. "I don't think he ever mentioned the name. Louise . . . what?"

We thanked Rod for his time and hospitality and headed out to Duffy's car. When we were far enough away from the front door, I looked at Duffy and asked, "Do you think anything he told us was true?"

Duffy got in on the driver's side. "I believe he is divorced," he said.

Chapter 8

I called Walt Kendig as Duffy headed back toward Mill Street in our quest to head back to New Jersey before the Tappan Zee fell down, which could be any minute. I'd promised I'd call him, so I did. Yes, we'd found out he was in Damien Mosley's high school class, but so were two hundred other people. The poor man seemed so happy to hear from me that it was just a touch pathetic.

"This is amazing!" he gushed. Duffy, who could no doubt hear Walt's voice despite my holding the phone to my ear, grimaced a little. "Duffy Madison and Rachel Goldman."

I decided not to debate his choice of billing and thanked him again for his help in our search for Damien Mosley. Walt seemed surprised somehow that we had not wrapped the whole thing up and found Damien, returned him to Pough-keepsie, and moved on to our next adventure before three in the afternoon.

"I thought for sure you'd be able to track him down," he said.

"Well, maybe we still can, but it's going to take more time," I told him. "Anyway, you were a big help, and we really appreciate your contribution. If we ever come back up to Poughkeepsie . . ." Maybe Duffy might come back to look for Damien Mosley, but I didn't see how this was going to help my writing at all, so he'd be doing any further digging on his own.

"Hang on," Walt said. Damn! Just when I thought I'd made a clean break of it. "I found something back at my office that might be of help to you. Do you want to come over here and see it?"

"What is it?" I asked, suppressing a sigh. I just wanted to go home and write something bad.

"A picture. Something that could give you an idea of Damien and what he was like."

A photograph of Damien Mosley would certainly go a long way to proving he was or was not actually the Duffy Madison now driving me away from Poughkeepsie. "Can you just send it to my phone?" I asked Walt.

"It's a real printed-out photograph," he said. "It's a little faded, and I don't think a scan would hold up well. You need to take a look. I mean, I don't want to tell you your business."

"My business is making stuff up," I told him, then looked at Duffy, who was frowning. "Walt says—"

"I heard him." Duffy made a right turn to begin his process of turning us in the opposite direction, back toward Walt's office. He'd do this by making three right turns rather than pulling into someone's driveway and then backing out in a K-turn or simply making a U-turn like any other normal American.

"We're on our way," I told Walt and hung up before he could be exultant at me. I just wasn't in the mood. I was tired of the detective life and wanted to go back to being a hack writer. I leaned back—I don't know why I always tend to move forward when I'm on the phone in a car—and moaned a little.

"What's the problem?" Duffy asked. "We might very well be on the verge of finding out something truly significant about Damien Mosley's disappearance."

I went back to closing my eyes. It just felt good. "I'm not an investigator, Duffy. I'm less interested in finding Damien than I am in finding my mojo."

It was very relaxing not to see anything but to feel the movement of the car as Duffy made his numerous right turns, then a left to get us back in the proper direction. "As we've discussed, I believe the two are intertwined. Your writer's block is bound to be relieved by finding the truth so you can accept that I am what I say I am."

I didn't open my eyes, but I did feel my teeth clench. Still, I managed to push between them, "I don't have writer's block. There is no such thing as writer's block. I'm still writing. What I have is a slump brought on by your messing with my head."

In my mind's eye, I could see the look on his face. If you believed him, I could have seen it before he *had* a face. "I am not messing with your head, Rachel."

That was enough; I opened my eyes and faced him. Duffy, of course, did not take his eyes off the road because he's Duffy, or a reasonable facsimile thereof, and Duffy would never do that.

"You are," I said. "You can't have it both ways, Duffy. If you're not messing with my head, then you are delusional. Those are the only two possibilities, and you've already told me you're not delusional, so what does that leave?"

There was no answer; we were already pulling up to Walt Kendig's place of business at Associated Accounting Services, as generic a name for a business as I could possibly imagine, and I have to name fake businesses all the time. Duffy parked the car across the street from the office, which was indicated by a sign in a third-floor window. There was a really dilapidated little MG, a two-seat sports car that had seen better days before 1974, its front right fender held on with duct tape, parked in front. I was glad we had gotten the address ahead of time, or I, personally, would have driven right by the unremarkable building and kept going until we'd gotten to Albany. Which I was guessing would be pretty far.

We got out of the car, Duffy changing his face from glum at having been challenged to businesslike and inquisitive. I imagine my face was going from frustrated to impatient but didn't have a mirror handy and was glad for it.

After trudging up the stairs (the building was only four stories and old enough not to have required an elevator) to Associated Accounting Services, I let Duffy lead me to the office door. I was still sort of longing for the lovely moment I'd spent in the car with my eyes closed. I resolved to sleep the whole way home. It had already been a long day, and it was still the middle of the afternoon.

"How far are we from Woodstock?" I asked Duffy suddenly. My father lives in Claremont, New York, near Woodstock, and if it was not very far from here, I could look forward to feeling guilty for not going to see him.

"About an hour," Duffy answered. "Why? Is there some reason you believe Damien Mosley might be there?"

We found the office door and opened it, so I didn't have to answer him. It wasn't a large office, but there were five or six people in cubicles in a sort of bullpen operation and a very bored-looking receptionist at the front desk.

She didn't get a chance to ask us what business we might have there for two reasons: (1) Walt Kendig appeared out of nowhere, undoubtedly having been watching out the window for us, and greeted us too warmly; and (2) she was applying nail polish and was very engrossed in her work. Black polish, if you were wondering. And Halloween wasn't even on the horizon yet.

"I'm so glad I caught you before you left!" Walt gushed. "I think you'll find this very interesting." He led us back toward his desk, third cubicle on the left, with the air of someone who was having way too much fun and knew it. "I found it after I talked to you because you reminded me of those days."

We didn't have to ask which days. We stood at Walt's desk, and he sat behind it, reaching for a folder.

"It was taken with a regular film camera, not a digital one," Walt said, seemingly apologizing for the poor visual quality of what we were about to see. It sort of made me wonder why we were bothering until I remembered Duffy and how I was about to discover that he was not Damien Mosley.

And that wasn't going to make me feel better, I knew.

"When was it taken, and where was it processed?" Duffy was the professional. I was the writer. We were each acting to type. I sat down in a spare chair because I was tired.

"Probably about a year before Damien left," Walt said. "And if I remember correctly, I had the roll developed at the CVS on South Road. Why does that matter?"

He handed the photograph to Duffy, who looked like he didn't want to touch it. It was evidence, even if there had been no crime committed, and Duffy was uncomfortable about contaminating the evidence. I knew he wished he had a pair of latex gloves in his pocket, or maybe he did and just didn't want to be seen for the anal retentive nut that he is.

"Everything matters in an investigation," he said. It's boilerplate; something he says when he doesn't have a reason for the nutty question he's asked but is afraid that if he doesn't ask it, he'll discover it is the key to the whole puzzle later. Duffy is haunted by something that happened to him as a young man, but I haven't decided what it was yet.

It didn't matter. Walt looked sufficiently impressed with the import of the moment. Besides, he had called us with this juicy piece of evidence and wanted (it was obvious) to be seen as a useful and helpful member of the team. Which was fine, since I was resigning from the team as soon as I got back to Adamstown. It was nice Duffy would have somebody to play with after I left.

"Wow," Walt said. "I could maybe check and see if they have records that go back that far."

"I don't think that will be necessary," Duffy said. "But if it becomes important, I will check with you."

Walt, awed, leaned in as Duffy turned his complete attention to the photograph. I was disengaged at this point but not so much that I didn't look at the desk surface to see what all the fuss was about.

It was, as advertised, a pretty ragged printed photograph on what I'm sure was promoted as premium stock, in a matte finish that actually made the image less sharp than it might have been. I was trying to show off how indifferent I could be about it all—writers are such children—but I had to lean over the desk to get anything approaching a good look.

The picture showed five people in bowling shirts, which was not a huge surprise. Walt's major connection to Damien Mosley appeared to be the bowling team, so any images he'd have would probably be related. The bowlers were standing around the ball return pointing to the screen over their heads, where presumably the score of their latest game was being displayed. It was too small a picture to make out the numbers and letters on the screen, but the team all looked pleased.

I recognized most of them. Walt, of course, was at the center, his arms around the shoulders of the two bowlers to his right and left, who were Louise Refsnyder (right) and Rod Wilkerson (left). Wearing a baseball cap on the far right was a man about Duffy's size and build, wearing a baseball cap (for a local minor league team, I was guessing, because the logo was not a Major League affiliate) that cast a shadow on the top half of his face and almost completely obscured his eyes.

"Rod's standing two people away from Louise," I told Duffy. "He said he didn't know her."

"We knew he was lying." Duffy shrugged.

"Rod said he didn't know Lou?" Walt sounded astonished. "They were pretty tight for a while before he married Brenda."

Duffy and I exchanged a look.

"That's Damien," Walt said, pointing at the man in the cap. He didn't know we'd visited with Rod, so it was a natural comment to make. I still found myself mentally rolling my eyes at him; of *course* that was Damien. Someone who looked like Duffy but would be frustrating enough not to let us see his face? Who else could it be?

At the far left was a woman, not perfectly slim but attractive, her dark hair parted in the middle and hanging to her shoulders. She was grinning but in an artificial way. It was easy to see she was doing her best to look happy. The fact that she was indifferent showed around the corners of her eyes.

"Who is that?" Duffy asked, indicating the woman.

Walt didn't even have to look. "That's Michelle," he said. "I forgot she was on the team until I found the picture."

Gee, thanks, Walt. That was way helpful.

Duffy looked at him a moment and asked, "Michelle?"

"Michelle Mosley. Damien's wife."

Chapter 9

"The strange part is that no one else had even mentioned Damien Mosley was married," Duffy was saying.

In the passenger seat of his car, I was doing my very best to seem asleep, but it wasn't doing any good. Duffy was rambling on anyway, and in a way I felt it was necessary to indulge him since I had gotten my way about driving home immediately after leaving Associated Accounting.

Duffy had naturally wanted to go back to everyone we had spoken to that day and demand an explanation. The fact that Damien Mosley was married to a woman named Michelle, whom Walt said left Poughkeepsie to live in Damien's West New York apartment a few weeks before Damien evaporated, had not come up in any of our conversations in Poughkeepsie until Walt had produced the photograph.

Duffy had asked Walt why he didn't tell us about Michelle before, and his response was that he figured we already knew. Because we (especially Duffy) should have, and he knew it.

That was why he wouldn't shut up even now on Rt. 287 heading back toward New Jersey.

"Well, you did all that research on him, and you didn't know he was married," I pointed out now.

I had vetoed the repeat visits to our Poughkeepsie sources for a number of reasons, all of which were that I wanted to go home. I'd argued that the traffic at the Tappan Zee Bridge would no doubt be horrific and would become more so with each minute we got closer to rush hour. And I noted that there was no reason follow-up couldn't be done on the telephone by Duffy after he had safely dropped me off at my home, where his fictional counterpart awaited to botch up another day of writing.

Duffy had argued that face-to-face confrontation was necessary, and I'd countered that his use of the word *confrontation* indicated he was acting emotionally and not rationally, not basing his actions on facts but feelings.

He started driving home at that moment. Sometimes it really helps in an argument if you invented the thought patterns of the person you're trying to convince.

"I'm aware of my shortcomings," Duffy told me now. I'd tell you exactly where we were on the drive, but I had my eyes closed on principle and did not open them. "Thanks for the reminder."

"Not what I meant." Now I'd opened my eyes, but I wasn't looking at the road signs strictly out of disinterest. Duffy was driving, and we'd get there when he got us there. I had no control. It didn't matter. Spring Valley, New York. "I'm saying, it seems like Damien and Michelle, or maybe just Michelle, took great care to cover up their marriage. Otherwise you would have found some evidence of it."

Duffy considered that while never taking his eyes off the windshield. "That is likely the case," he said. The man has an ego, but in this instance (particularly since I'd said it first) I had to agree with him.

"Look, Duffy. I got involved in this because I wanted to see if there was any evidence that you are or ever were Damien Mosley. Instead, we spent a day looking for Damien Mosley and finding out he could bowl and was married, probably cheating on his wife, and that he had a second apartment in West New York. None of that helps me with what *I* wanted to get out of this. So if you want to keep on searching for Damien, I'm afraid you're going to be on your own from here, okay? I'm a novelist, not Doctor Watson."

"As I recall, Watson did chronicle all of Sherlock Holmes's adventures," Duffy noted. "But I take your point. Thank you for coming with me today, Rachel. You were invaluable. I'll take it from here."

I heard him say the words, and I knew he meant them. He would go on searching for Damien Mosley, and he probably would find the guy. Duffy was good at what he did. But he wouldn't concentrate on proving or disproving his theory that I'd concocted him straight out of my head and he'd come into being at the exact time I'd started writing the character in my novels. If I needed proof of that to write something decent again, I'd have to find it myself.

Well, actually Paula would have to find it for me, but that was almost the same thing.

While I was still there in the car, though, Duffy wanted to hash over more of the details. "I'll have to check the address Rod Wilkerson gave us in West New York and see if anyone named Michelle is living there now. Rod said Damien's mother willed him the apartment, which would indicate that she is deceased and that the space is owned like a co-op or a condominium; the real estate records will be public and easy to find. But none of the people we met today seems to know the surname Michelle Mosley was born with, and that will slow down my progress."

Just as I was starting to wonder why I was in the car at all if he was going to just spout things he was thinking, Duffy asked, "What makes a woman decide to change her name when she marries, or not to do so?"

It was touching that Duffy came to me for all questions about women, but if he started asking me about his relationship with Emily Needleman, I had already decided to make that an off-limits topic. "Tradition, I guess," I told him. "Some women feel bound to that idea, and others don't. You have to remember that I've never been married, Duffy."

"No, but surely you've thought about it."

"Actually, I haven't. When it becomes an issue, I'll let you know."

"Do you think there is any significance to Michelle taking Damien's name when they married?" That would be more the point to Duffy. Whether or not I would change my name, or get married, or have a life outside of helping him find missing people, was not irrelevant but definitely secondary.

"I have no idea," I said. "We really have no sense of who Michelle is or what their marriage was like, other than Louise saying he cheated on her a couple of times, and then she and Damien broke up right before Damien left." I preferred the term *left* to *vanished* or *disappeared*. Don't even get me started on *went missing*, which doesn't actually mean anything. Writers care about words.

"That is important, don't you think?" Duffy asked. We were about to get in line for everyone's favorite death trap of a bridge. "If Damien was having a physical relationship with Louise Refsnyder, that would indicate his marriage to Michelle was not very strong, wouldn't it?"

There are times I really do think Duffy just came to being five years ago because his responses, particularly when dealing with adult relationships, come from a place of such innocence and wonder that it's like he's experiencing it all for the first time and needs a parent to explain.

"Everybody's marriage is different," I told him. "Some people would consider that an irreparable breach of trust. Others would shrug their shoulders. I've heard of people who have open marriages and sleep with other people as a matter of course. I don't know anything about these two, so I can't say what it means. The real question at this point is whether we believe Louise about her relationship with Damien. She isn't necessarily the most reliable witness."

Duffy's eyebrows rose. "You think she was lying?" he asked.

The traffic on the Tappan Zee wasn't as bad this time, oddly. I guess more people wanted to get into New York than New Jersey, which was something of a stumper to me. We were moving slowly, but we were moving. "I don't know if she was lying, but just because she was flirting with you doesn't mean she's reliable, Duffy. In fact, it makes me wonder if maybe she was distracting you because she knew something she didn't want you to find out."

Duffy's response almost made me laugh out loud. "She was flirting? With *me*?"

"She wasn't flirting with me," I told him.

"I did not notice anything. Are you certain?"

"If she were any more obvious, I would have had to leave the room and give you two some privacy," I said.

Duffy actually looked a little nauseated. "You think she wanted to sleep with me?" His voice rose in pitch out of the baritone range and into the lower areas of tenor.

"No, I think she wanted to distract you. But from your reaction, I'd say she distracted me and missed her target completely." We made it back past the sign welcoming us to New Jersey, and I relaxed back into my seat again.

"It's distressing that I missed the signals." Duffy looked upset with himself, shaking his head just a bit and pulling his lips into his mouth then letting them out. "I'm glad you were there."

The crazy thing is that I didn't feel the trap going up around me; I heard what he'd said as a compliment. "Well, so am I," I told him. And that was a mistake.

"It would be a miscalculation for me to think I can handle this case on my own." Duffy drew in a deep breath to indicate he was thinking.

I'm not stupid. This time I saw the kind of case he was building and did my best to sidestep it. "I don't think so," I said quickly. "You're perfectly capable of finding missing people without me. You've done it plenty of times."

"Yes, but I had the authority of the prosecutor's office behind me and a support staff that could handle things. I had Ben Preston along on almost every interview, and he could point out the things I missed. This case doesn't have that official stamp on it. It's just you and me." He chewed on his lower lip.

It was going to be necessary to bring him down to earth, and the landing might not be a soft one. "Duffy," I said, "you have to understand. I'm not going to be helping on this case. I have my own work to do, and I don't see how finding Damien Mosley, if he's findable anymore, is going to serve the purpose I had coming into this. Even if we find him, I'll still wonder if there's someone else who got knocked on the head or something and became you. So if you're going to devote yourself to this investigation—and I can see by the look in your eye that you are—it will have to be without my help. Okay?"

The GPS, which was completely unnecessary at this point, indicated we still had about a forty-five-minute drive ahead of us, and judging from Duffy's expression, it was going to be a quiet one.

Which was what I had wanted in the first place.

*   *   *

Paula had not been working in my house that day, so it was peaceful and empty when Duffy dropped me off, and we exchanged the usual pleasantries about seeing each other soon. I opened the front door and went inside as I heard the tires of Duffy's car backing up on the gravel in my driveway.

The beast, which was what I'd decided to call my new manuscript (not as a title but as a description), awaited.

It was just after five when I walked into my kitchen and got out some leftover chicken. Duffy loses track of time when he's on the trail and rarely eats; I went along for his ride today, and I was famished. I put the chicken in the oven and turned it on because I believe in delayed gratification and because the microwave makes chicken gummy. I got out a packet of microwave rice because I was hungry right now, and the microwave doesn't hurt rice at all.

I sat at the table, not microwaving the rice (just by itself would be bland) and not getting up to chop up vegetables to put into the rice, maybe with some chicken broth that would make it less boring. I didn't do that because I was writing. If you were in the room, you'd swear I was doing no such thing.

The thing about writing fiction is that unless you're at your keyboard clicking away, nobody can see you do it. They see you sitting at a table staring off into space and think you're stoned or lazy when in fact you're trying desperately to come up with a plot point nobody's ever seen before or help your character out of an incredibly difficult situation that you pushed him into the last time you couldn't think of something for him to do.

But today's events kept getting in the way of the perfectly awful fictional ones I'd been concocting. A female witness I was writing had turned into Louise Refsnyder. Angela Mosconi was starting to seem more and more like someone who should be named Emily Needleman. The dead man at the bottom of the cliff? Maybe he'd be a missing bartender identifiable only by his bowling shirt, and he'd have a secret wife.

Now it was getting complicated: Had I really invented Duffy out of the sky and given him life, or was I now a figment of *his* imagination?

I put the rice away and turned off the oven, then I called the local Thai place and put in a delivery order. The last thing I wanted to do was get into another car, even if it was my own.

The woman on the phone said it would take about forty-five minutes for the food to show up, which was odd since the restaurant was maybe six minutes from my house, but I let it go given the time of day. Rush hour. Lots of takeout orders.

I dragged myself into my office and procrastinated for a while by checking my e-mails, none of which—thankfully—had anything to do with Damien Mosley, Louise, Walt, Rod, Michelle, or anyone else who might be involved with Damien's leaving and not coming back.

My mother e-mailed from her home in Colorado. She had taken up hot yoga and thought it would do me a world of good. Mom did not explain the reasoning behind her claim. Maybe she just thought hot yoga would do *everybody* a world of good.

I had not received an e-mail from my father today, which wasn't terribly notable, but he had posted the cover of my latest Duffy novel to his Facebook page in anticipation of its release a mere four months from now. Dad likes to brag to his buddies on the Wiffle ball team (my father plays Wiffle ball competitively), and yes, he has a Facebook page. Probably a sign it's time to move on to the next social media phenomenon.

The rest of the incoming lot was unremarkable. Neither my agent nor my editor had gotten in touch, which didn't mean a thing at all during this stage in the creative process. They just let me write and wait until there's something to talk about. Writers are supposed to love autonomy. I wouldn't mind a little guidance, but then I wouldn't want anyone telling me what to write, either.

Writers are crazy, or hadn't you noticed?

The guy came with the Thai food, and I tipped him generously. I tip based on quality of service and in proportion to how hungry I am, so it's something of a wonder that I didn't insist he take my sofa home with him, too. I practically ran the bag into the kitchen, got a beer out of the fridge, and tucked in.

That, naturally, is when my phone rang.

Brian Coltrane is one of my closest friends and has been there for me on many an occasion when I have needed him. But now I was really hungry and trying to decide whether the pad thai was more important than whatever Brian had on his mind. On the other hand, he was one of my closest friends and had heard me chew before. I put the call on speaker so I could eat with both hands.

"Hey. What's up?"

"Are you eating?" Apparently, the loud slurping and the strained quality of my voice through noodles had tipped Brian off. He's an astute fellow.

"No. Why do you ask?" I leaned over a little so he could hear me chew more clearly.

"No idea. So how did the trip to Poughkeepsie with the lunatic go today?" I'd told Brian about the field trip with Duffy because I generally tell Brian everything and so the police would have somewhere to start looking if Duffy actually had turned out to be a homicidal maniac, which I didn't really believe would happen but have decided I should consider a possibility. The man thinks I created him and that he was in his late twenties when he was born. You can't be too careful.

If Brian was just calling to catch up on my adventures, I could call him back after inhaling the rest of my dinner, but then I looked down and saw there was very little left. Did I mention I was a bit peckish?

"We talked to some people, but I don't know if we have any real leads on where this guy might have gone or if he magically became Duffy Madison five years ago," I reported. "Did find out he was married, though, and he had a place in West New York."

"The whole thing is a wild-goose chase." Brian is, let's say, a bit skeptical about Duffy, but then he wasn't there when Duffy actually did save my life. The fact that Duffy had a hand in endangering my life in the first place wasn't something we discussed. "You should stay away from that guy, Rach."

"And here I was lamenting how I hadn't heard from my father today," I said, sucking up the last of my dinner, which I now understood had been underordered. I got up and rummaged in the freezer for some ice cream. It was that kind of evening. "Now my day is complete."

"Hey. I've met the man, and he seems perfectly reasonable, except that he's crazy," Brian said. "I worry about you."

"You get this way when you're between girlfriends," I reminded him. "You're actually not my big brother."

There was a smile in Brian's voice. How can you hear when someone's smiling? But you can. "I might not be between girlfriends anymore," he said.

The conversation drifted away from my problems, Duffy's psychosis, and Damien Mosley's disappearance in order to concentrate on the really important issue, this girl Brian had met at the supermarket the day before. He's not the kind of guy who trolls the produce aisle looking for women, but he is good-looking, and women do buy kale, so do the math.

"Her name's Julie, and she works for a software marketing firm in the city," he reported. Apparently, Julie was funny and smart and adorable, and by the time Brian was finished describing her, I practically wanted to adopt her. He has a tendency to start relationships wearing rose-colored glasses. It is not something I've never done, so I indulge his early delusions. Three months from now, Julie would no doubt be the daughter of Beelzebub, and I would be sweeping pieces of my friend off the kitchen floor. We all have our rituals.

I congratulated him on his good fortune and good taste, being careful not to overpraise the woman I'd never met for fear my words would be recalled verbatim when things went inevitably south. And just when I was getting back to my own travails—I think we were up to the issue of crumbling infrastructure—I heard the tone that indicates someone is trying to call you while you're on the line. I asked Brian to hang on and pushed the flash button.

I already knew the call was from Duffy and girded myself for having to explain again why I would not be assisting in his investigation. But he decided to forego pleasantries (not unusual for Duffy) and jumped right in.

"I believe Damien Mosley is dead," he said.

Chapter 10

The last person I had wanted to walk through my door arrived at about six thirty. Duffy came in and walked to my office, which is where he thinks we do our serious thinking. It is the most cramped and unkempt room in my house, and I normally don't let strangers in before verifying they've been properly vaccinated against communicable diseases.

"Okay, you had your dramatic moment," I said, sinking into my Captain Kirk–style office chair. If I could have pushed a button and asked Scotty for warp speed, I'd have done so, but alas, it was just a swivel chair with arms. "What makes you think Damien Mosley is dead, and more to the point, why is it any of my business now that I've told you I'm not involved in your investigation anymore?"

I know what you're thinking: I was going to be part of Duffy's search for Damien Mosley, and I knew it. Part of the hunt was my idea, more or less, to prove that Duffy wasn't Duffy before I started writing Duffy, that he had in fact read at least one of my books at some point and had, for whatever reasons of physical or psychological trauma, taken on the identity of my character. And it was in my best interest to prove just that by showing that before Damien vanished, Duffy might very well have been him.

Yes, I knew that. And my allowing Duffy to come to my house (after trying unsuccessfully to get Brian, who had a date with Julie, to come over to referee) was a sign that I was aware I'd be involved. But I was worn out from a day of grilling people about a guy who'd fallen off the edge of the earth five years before, and I was looking forward to writing a thousand words without actually knowing what they were going to be yet. I don't write well when I'm tired, and I was already not writing well before I was tired.

So I was being, perhaps, difficult.

And Duffy did look a little wounded after I'd suggested I wasn't going to be his partner-in-not-crime anymore. It made me feel a trifle guilty, but the whole tired thing was winning out at this point.

"I thought you would find this particular development intriguing enough to spark your interest in the case again," he said, trying to find an unoccupied spot on my ancient leather sofa and moving some papers out of the way. I probably should have thrown them out in 2011. "I made a few phone calls when I got home, and I am convinced that Damien Mosley died five years ago."

"Why? I know you, and you need facts to make a statement like that. You want me to ask, so I'm asking. What's the proof?"

"I was unable to find Damien's wife Michelle," he began, which didn't sound like proof at all. I decided—against my cranky nature—to let that go because I knew Duffy would keep talking anyway, and he did not disappoint. "I have still been unable to find any records of a marriage or even her maiden name. So she has not been of any help to this point.

"But"—and I'd known there would be a *but*—"I have tracked down some of the records on Damien's apartment in West New York, which are very interesting. The property was rented by a Dorothy Mosley in the late 1990s, and when the building went co-op, she bought the property and rented it as a profit source for ten years. Then apparently Mrs. Mosley moved into the apartment in 2002 and stayed there until exactly five years ago, when she supposedly willed it to her son."

"Supposedly?" I asked. "You have some reason to think she didn't?"

"There is no record of her dying, so she couldn't have willed it to him," Duffy answered. He shifted on the sofa a bit, trying to find a comfortable spot. But if one was not a stack of papers or an advance reader copy of one of my books, there was no refuge on that couch. "If they had an agreement about the ownership of the property, it was never filed formally, because there is no public record. The apartment is still legally in Dorothy's name, but as far as I can see, no one has lived there in at least two years. Not even as a vacation rental."

This didn't seem to be leading to proof that Damien was dead, but I know Duffy's methods, and he was building toward that, making his case airtight and convincing. I did not have to ask a question about that. I did wonder about the specifics, though, and besides, I was aware he was waiting for his cue.

"Who's making the payments?" I asked. "Even if the apartment was paid off years ago, there's still property tax and co-op fees, maintenance, that sort of thing. Someone has to be paying those bills, and you said you didn't have any trace of Dorothy Mosley alive or dead. So I'm guessing it's not her."

"You're right," Duffy said, pointing at me like a smart pupil. "What's interesting is that Dorothy apparently set up a trust five years ago, just a few weeks before Damien vanished, that pays all the fees and necessities for the West New York apartment. I don't know where her money came from, but there has been no problem keeping up with the bills there."

I sat back and let the chair tilt so I could look at the ceiling fan, which was not on at the moment. It's a way I think. "The timing is the really interesting part, isn't it? It seems like she knew she wouldn't be at the apartment and maybe that Damien or someone else would be, so she had to keep paying for it."

"Precisely." Duffy gave up the whole couch thing, probably acting on a request from his butt, and ran his hands through his hair. I gave him that mannerism because I wanted him to have a signature move and remind my readers, many of whom are female, that Duffy has very thick hair. You should see some of the letters I get. "That indicates intent. This isn't just a big coincidence, but there's more."

For the record, I had known there was going to be more. I'd just like that noted.

"Our friend Sgt. Dougherty was not actually working on the Poughkeepsie city police force five years ago," Duffy said. "He was then working for the town of Poughkeepsie, which is adjacent to the city but a separate municipality."

"I know," I said. "Who wouldn't want to name two things right next to each other Poughkeepsie?"

He ignored me, which was just as well because I was only trying to amuse myself at this point. I knew he'd start lecturing again, and he wasted no time at all.

"So the sergeant, through no fault of his own, has no personal recollection of the investigation, if there was one, into Damien Mosley's disappearance." Duffy let his head hang down, stretching the neck muscles and giving him the appearance of someone who found the floor absolutely astonishing. "I looked into the public records of what actually did occur, with a little help from Ben Preston's access into law enforcement sites." Ben, the investigator with whom Duffy worked in Bergen County, would no doubt have allowed the use of his passwords for an inquiry like this one, but it was just as likely that Duffy had not asked and merely knew Ben's passwords from previous use. It didn't matter.

"So was there some major mess-up in the way they looked for Damien?" I asked. I didn't actually say *mess-up*. I used another term. But I don't know you well enough to use that kind of language with you.

Duffy didn't seem to care. "No, but only because they didn't really look for him at all. They filled out the proper paperwork and authorized his landlord to sell his belongings in order to get back some of the money he was owed in rent after the police made a rather halfhearted attempt to locate Damien, calling his phone a few times. The necessary forms were delivered to his address, evicting him from the premises, and since he never showed up to contest the proceedings, everything went very smoothly."

I was getting even wearier. It had been a ridiculously long day, and I'd never gotten to eat my ice cream. It was time to give Duffy his moment and cut to the chase.

"So if the Poughkeepsie police didn't actually look for Damien, and there's no record that he lived in West New York, with or without a wife, what makes you think he's dead and not just working for an insurance company in Madison, Wisconsin?"

Duffy, clearly having been waiting to savor this moment, stopped and turned right toward me to make maximum eye contact. "Because he didn't vanish from Poughkeepsie. I think he vanished from West New York, and he did so because he died."

I was about to note that he hadn't actually answered my question, but Duffy didn't give me the chance. "At virtually the exact time Damien Mosley vanished, police in North Bergen, adjacent to West New York, were called about something seen at the bottom of a drop in James Braddock Park. The caller, who remained anonymous, couldn't reach whatever it was but thought it looked wrong. Police investigated and found the body of a man, roughly in his late twenties and of the right build and height to be Damien Mosley."

A man dead at the bottom of a hill. A park in New Jersey. Duffy Madison investigating the scene. It was too much. My stomach churned a little, and my voice was oddly dry when I looked at Duffy and tried to speak.

"Did . . ." I cleared my throat. "Did the man fall onto a fence post and get impaled?" I asked.

Duffy didn't turn his head, but his eyes looked around the room as if searching for the sane person he'd known was here a moment ago. "No," he said slowly. "He tripped on wet grass and hit his head on a rock after tumbling down a hill. Why?"

Okay, so I hadn't written about Damien Mosley's—or somebody's—death five years after it happened without having heard about it first. That is what in my world constitutes a "relief."

"Nothing," I answered, waving a hand to tell him to go on. "So I'm guessing you think the man in the park was Damien Mosley. What makes you think that?"

"As I said, the physical description fits," Duffy said, having shaken off my bizarre behavior. "And the timing fits. There are no fingerprints on record for Damien because he never had a job that required them and was never in the military. Dental records are inconclusive and haven't been checked anyway because the North Bergen police never heard of Damien Mosley before tonight. But there is one thing."

Wait. The North Bergen police had never heard of Damien *before tonight*? "You called the cops in North Bergen already?" I asked.

Duffy looked startled. "Of course. I believe I might have been able to help solve a case they've had open for five years. Why would I not call them?"

I swiveled back and forth in my chair, a nervous habit I developed at the age of four when I visited my father in his office. "Don't you see, Duffy?" I said. "You're making huge leaps of logic here because you *want* this dead guy to be Damien Mosley. You want to prove to me that he was never you, or you were never him, or something. So based on a few coincidences and your own prejudices, you called the North Bergen police tonight and told them your theory. What did they say?"

Duffy stood and stared at me. "I don't know where to begin," he said. "Rachel, you are making accusations that go against my entire method of operating, not just in my work but in life." He didn't seem offended so much as amazed I would say such things. How could I get such a wacky idea?

"What did the North Bergen cops say?" I repeated.

A squint, but no movement. "That they'll get to work immediately on getting the paperwork ready to exhume the body from the anonymous grave the John Doe was placed in five years ago," he said. "Sgt. Johnstone remembered the case and seemed quite excited that they might finally be able to put a name to the body."

That seemed really unlikely. "Just based on your word and a few coincidental details, they're going to authorize an exhumation? What are you leaving out that you haven't told me yet, Duffy?"

"I haven't gotten the chance to tell you everything," he countered. "You decided to attack my method."

"Okay, I've stopped. Now tell me what you've been holding back."

Duffy sighed, and his shoulders rose and fell with the effort, a theatrical flourish he added just to reiterate how wrong I had been about him. "A study of the photographs taken from the scene on the night the body was found indicate Damien Mosley's car was parked less than forty yards from the scene," he said.

Chapter 11

"An exhumation?" Ben Preston looked incredulous, as any sane person would. "You ordered an exhumation in North Bergen, Duffy? That's not even our county."

I'd insisted that we call Ben, the investigator to whom Duffy reports, to get him up to speed on the events of what was now officially the longest day I'd ever spent in my life. Duffy had argued that the case as he saw it was outside Ben's jurisdiction—which was undeniable—but I'd come back that Duffy was a consultant to Ben in the Bergen County Prosecutor's Office and that he should be informed whenever Duffy had any dealings with law enforcement.

But the truth was, I just needed another person who wasn't Duffy in the room.

It had taken about ten minutes to convince Duffy I was right—a rarity—and another half hour or so for Ben to make it to my house, which he had visited before. Ben and I went out on a date once, and that had proved to be the wrong thing for both of us. At least then. He was still attractive and kind of self-effacing, but at the moment I'd just called him to be Duffy's boss and my relief.

"I did not order an exhumation, Ben." We had moved to my living room because if two was a crowd in my office, three people would constitute the stateroom scene in the Marx Brothers' *A Night at the Opera*, and if you haven't seen that, you should. Duffy stood next to the coffee table, which I usually used as a footrest while watching TV, and Ben was sitting in the easy chair while I took up a position on the sofa, where it was quite possible I would fall asleep soon. "I requested that they consider asking for one because I believe I might have found the solution to an open case they have."

We'd gotten Ben current with the case of Damien Mosley without mentioning my interest in it, saying just that it had something to do with the book I was writing. Obviously, Ben knows Duffy shares his name with the character in my novels, and he has a vague idea that there's more to it, but we hadn't actually made clear exactly how closely Duffy thinks he's connected. I don't want him to lose his job, and I don't want Ben to think either of us is insane. Mostly me.

"So you saw this Mosley guy's car in a picture of the scene where a body was found," Ben said. He was talking mostly to himself. I considered asking if he wanted a glass of wine, but somehow that didn't seem strong enough fortification for the kind of conference we were having. Duffy doesn't drink. I'm not sure Duffy is human. See previous comments. "The guy slipped and fell on a rock, and that's just about the same time your friend Mosley went into the wind." Ben likes to talk like a cop. He's a county investigator who used to be a police officer, like many of them were at one time. He'd had to go on disability leave, and I think he still misses it, wonders what life would be like if he'd managed to stay healthy.

I made a mental note to consider writing a series about a county investigator haunted by his past as a police officer. The Duffy books can't last forever, which would be very bad news for the man who had called all of us together tonight.

"That's right, Ben," he said. "If you add up the timing and the proximity of the car—"

"You get a series of circumstances," Ben said, spreading his hands in a futile attempt to calm Duffy down. "Yeah, if you want to interpret it that way, you get the possibility that this body was Mosley. But an exhumation, especially when there's no family involved, is expensive and complicated. You know that, Duffy. What do you think the North Bergen cops will do?"

"They'll get in touch with the county," Duffy said. And then he turned toward me. "You know some people in the prosecutor's office here, don't you, Rachel?"

"Yes, but North Bergen is in Hudson County," I reminded him. It was odd that Duffy wouldn't know that, or remember it. "I don't know anybody there." I was just as happy because I had no desire to use up my contacts in the county prosecutor's office on something this flimsy, asking for an exhumation of a body when it hadn't even been suggested a crime had been committed.

"That's true," Duffy said, looking baffled. Duffy rarely looks baffled. Usually he's so sure of himself, you want to smack him, and he's almost always right. I wondered whether some memories of his past life, his real life, were seeping into his head, confusing him.

Ben watched the dynamic between the two of us. He defers to Duffy a lot of the time, but he actually is Duffy's boss. And Ben is not a bad investigator by any means. What he saw when he looked from Duffy's face to mine must have told him something, but I couldn't for the life of me imagine what, largely because I didn't know what we were communicating to each other myself.

"What will an exhumation accomplish?" he asked Duffy after a moment. "We don't have any DNA of Mosley that I know about. What are you going to match?"

"We can go to the apartment in West New York and find a sample of hair or something," Duffy suggested. "No one has lived there since that night. We might find a match."

He was really grasping at straws. "Duffy," I said. "You couldn't prove any DNA you found in the apartment was Damien's. I don't even understand why the North Bergen police didn't know who the man was on the night the body was found. There was no identification in his wallet?"

"There was no wallet," Duffy answered. "Either he didn't have it with him, or someone took it before the EMS arrived."

Ben's forehead crinkled, which I had found endearing for a brief period. Now it just meant something was bothering him. "I don't get it, Duffy," he said. "What is it about this case that's so fascinating to you? Nobody called you in; you're not working it. How did you get interested in this guy to begin with?"

I hadn't actually worked this out with Duffy ahead of time, but I knew he wouldn't just launch into the truth in this case.

"Rachel's assistant Paula found the man had the same initials as I do and that he disappeared at the same time I first came into your office and began working on cases," Duffy told Ben. "She believes that I might have somehow been Damien Mosley previously, and some trauma made me believe I am Duffy Madison."

Okay, so maybe I didn't know he wouldn't do that.

Ben's reaction was not what I would have expected. He nodded as if that was exactly what he'd been thinking all the time. "So this is about your using Duffy's name in your books," he said to me.

"No." I tried not to sound like a third-grade teacher who had already explained the concept of multiplication tables to her students five times. "I don't just use Duffy's name in my books. I created the character years before I knew anything about this man, and I believe that he somehow found out about the books and became the character for his own reasons, but he doesn't remember." Since we were all putting our cards on the table, I could go ahead and show them the two pairs I had in my hand.

Ben processed that, although I knew for a fact he'd at least sort of heard it before. Then he shook his head and looked at Duffy. "So you're chasing after this guy because you think he might have been you?" I didn't blame him for being overwhelmed by the concept—I'd been living with it for months, and it still caused me migraines—but Ben seemed almost like he was trying not to understand.

"No," Duffy answered, "I do not believe that I ever went by the name Damien Mosley. I am attempting to convince Rachel of the same so she can reach the same conclusion I have—that I actually am the person she created."

I'll give Ben Preston credit: He did not react as I had when Duffy first surfaced with his nutty theory. I had hung up and disconnected my phone, then practically had him thrown out of a book signing I was doing before I was forced to talk to the man by the county prosecutor. Instead, Ben let his eyes widen a bit (probably because he couldn't control them sufficiently) and let out his breath. He never broke eye contact with Duffy. Truly, it was an impressive act.

"You're the character Rachel created five years ago?" he said with an even tone, as if he were asking Duffy whether he'd gotten whole milk or two-percent when he went out to the convenience store. "But you're much older than that." Not necessarily the argument I would have led with, but certainly a valid one.

"I have no coherent memory before that time," Duffy said. "Since Rachel never wrote me as a child or a teenager, I believe this is the stage of life at which I began."

Ben looked at me, either wanting help or at least an anchor in the real world. Then he shook his head as if trying to get water out of his hair after a swim. "One thing at a time," he said. "Damien Mosley. You're trying to solve his disappearance why?"

I decided to jump in ahead of Duffy, whose explanation would no doubt have been so ethereal and incomprehensible that it would have sent Ben to bed for three days. "Because he wants to prove to me that he wasn't Damien Mosley." I turned toward Duffy. "You win," I said. "I believe you. Damien Mosley was an entirely different person. Okay? Can I go sleep now?"

Duffy looked at his watch. "It's eight thirty."

"Let's say I've had a long day. Do you accept my concession? I no longer believe you used to be Damien Mosley." And with the presence of a body and a car that had indeed been registered to a man with that name, my claim was almost true. "So let's stop looking for him. You can go back to working with Ben when he needs you, and I can go back to making up stuff for *my* Duffy Madison to do. How's that sound?"

Duffy looked oddly disappointed. I settled back into my sofa cushion, now determined to go to sleep whether these two guys left or not. I didn't close my eyes, but that was definitely in my short-term plans. Ben, undoubtedly wondering what planet he had accidentally been transported to, leaned forward in the armchair and squinted, probably trying to see Duffy more clearly because this version was about as blurry as you could get.

"I have the theory about Damien's case, and I believe it's necessary to see it through," Duffy answered. "I don't know if the North Bergen police or the Hudson County prosecutor will agree to an exhumation, but I do believe I can gain access to the original medical examiner's report. I imagine that will indicate that blunt force trauma was the cause of death."

"Will that end your investigation?" Ben asked. He could approach the issue from a professional viewpoint, and he had worked with Duffy—this Duffy—more than I had.

"Now that they know there might be a connection, it is possible the police will be able to make a positive identification," Duffy answered. "If that is done, my investigation will be complete."

"Good," I mumbled as I settled back more deeply. "Let me know how that works out." My words were just a little slurred, and I hadn't actually had more than the one beer.

Ben must have gotten the hint, especially now that my eyes were starting to close. Or the lights in the living room were dimming for no reason. Ben stood up. "I think I'll be moving on. Come on, Duffy. Rachel needs to sleep."

Then it occurred to me that Rachel needed something else entirely. I sat up, and I wasn't happy about it. "What Rachel really needs is to write a thousand words tonight," I said. "So give me a call when you know what's going on with Damien Mosley, okay?"

Duffy was persuaded to head for the door over his protestations that this consultation was helping him sort out his thoughts. But Ben, who knows how to handle the man, said they could go to the Adamstown Diner and talk some more. Ben was rising in my estimation.

Once they left, I dragged my weary butt into my office and faced the blank screen, the thing that most offends the eyes of a writer. I started by reading over the pages I'd written the day before, which is supposed to help me improve them and then gain momentum going into today's installment. This time I just wanted to put my head down on my keyboard and let *ddddddddddddddddddddddd* a thousand times be my contribution for the day.

Instead, I started plowing through. I won't tell you any more of the plot I was concocting because one of these days you'll be walking by it in a bookstore, but suffice it to say that there are days when the words just flow out of you, when you can't possibly put a finger wrong and every idea that comes to mind is absolutely fresh and brilliant.

This was not one of those days.

I'd been struggling with the pages for about an hour and a half and was getting somewhere in my word count but not much of anywhere in my story when my cell phone rang. Caller ID indicated it was Ben Preston on the other end of the satellite signal (I like to keep up to date; anyone can say "the other end of the line"), so I hit the accept button and said hello.

"What have you done to Duffy?" he demanded almost immediately. "The man is right on the edge of crazy."

"On the edge?" I asked. "He jumped over the edge a while ago, I'd say. What's especially crazy about him now?"

"Well, he thinks you made him up," Ben reminded me. That was right; it was news to him. "That ain't nothing."

I looked over that last paragraph. I'd used the word *control* three times. Two of them had to go, and a thesaurus is cheating. I groaned a bit but not loudly enough for Ben to hear. "Yeah, I wasn't going to mention that," I told him. "But Duffy wasn't going to lie about it. You know Duffy."

"I thought I did," Ben groused.

I substituted *manipulate* for one of the *control*s. That left one to replace. "Don't get peevish," I told Ben. "You should consider it a plus that Duffy didn't try to cover up his nuts-ness."

"To some extent I'd prefer it," Ben told me. "That would mean he knew it sounded crazy. But he seems to believe it's a logical, natural conclusion to reach, and he can't understand why we're not all on board with it."

"I thought after I told him that the Damien Mosley thing wouldn't make a difference, he'd lighten up," I said. "I won't push him on the whole creator idea anymore, and maybe he'll just settle into it."

"But then we'll never know who he really is," Ben pointed out.

Manipulate, control . . . *manage*! Now I was getting somewhere! But did *manage* sound too much like *manipulate*? Hard to say. If this guy wasn't insisting on having a conversation, it would be easier to concentrate.

"I don't know if it matters anymore," I said. "He's Duffy Madison now." And if I thought about him less, I could think about my own Duffy more. Selfish? Moi?

"Of course it matters. The man is working for the prosecutor's office. Now with this information in my lap, I should be talking to my boss right now and recommending we refrain from hiring our missing persons consultant because I have very good reason to think he might be suffering from a severe mental illness."

That was true. Duffy's revelation to Ben could mean he'd lose his means of employment. I honestly didn't know if that would cripple him financially based on the fact that it didn't seem to be bothering him now. But I knew for a fact that not working or having an outlet for his constantly striving mind would kill the man. He *needed* the work.

"You can't do that," I breathed all at once.

"I don't want to," Ben admitted. "But if it gets past me to the prosecutor or to my supervisor, Bill Petrosky, it wouldn't just be Duffy's job that would be in jeopardy."

I decided *manipulate* and *manage* were different enough and started thinking about what would come next. I had 224 more words to write today, something that would take less than fifteen minutes if I actually had an idea. The way I was feeling tonight, we could be talking about the sun coming up before I was finished. But the thousand words were not negotiable.

"Can you hold off for a little while?" I sort of begged. "Maybe if Duffy sees that this Damien Mosley thing all comes together, that the guy fell down and hit his head and he really never was Duffy, he'll just stop talking about it entirely, and everything can go back to what passes for normal."

Ben let out a long breath. "Rachel, you know how much I trust Duffy. You know I think he's the best I've ever seen at what he does. But if he really and truly believes he came to life because you started writing about a guy like him, I honestly don't know if I can work with him again."

"Well, you're not actually working with him now," I said. "You don't have a missing person case you need to consult on, right? That's what's making Duffy so crazy right now, that he's out of work. Until you get another case you'd call him in on, there's no reason to talk to your boss, right?"

Writers are contractors. We work for ourselves and then try to sell our work to someone who has—what do you call it— money. Duffy was essentially working under the same kind of arrangement for the prosecutor, in that he wasn't a salaried employee and only worked for a fee when a case on which he was needed arose. So technically there was no reason for Ben to talk to Petrosky about Duffy until the issue of hiring him was brought up. It wasn't much in the way of an argument, but it was all I had.

It took a while until Ben answered. "I guess not," he said, but he didn't sound like he believed himself.

"Good. Let's hope nobody is reported missing in Bergen County for a while."

It was early in the book, time to get fictional Duffy into more trouble as the plot progressed. That's the way it works— you give your character a problem and then continue to make it worse until it looks like things are just about impossible to fix. Then you come up with a way for the character to fix it.

Unless you're writing something depressing, which I'm told can be very lucrative.

"I always hope that," Ben said. He sounded tired, and I knew I was tired. "Rachel. Can I come talk to you tomorrow night, maybe? So we can maybe figure out this Duffy thing. About how you brought him to life with your word processor."

"I'll bet you use that line on all the girls," I said.

"Pretty much."

"Does it work for you?"

"Well, let's see. Dinner tomorrow? I'm buying."

So we were back to that, were we? Once again I was confused whether Ben was asking me out or wanted to discuss business with me. I'd have to ask Paula tomorrow. "Sure," I said. We decided he'd pick me up at seven.

I wrote the 224 more words, mostly dialogue, which meant that I could keep plot points coming and have a general feel for the characters even if Duffy was continuing to elude me. It took about a half hour, which is longer than it should, but I was so tired that I had already decided to sleep until Thursday, assuming I could remember which day of the week today might be.

I did not read today's writing over. For one thing, I was sure it was truly awful, and just as a matter of policy, I don't ever do that. I'd read them tomorrow if I could summon the courage.

Instead, realizing that I was exhausted but not as sleepy as I should have been, I searched my shelves for a paperback I could take to bed with me. I usually don't read other people's fiction when I'm writing because I'm paranoid about their voices or ideas creeping into my writing, but I didn't think I'd get through a whole page tonight before I was asleep, and I wouldn't remember a word of what I'd read the next morning.

But I couldn't find anything that piqued my interest at the moment. I'm a very picky reader, which is one of the reasons I started writing Duffy books, because they were the kind of books I wanted to read, and nobody else was writing them. Sometimes one has to take matters into one's hands.

Right now I couldn't find anything I felt like taking into my hands, so I spent about a half hour working against the problem I'd been grappling with all day. I'd concluded, with Duffy's help, that Damien Mosley was not the bridge to early Duffy Madison, so I'd have to find another way to solve the mystery of who this crazy man was before he'd showed up on the Bergen County prosecutor's doorstep five years ago to help out with cases of people who vanished.

In short, Duffy wasn't going to be any help in finding himself, so I'd have to find him on my own. And even saying that sounds weird to me now.

When living Duffy had first surfaced at my house, Paula had done her usual thorough job of research but had been unable to trace him back past Oberlin College and then an oblique reference with an unhelpful photograph—not unlike the one I'd seen today of Damien Mosley—in his high school yearbook. Assuming this Duffy was that Duffy. It's not impossible there could be a number in the United States alone.

But now that I knew a little more about Poughkeepsie, where I had arbitrarily written that Duffy had grown up and where that high school picture was taken, I could make a few more specific searches, get sleepy, and then leave notes for Paula to follow up on in the morning.

It was a plan. Sort of.

The high school records Paula had left me did not give a street address for Duffy or the names of his parents. He had been in only one student organization, the Classics Society, and the one member from his class Paula had located didn't remember him. That was odd; it was a very small group, and you'd think Duffy would stand out even among earnest Latin geeks.

Luckily, Paula had left me a pixel trail. Her search for Duffy in adolescence had gone through an online reunion-based website that scanned and displayed every page of the yearbook for each class in question. Paula had obtained a password, probably by posing as a member of Duffy's graduating class—these sites don't really care about security that much—and that gave me access to the yearbook.

Now I could search for all the members of the Classics Society and see if there were other references or surviving classmates Paula had not contacted. She's incredibly thorough, but maybe I could run some of the names of the missing past people I'd met in Poughkeepsie today and get a line on where their wandering classmates had wandered.

But as it turned out, I wouldn't have to do that. A quick glance through the yearbook found seven members of the

Classics Society, mostly through a photograph in the "clubs and associations" section that listed all the members in the picture and the one (Duffy Madison) who "was absent on Picture Day."

Big surprise.

The other six members included the woman Paula had spoken to on the phone and four classmates whose names I made sure to print out and store in a file. But the last one was the person I found most interesting, and I made sure to leave a note for Paula to follow up on the next morning, after letting herself in very quietly.

That member was Louise Mendenhaus, whom the photograph confirmed I knew better as Louise Refsnyder.

Armed with that information, I went to bed and slept like a log. Assuming logs sleep.

Chapter 12

"So this Louise looked your Duffy right in the face and didn't recognize him from high school?" Brian Coltrane looked up from his turkey club and French fries with a wry grin on his face, which is Brian's default expression. But I love him like a brother anyway.

"She didn't react except to say that Duffy looked something like Damien Mosley," I said. "But she said he wasn't a dead ringer for Damien, and we're pretty sure Damien ended up in a ditch with a great big bump on his head, so I don't know what to make of it."

I had gone to the Plaza Diner for my semiweekly (that's the one that means twice a week, right?) lunch with Brian and had brought my best intentions to order a salad with me.

So I sat there with a grilled cheese on rye and stole a fry from Brian's plate, knowing full well he'd do the same with my onion rings. Don't judge unless you have the willpower of a demigod.

"Best thing to do is confront Duffy with the picture," Brian said. "Place it right in front of him and get him to explain it."

"That's the thing—he *won't* explain it," I argued. "Any-time I've tried something like that on him, he just shrugs and tells me he has no idea what it all means. He is just what he is, and I'm supposed to take it on face value." I was stealing a larger percentage of fries to Brian's theft of onion rings, but onion rings are larger and therefore count more—you should pardon the expression—heavily.

"So what are you going to do?" Brian thinks he's clever and that he can manipulate me into thinking of a solution on my own. I had beaten him to the punch by coming up with a plan before I'd left my house, but that sort of played into his strategy, and . . . what was I talking about?

"I'm already doing it," I said triumphantly, when I probably should have been less smug. "I've got Paula on the case."

Brian snagged a ring and dropped his eyebrows down a little. "You've done that before," he reminded me, possibly thinking I had fallen into the same amnesia pit from which Duffy had first emerged. "Paula looked for Duffy and came up with Damien Mosley."

"That much is true, inspector," I said, for once paying attention to my own food. "But now she's armed with more information—namely, that Louise Refsnyder, or Menden-haus, or something, was lying when she pretended not to know Duffy. That gives us something to work with. She also didn't know that Louise has a different last name these days than she did in high school." You can get your grilled cheese any way you like, but for me, it's not worth it if it's not on real rye bread. Or a bagel. Bagels are good, too.

"Amazing, Holmes!" Brian was nothing if not quick on the uptake. "So what has she come up with so far?"

"Nothing, but it's only been a couple of hours. Give the woman time."

Brian put down the quarter of the sandwich he was eating, apparently to show his concern for me. "So how's the writing going?"

Let me be clear: Writers love to discuss their work. Indeed, we'd rather talk about things we've written than write something new, and it's not even a close competition. But when people who aren't close friends ask, "How's the writing going?" or "How's the book doing?" (I still don't have an answer for that one—how's the book doing *what*?) or my personal favorite at cocktail parties (which I never attend), "So, still writing?" the effect is more condescending than interested. Still writing? No, I've decided to give it up and go into animal husbandry. So, are you still a neurosurgeon?

But when Brian, who knows me well despite never having read any of my books at all (his tastes run to news websites and graphic novels), asks how my writing is going, it's because he knows that lately it hasn't been going well at all. He knows that because I've told him. So I don't take it as an insult.

"Okay," I said. "So tell me about Julie."

"Don't try to dodge the question," Brian said, taking two onion rings just to prove his point. "Has spending the time with Duffy cured you of your character problem?"

I'd thought character problems were what happened when a political candidate was found in a hotel with someone other than the person they were supposed to be in a hotel with, but that would have been yet another dodge, and Brian would know it. "Not really," I said. "I think it might be making it worse. I keep wondering if real Duffy would do what I'm making fictional Duffy do. I'm worried that if I write something bad that happens to Duffy, something bad will happen to Duffy. I'm stuck because I'm getting to be just as crazy as he is, Brian."

You would think that such an emotional self-discovery would obliterate one's appetite for French fries. You would be wrong.

"You're not crazy," my friend assured me. "You're letting his crazy influence you. And you have two choices: You can dig in and really find out where this guy came from, or you can decide it doesn't matter and move on with your work."

That was clear, it was concise, and it was true. I took a fry and bit it in half. Ketchup just confuses the issue.

"If that's the way you're going to be, I don't see any point in discussing this with you," I said.

Brian smiled. "I got through. Good. Now let me tell you about Julie." He did, at length, and I even got a second soda despite the Plaza's inability to make a decent diet cola.

*   *   *

"Louise Mendenhaus got married three years ago to a guy named Jared Refsnyder," Paula told me even before I could take off my jacket. I had just gotten back from the Plaza, and my assistant was bursting with the work she'd been doing while I was gone. "They were divorced less than six months later."

"Sort of makes you wonder why they bothered with the wedding in the first place," I said as I settled into my work chair.

"Because Louise was pregnant," Paula said without a beat. "She lost the baby less than a month after the wedding, and it appears there didn't seem to be a point to staying together after that."

I sincerely hoped there was never anything personal I felt the need to hide from Paula. "How do you find out all this stuff?" I asked her.

"You'd be amazed what people feel obligated to share on Facebook," she said.

"Yes, I would. I assume you have more." I gestured for her to continue, like she was going to need encouragement. If Paula wasn't a great assistant, she would have a bright future as a gossip. The money would be about the same.

Paula didn't even acknowledge my compliment; of course she had more to tell me. She was Paula. "The thing is, Jared was not from Poughkeepsie. He was a guy Louise knew from her waiting tables at the bar, and he came in twice a week because he was a short-haul truck driver running a route from Albany to Atlantic City. They hit it off, so to speak, when Jared was en route one summer and then got married just long enough to get divorced by the end of the year."

"What does that tell us about Duffy?" I asked.

"Virtually nothing," Paula said. "But I thought it was interesting."

In a general way she was right, but I was sort of goal-oriented at the moment. "Our project is to find out where our living Duffy came from," I reminded Paula. "What does Louise's brief marriage have to do with that?"

"Not that much, but Louise is probably important," Paula said in an attempt to rebound. "She was in that club with Duffy, which we can confirm through the yearbook, but she doesn't recognize present-day Duffy, who can't look *that* different. So I looked into how many boyfriends Louise might have had in high school."

"Okay, now you *are* scaring me."

"Follow me on this," Paula said, pulling the pencil from behind her ear and using it to gesture for emphasis. "Louise Mendenhaus wasn't the most popular girl in school. She wasn't voted most likely to do anything in particular. She was in two clubs: the Classics Society and the Honor Society. She was, for lack of a better term, a nerd."

That didn't jibe with the Louise I'd met the day before. "Where did she go to college?" I asked. There is never the possibility that Paula won't know, so it's not rude to assume she will. It's very convenient.

As I expected, Paula did not find it necessary to refer to the notepad in her hand. "That's the interesting part," she said. "Louise didn't go to college."

"We can assume her grades were good because she was in the Honor Society. There's no reason to think she had to work to keep her family in food and shelter, is there?"

Paula shook her head. "No. They're not wealthy, but her mom was a bank teller until two years ago, and her father worked for IBM nearby, not as an executive exactly but selling computer parts to hardware manufacturers. They were doing okay, and they could have at least helped with college if she'd wanted to go. I don't have hard data on it yet, but it doesn't even appear she applied to schools. She took the SATs, according to the Educational Testing Service in Princeton, and while they wouldn't give me her scores, they were willing to say they had no record of her giving access to those scores to any college anywhere, ever."

That didn't add up. "Why does a girl who worked hard enough to get good grades give up the chance to go to college and go to work waiting tables at a strip club?" I asked myself.

Luckily, Paula didn't know I wasn't exactly talking to her, so she answered me. "It's a good question. But that brings me back to how many boyfriends she might have had."

My expression must have been one of bafflement, and I added to it by saying, "Of course it does."

Paula never sits in my office. For one thing, as I've noted, there is no logical place other than my chair to do so. That is semi-intentional in that when I'm writing, I don't want to have extended conversations with anyone (mostly Paula, because usually there's nobody else around). But lately I've noticed I was having a number of long talks in this room and was starting to feel guilty about sitting when she was standing. Paula did not know that and probably wouldn't have cared. She didn't pace like Duffy does. She tends to lean on the doorjamb from the hallway into my office, and that's what she was doing now after having stood in the center of the room for a while. It gives her that casual look as if she's brainstorming when in fact she already knows everything there is to know in the universe. I'm on to her game.

"Think about it," she said, as if I hadn't been doing so. "Duffy is in the Classics Society, which we know from the yearbook and from one other member, although she didn't exactly remember him. Louise is in the Classics Society, and she looks straight into Duffy's face years later and comments only that he resembles Damien Mosley."

"We're back to the idea that Duffy is Damien Mosley?" I was in way over my head and forgetting how to swim.

"Not at all. We can be pretty sure Damien is dead because Duffy is never wrong about stuff like that." That was true. Paula actually has read all my books and knows Duffy in some ways better than I do because she keeps the Duffy Bible. "But let's just take a minute to consider: If you knew someone casually in high school, even just a little bit, you'd probably recognize him even after fifteen years, right? Maybe you wouldn't be able to remember his name off the top of your head, but if someone mentioned it to you, there's no way you'd blank on it entirely."

"So you're saying Duffy and Louise *didn't* go to high school together." Now I was forgetting how to dog paddle, and there wasn't much time left for me. It made me sad. To drown so young.

"No, I'm saying this: Under what circumstances would you flat out lie to someone about a guy you knew in high school? What would make you insist you'd never even heard of him?"

I thought about that, and with everything Paula had said, it hit me right between the eyes. "If he was some guy I dated in high school and I was embarrassed that he dumped me."

"Bingo," she said.

Chapter 13

Paula's reasoning was logical, but her evidence would have needed an airline ticket to get within driving distance of circumstantial. We both knew that, but we also figured we knew Louise's motivations.

That didn't get us anywhere until we could prove something.

We brainstormed for about an hour. I actually walked into Paula's office so she could sit down. I could, too, because Paula has an extra chair in her office that is not covered in papers and assorted detritus. Paula is annoyingly organized, but I try not to hold it against her because it is on my behalf.

What we (mostly Paula) came up with was this: She would dig into Louise Refsnyder's (née Mendenhaus) background some more, specifically to see if she could locate the ex-husband who probably didn't know her that well, just to cover our bases. Paula would also see if anyone else named "Madison" had graduated from Poughkeepsie high school for ten years before or after Duffy did, on the off chance that he'd had a sibling or a cousin we hadn't considered before.

I knew he wouldn't. I wrote Duffy as an only child. His parents were currently living in Oslo, Norway, for reasons I can't actually remember other than it kept them out of a particular story where their proximity would have been a problem for me. I told Paula to check into that possibility. Who knew? The idea that Duffy Madison would have rung my doorbell the night before would have seemed absurd a year ago. Now I barely flinched when I saw his name on my caller ID.

My role in our reconstituted efforts to track down the "real" Duffy Madison would be somewhat more focused and a little uncomfortable on my part.

First, I called my buddy Walt Kendig in Poughkeepsie. This was going to be a recurring theme now that we had some new information on both Louise Refsnyder and Damien Mosley.

Walt, of course, sounded thrilled to be hearing from me. The idea that people think authors are celebrities is a source of both ego boost and astonishment for me. I love people who write; some of my best friends really and truly are authors. But I know the job, and I know the routine. The idea that anybody would think what I do is in the least glamorous borders on hilarious.

I told Walt I had some news about Damien because I thought that was the easier way into the conversation. Just asking whether Louise had dated Duffy in high school would have been counterproductive: Walt said he had not socialized with any of the members of his bowling team before he'd been recruited by the bartender at Rapscallion's, a guy named Barry, who he said later bought the business before leaving town a few years after that.

After I'd explained Duffy's discovery, there was a long pause allowing Walt to absorb the information that his friend was probably dead.

"So he fell down on a rock, huh?" Walt said. "Tough break." Some people absorb things faster than others; Walt absorbed as quickly as SpongeBob SquarePants.

"Yeah," I said. I was apparently having a harder time with the news than Walt, and I'd never actually met Damien Mosley.

"So I guess that closes the case, huh?" Walt sounded a little disappointed. He was losing his connection to the amazing people he'd met only the day before.

Might as well give him a ray of hope. "If the investigator was anybody except Duffy Madison," I said. "He's going to work this until there's absolutely no shred of doubt that the guy at the bottom of the hill was Damien and that he definitely died because he fell and suffered the trauma to his head." Crime fiction writers know not to say, "hit his head on a rock." We are way more precise than that.

"Well, is there anything else I can do to help?" Walt asked. I had a sudden urge to scratch him behind the ears and tell him he was a good boy, but technology has not yet devised ear-scratching phone technology. There's your ticket to millions, app developers. You're welcome.

"I did want to ask you about Louise Refsnyder," I said, as if there were some connection between my inquiry and Damien's death, which there wasn't. "Did she ever discuss her old boyfriends with you?" I purposely didn't say anything more than that because I figured Walt was the kind of guy who wouldn't ask why I'd brought up the subject. I let him make connections in his own head because there weren't any in the real world.

He must have come up with an interesting train of thought. "You mean her ex-husband?" he asked. "I don't think they were together very long."

Before he could ask the dreaded "why" question, I jumped in as I heard the doorbell ring. Paula got up from her desk to investigate. "No, I meant further back. High school. Did she mention a high school boyfriend?"

I could practically hear Walt thinking. What I did hear was my front door open and the muffled sound of voices in my front hallway. "I don't remember anything about a high school boyfriend," Walt said. "Sorry."

Before I could ask another question, Paula ushered Duffy into my office and, standing behind him, shrugged her shoulders to indicate she hadn't been able to dissuade him from coming in. I nodded my acceptance, and Paula retreated to her own lair.

"Don't worry about it," I told Walt. "If you think of anything else, please get back to me, okay?" I purposely didn't use Walt's name to avoid making Duffy suspicious.

I hung up, and Duffy looked at me.

"Damien Mosley was murdered," he said.

Chapter 14

There are few things Duffy Madison enjoys as much as a dramatic pronouncement. He likes to shake things up, and he is an emotional guy, so when he comes across a fact that he believes leads to a "eureka" moment, he tends to play it up to the hilt.

Of course, I had a few reasons for writing Duffy that way. For one, I didn't want him to perfectly fit the calculating, almost stoic Sherlock Holmes model; Duffy was going to care desperately about the people he was trying to help. For another, a writer is pretty much always looking for a nice jolting end of a chapter, a way to bring one small piece of the story to a conclusion while enticing the reader to continue turning pages. Losing the reader's interest is the worst thing an author can do.

So when Duffy dropped his "murder" bomb in my lap, I had time to consider my reaction because I more or less expected him to be didactic and a touch melodramatic. He had shown up unannounced and had not waited, as he normally would have, outside my office door for permission to enter.

Also, he hadn't asked me about the phone call I was ending, one I would bet cash money he knew was about him.

These were all signs Duffy was going to try for a rise out of me. The real question was whether I should give it to him. I decided against.

"What makes you think so?" I asked.

I'm fairly sure I heard Paula chuckle just a bit from her office across the hall, but Duffy did not react to the sound. He was still trying to get a bigger reaction out of me. I've found since this version of Duffy emerged from nowhere that it's productive not to feed his ego all the time because it forces him to try to impress you even more.

"Ah!" Duffy held a finger up in the air. He seemed positively invigorated by the possibility of a murder investigation. It's the Holmes thing again; every crime fiction writer in the world is influenced one way or another. "The North Bergen police were kind enough to supply me with the original photographs taken at the scene of Damien Mosley's death, and I have observed some details they did not take into account originally."

("Observed" isn't blatantly British, but it is very Sherlock. He'll often admonish his best friend, "You see, Watson, but you do not *observe*." You have to wonder why anybody wants to hang around with this guy.)

I knew that Duffy wanted me to ask about the pictures, which I was certain he had on his person somewhere. I didn't want to torture the poor man, but I did want to make a point that I thought needed reiterating.

"Duffy, you remember I told you I was no longer on this case with you, right?" I said. "I'm not an investigator or a cop, and all I want to do right now is figure out how to write my next book. I don't understand why you came here with this lead. Why not go to Ben or someone in North Bergen?"

Duffy's eyes flashed just for a moment with absolute astonishment. How could *anyone* pass up the opportunity to investigate a juicy murder with him? Why wasn't I as engaged in Damien Mosley's supposed murder—although if Duffy said it was a murder, I had little doubt that's what it was—as he was? Duffy hasn't had much experience with women that I know about (although it would be worth looking into the idea of him having dated Louise Refsnyder), so sometimes he really does find me baffling.

"Ben is a fine investigator, but he has no jurisdiction in North Bergen," Duffy stammered for a moment.

"Neither do I."

Duffy regained his composure. "The North Bergen police have been informed, and Detective Lowenstein is considering his options, including the possibility of exhuming Damien's body for a more detailed examination."

Okay, I'd tortured him long enough. "Why don't you think the ME did a thorough job the first time?" I asked. "What did you see in those photographs?"

Yes, I knew what I was in for: Duffy reached into his jacket pocket and pulled out an envelope. Lucky me, I was going to have a guided tour of the scene where a man who might have been Damien Mosley died, possibly having been murdered. Then I could go back to my own story about a guy being impaled on a fence after falling off his bicycle.

Crime fiction writers live rich, full lives. They just mostly take place in our heads.

Duffy looked for a flat surface on which to spread out what I was sure would be somewhat gruesome prints of digital photographs. But we were in my office, which meant there was no such open space to be found.

"Perhaps we should move to the dining room table," he suggested.

I followed him into my dining room, musing as I do periodically on the wisdom of allowing a crazy person into my home often enough that he could lead the way from one room to another. But I walked on behind and waited while Duffy painstakingly arranged the pictures on my dining room table, where I do occasionally eat actual food. I couldn't wait to see photographs of a guy with his head bashed in on that surface.

Duffy had laid out the photos as they were numbered on the back by whoever had filed them away in North Bergen. I wasn't sure there was any rhyme or reason to the numbering, but Duffy clearly was, and I figured he worked more often in this sort of area than I did. He pointed at the first—top left, with twelve pictures arranged in four rows of three each—image.

"This one shows the area from which Damien fell," he said.

I was pleased to note there was no body visible in the picture, although my peripheral vision had noticed more than one shot with a man facedown in the mud to come later in this gruesome collage. So I worked to maintain my focus on the picture Duffy was indicating.

It looked to me like a fairly low-angle shot of a dirt road with grass to the right side and a hill, or the top of a hill, directly ahead. There were footprints on the dirt going in pretty much every direction and yellow police crime scene tape wrapped on a few trees around the site, isolating it from the rest of the park.

"So, land. Right?" I said.

Duffy, now accustomed to my enthusiastic approach to crime busting, did not miss a beat. He pointed at a spot, shiny and white, on the photograph. It looked to me like maybe a tooth in the grass, and I definitely did not want to see that. Not that I have anything against teeth per se, but I didn't want to think about the implications of finding one in this particular spot under these circumstances.

"This is the significant area," Duffy said. As if the pointing hadn't made that clear. But he didn't go on.

"Why?" I asked. I realized questions were simply enablers for a born lecturer like Duffy, but now he'd actually gotten me thinking about the scene. I hadn't noticed anything all that significant.

"Do you know what that white object is?" he said. Duffy has an annoying habit (I know, you're amazed) of answering questions with questions so he can feel he's actually teaching me how to solve crimes. I don't want to know how to solve crimes. I want to know how to write my way through a slump.

"It looks like a tooth," I answered.

"It's not," he said. That was probably a relief. "The photograph is not especially clear in that area. What you're seeing is actually smoothed grass, a spot where a shoe slipped and skidded, just a little bit."

I was glad it wasn't a tooth, but I didn't see how that was going to be significant. "We already knew Damien fell down the hill here," I reminded Duffy. "So he slipped and then he fell. How does that make it murder? You don't even know if it's Damien's shoe that matted down the grass there. Anybody's foot could have done that, even one of the crime scene investigators."

Duffy smiled. I'd given him the exact response he'd wanted, which meant that I was definitely wrong. He loves showing people where they made mistakes so he can correct them. Why had I made up this character? Well, largely because it never occurred to me we'd actually meet. It was becoming clear I'd been very shortsighted in that regard.

"It's true that other people had walked through this area before the crime scene tape was put up," Duffy said. "There was the young jogger who made the nine-one-one call and the uniformed police officers who had responded. But that skid wasn't made by Damien Mosley's shoe because Damien, as you'll see in subsequent photographs, wasn't wearing shoes."

Huh? "Who goes out for a walk in the park at night barefoot?" I asked. It was really thinking out loud, but Duffy believes every question ever asked is directed specifically at him, so he answered. If I was being honest, I'd expected nothing else.

"That is a good question," Duffy said, "but the theory is borne out in this picture here." He indicated the one immediately to the first photo's right, a close-up of some mud nearer the edge where Damien—or somebody—had dropped to his death. "See this footprint? It's very deep, as if the man standing there was trying very hard to hold his position. But it is also clearly that of a barefoot man; at least three toes are distinctly indicated."

That was true. Assuming Damien was the person who died here, he had definitely not been wearing shoes when standing on that precipice. "Were there any shoes found nearby?" I asked.

"Very good, Rachel!" Duffy gushed. "Yes. A pair of New Balance running shoes was found seventy-eight yards south of the edge we're looking at now, and the size of those shoes is a match for the footprints found here. The owner of those shoes, which had athletic socks stuffed into their toes, was the man who fell to his death here. Damien Mosley."

I chose not to argue the point with him at that moment, but we still did not have a positive identification of the man who died that night. Duffy wanted it to be Damien for his own reasons, which might have been clouding his judgment. When there were facts, I'd make my case if necessary. (Hey. Duffy's character didn't come from nowhere.)

"Why do you think he took off his shoes?" I asked. Duffy had a theory for everything.

"My best guess is that whoever killed him forced him to do so. We don't have photographs from the area where the shoes were found, but there are small dots of blood here and there on the path, see, like here and here. Very small, but indicative that Damien had cuts on his feet from the rough surface. He did not decide to walk this way without shoes; someone was directing him. But that is just a guess."

"I'm still not getting murder from this, Duffy," I said. "A guy takes off his shoes, walks around in a park, falls down, and hits hit head. It's odd, I'll grant you, but so far I'm not seeing how it's criminal."

Duffy pointed to the third photograph. "This is where it gets interesting," he said. I didn't see how; it was a picture of the same scene from a medium distance. All I saw were trees and dirt and grass and the trunk of one police cruiser on the right side. But I knew better than to comment on how truly fascinating the picture was, because Duffy certainly wanted me to so he could show off the crucial detail I had missed. It's kind of a really sick parlor game.

Not wishing to be embarrassed, I studied the photograph more closely. I remembered that the photographer was not Duffy, so the angle of the shot might not be relevant to what it was I should be noticing. The lens had been aimed mostly at the ground leading up to the fall, but not so closely that you expected to see the photographer's shoes. He or she had shot the picture almost straight from eye level, so the dirt and grass were there but so was a hint of the sky (fairly dark) and the trees in the wooded area to the left of the drop. I wondered if a magnifying glass would have revealed something especially significant, but I didn't have one except as an app on my phone. But I didn't activate it because my phone was back in my office, and I didn't want to make a show of it.

Besides, I was pretty sure I wasn't going to see what Duffy had seen anyway.

I was just about to throw my hands up and concede defeat when it occurred to me to examine the police car that took up only a small fraction of the frame. Could Duffy think a cop was involved in Damien's death? But all that appeared on the picture was a standard white car trunk, license plate not visible. I couldn't see the back window, and the bumper, not surprisingly, was free of stickers. It was a cop car, no frills.

"I give up," I sighed. "I don't see anything that points to a murder. The only interesting thing in the whole picture is that one tree branch." I pointed to a tree in the background of the photograph. "It's bent funny."

Duffy did not respond with the derisive laughter I had expected in my low-esteem-afflicted writer's mind. Instead, he beamed at me and nodded his head approvingly. "Very good indeed," he said. "That is the significant feature."

"It is?" He'd caught me by surprise.

"Of course. Your eye was drawn to the branch. Otherwise this is a pretty standard crime scene photograph without any noticeable abnormalities. Look at the way that branch has broken. What do you think could have caused that?"

Still reeling from being correct, I leaned over to look closely at the photograph again. "A really fat bird?" I asked.

Duffy clicked his tongue. "Think, Rachel. Look at the other trees and even the other branches on that tree. None of them appears in any way abnormal. Some of the branches are thinner and would have been weaker than the one in question, so we can rule out damage from a storm or any phenomenon that would have affected them all equally. So what can we surmise from that?"

My mind was focused on the idea that I'd never use the word *surmise* for anyone but Duffy in dialogue, so I wasn't going to have a satisfactory answer for him. "Don't try to teach me, Duffy. Just tell me what I'm looking at."

"It's the angle and the kind of damage done." Duffy was still leading me to an answer instead of just giving it to me. He would have made a really annoying college professor, but his students might have had a chance to learn something. "What does that kind of damage to a healthy branch?"

Okay, in order to make this scene end in time for the following Thanksgiving, I would have to think harder. This was about Duffy's claim that Damien Mosley (or whoever was at the bottom of the ditch) had been murdered. It wasn't about trees or their nature, of which I knew nothing. If I were writing this scene and wanted to prove a murder had been committed, what would I use to break a tree branch in a crime scene photograph?

"A bullet?" I said.

For a moment, I thought Duffy might actually kiss me on the cheek, but he managed to suppress the impulse. He did clap his hands and point at me. "Exactly," he said. "There would be no point in going to check the scene again now because it has been years, but the photograph indicates that someone shot from a low angle toward a high angle, as if trying to hit someone's head from a supine position, missed his target, and instead hit a tree branch quite a distance away."

That sounded like an enormous leap of logic to me, but Duffy is always right about this stuff, and besides, I had clearly guessed correctly, so it was really my victory. "So you think someone tried to shoot Damien, missed, and then instead of taking another shot, he pushed the guy over a cliff?"

"That is one possibility. Another is that a second bullet actually lodged in Damien's skull, and because of the extensive damage done by the rock on which he landed, the medical examiner did not think to look or did not find a remnant if the bullet passed through. It seemed obvious enough that Damien had fallen and hit his head. There was no reason to search for another cause of death."

It sounded so logical when he said it. If I had written something that preposterous or suggested a county ME was that incompetent, my editor would be all over me with notes about implausibility, and Sol would be right. As Joseph Mankiewicz, the writer and director of *All About Eve*, once said, "The difference between life and the movies is that a script has to make sense, and life doesn't."

"So what do you think you should do about it?" I said. "Do you think the North Bergen cops will push for an exhumation based on that picture?" He hadn't mentioned any of the others, and I didn't want to look at them.

"I'm not sure," Duffy admitted. "What I see as clear evidence, they might view as speculation. I'd like to gather more information." That sounded vaguely ominous.

"I'm not going to the scene of the crime so you can try to dig five-year-old bullets out of a tree, Duffy. I have fictional things to make up for you to do." Might as well embrace the crazy.

He spread his hands to deflect any misunderstanding. "I have no intention of asking you to do that."

"Good." But I knew something else was coming. It was in his tone.

"What I would ask is that you join me in a visit to Damien Mosley's apartment in West New York," Duffy said.

I shook my head reflexively. "No, not this time. Whatever you think you can find in an apartment that nobody's lived in for years is your problem, Duffy. I have to write a thousand words today, and that means I have to get my head in the game. I don't have time to traipse out to West New York with you. I wouldn't be any help, anyway."

"I disagree. You have a good eye for abnormality that can be quite useful."

I didn't point out that I felt my eye for abnormality was the quality that helped me create Duffy Madison. That would have been cruel, if accurate. I had been looking for a character who was not like everybody else, and Duffy was clearly that.

"You know what you're looking for," I encouraged him. "You brought that picture of the bent tree branch. I never would have thought to look at that if you hadn't led me to it. Trust your talents, Duffy."

He stood up and started gathering the photographs from my dining room table. "Of course," he said quietly. "I understand. You are a busy woman, and you have obligations." He slid the pictures back into the envelope and sealed it. "It's just that I am used to working with a partner, and Ben is not able to fill that role for me on this case. It feels a little odd, that's all. Sorry to trouble you."

If you think fictional characters can't successfully employ passive aggression, you won't ever understand why I found myself in Duffy's car heading to West New York. But I made him promise I would be back by five. I needed to write the thousand words and be ready to go by seven.

I had a date.

Chapter 15

"This building was extensively renovated as the area became more valuable in the real estate market," Duffy explained. "It is an eighty-year-old structure, but you would never know that now."

What he said was true: The six-story apartment building where Damien Mosley had apparently never actually lived had been given an extensive makeover, which was not terribly surprising. The Hudson River banks on the New Jersey side, now known in local real estate jargon as "The Gold Coast," offered views of the Manhattan skyline that people in Manhattan couldn't get, so those willing to defile themselves to the point of living in the Garden State were happy to pay the outrageous prices for up-and-coming areas like this one, which was just starting to gentrify.

It was a lovely building now, true to its heritage but clean and inviting. The brick was old but had clearly been very recently steamed to bring out its color. The windows were gleaming in the afternoon sun. The doorman at the front entrance looked at us with an air of consternation. No doubt we were ruining the ambience.

Duffy walked up to him. "I am a consultant investigator for the county prosecutor's office," he said. It was true, but not in this county. I assumed Duffy saw no need to include that piece of information. "My associate and I would appreciate it if you would allow us entrance to an apartment in this building where we believe a crime has been committed."

The doorman was wearing a long coat, thankfully not wool, and a matching hat that were supposed to make him seem almost regal, or at least verging on butler-quality servant. Instead, he looked mostly like the guy on the label of Beefeater Gin, and his accent was pure Bayonne.

"You got ID?" he asked. "Anybody could walk up here and say they're investigating for the county. Let's see a badge."

That was a problem since Duffy was a consultant and not an officer of the county, especially not this one. "Consultants are not given badges, but I have a business card," Duffy said, reaching into his pocket for his wallet.

The doorman held up a hand. "Don't bother. You can get business cards from VistaPrint for free. Doesn't mean anything." He was a very good doorman, I thought. If I lived in this building, I'd give him an excellent tip at Christmas time. And if I lived in this building, I could probably afford it.

"I can give you the name of a contact at the prosecutor's office to vouch for my credentials," Duffy said, still pulling out his wallet. He extracted a business card from his wallet.

And handed it to the man wrapped in a twenty-dollar bill.

There was no acknowledgment of the bribe from the doorman at all. He shoved it into his coat pocket before a resident of the building could come out and see him compromising her security for the price of a light dinner at TGI Friday's. "That won't be necessary, sir," he said with a sudden change in inflection. "Which apartment is in question?"

My hypothetical tip declined by half.

"Apartment Four-D," Duffy said. "Leased to Mrs. Dorothy Mosley."

The doorman's eyes registered quick surprise. "Oh, that one," he said. "Nobody's lived there for years." He opened the front door for us. "Third door on the right out of the elevator."

We had almost passed him in the doorway when I swear I heard him mumble to himself, "Could have gotten into that one for ten bucks."

Duffy Madison stifled a laugh.

We didn't talk while riding the elevator—and thank goodness this old structure had one, because they weren't necessarily mandatory by law in those days—but with the key the doorman had given us, we got into the apartment without any trouble at all.

The unit itself had probably been upgraded when the building went co-op, so the walls were clean and straight. They had been painted probably in the past few years but not in the past six months.

For a place that hadn't been occupied for years, it was not as dusty and depressing as one (me) might think. Dorothy must have had an agreement with someone to come in and clean periodically, or it would have been obvious, and it wasn't.

But one glance around the place told you there had been no occupant for a while, definitely. Everything was left in place. There were no dishes in the sink or in a drainer next to the sink. There was no newspaper open to the crossword puzzle. There were no cords for chargers plugged into the outlets, waiting for a smartphone that would undoubtedly come home dead as a doornail.

That struck me. "Did anybody ever find Damien's cell phone?" I asked Duffy, who had started opening kitchen cabinets, which had dishes and cooking implements but no packages of food, perishable or otherwise.

"Not that I know of," he answered. "It wasn't in the file. No wallet was found. I asked about the car at the scene of what North Bergen insists on calling the 'accident,' and they said there was no registration in the glove compartment, but the license plate and VIN number indicate it was Damien Mosley's car. It was never reported missing or stolen because Damien lay dead at the bottom of the drop. It was finally towed from the spot to a police pound three weeks after the incident and sold at auction a year later. It never occurred to them it was there because its owner was the John Doe they were trying to identify."

"You'd think that would be their first assumption," I said while opening a closet in the hallway. Cleaning supplies, brooms, a vacuum cleaner. Nothing personal and nothing anyone would have been using recently except whoever was doing the periodic straightening up.

"Yes, normally," Duffy said. "But five years ago, when a body came back with no fingerprints on file, the obvious move would have been to go to dental records. But it seems Damien Mosley never had so much as a cavity in his life. His teeth were in perfect shape. Dentists don't autograph their work, so they had no idea where to look. The car seemed a separate issue. No one in the department then put two and two together."

"What are we looking for?" I asked him. There was still time to get home and do some work before Ben came to pick me up. I'd asked Paula, and she laughed and assured me this was a date. I had no doubt she would lay out clothes on my bed for me to wear tonight. Paula dates more than I do, but then the pope probably dates more than I do.

"Whatever seems unusual," was the reply. Which didn't help at all.

I walked slowly toward what clearly were the bedrooms. There were two, and that made me wonder more about how much this place must have cost to buy than who might have slept there. This is the toll of living in a high-rent area. Of course I own my house, or the bank does, but in my business, you're never more than one contract away from being unemployed.

"I can't tell from looking around whether this place was Dorothy's or Damien's," I said a little louder. "It's almost completely impersonal."

"But not totally abandoned," Duffy said. "Someone lived here, but they did not live here recently. And it's not like it was being readied to sell; it would look more generic than this. There are paintings on the wall. There are area rugs. It's just that nothing has been used in a while."

"Why would someone keep a place that could sell for a lot of money off the market if they weren't living here?" I asked him. I looked in the bathroom, first door on the right. Clean. Perfect. Like a hotel room. There were things in the medicine cabinet but no prescriptions that would have named labels.

"That is an excellent question," Duffy admitted. "The assumption must be that it was expected someone would be living here, but those plans went awry. And once I can get some bank records on Damien Mosley or his mother, it might be possible to determine who created the trust to cover the maintenance fees here after the mortgage was paid off, and how long it is instructed to do so."

I walked into the first bedroom, clearly the master, which required that I yell out to Duffy. "Why can't you find Dorothy Mosley?" I asked. "She didn't vanish like her son, did she?"

"Mrs. Mosley has proven to be more elusive than I might have anticipated," he called in to me. "But it is more difficult to do research when one does not have the authority of the government behind him. I am working in foreign territory for me, as you must know. I've never investigated privately, and Ben can't do much to help."

The bedroom was very neat but wasn't being obnoxious about it. There was a chenille bedspread, white, on the queen-size mattress set in a white wooden frame with a matching headboard that incorporated two shelves, one above each pillow. The shelves held books that told me nothing about the person (or people) who slept here. Classics, nonfiction that ran mostly to biographies of American presidents, and some travel guides to places like Rome, Amsterdam, Barcelona, and Bali.

"I think this place was decorated by Central Casting," I told Duffy, assuming he could still hear me. "There's no hint of personality."

"On the contrary," he called in, which indicated my voice was carrying. "We are seeing a great deal of information about the person who lived here."

We were? I wasn't seeing it. But then, it's always been an advantage in this world to have been born fictional. It gave him observational powers that no real human could have. I knew Duffy would explain exactly what we were learning in excruciating detail later, so I didn't ask the question now.

The closet in the bedroom yielded a little more. There was clothing for a woman and probably not one old enough to be Damien Mosley's mother, judging from the styles. Nothing flashy and not very much: black-and-gray pants, plain-white and light-gray blouses, buttoned up, no incredibly high heels, skirts. Enough clothing for exactly two days. Either she hadn't owned very much, hadn't kept it here, or there was a colossal unpaid bill for merchandise left unclaimed at a local dry cleaner.

There was no hairbrush. No laundry (although that made sense, given the obvious cleaning service and the time elapsed). No obvious impulse purchases. No winter coat or outerwear of any kind. Was there a closet in the front room or the hallway where such things might be kept? Did she only live here during warm weather? It was like the *idea* of a woman resided here.

Duffy appeared in the doorway. "What have you discovered?" You've got to love the guy: He assumed I had found stuff out and seemed almost annoyed that I hadn't told him yet.

"That I'm a lousy detective and you had no need to bring me here," I said. "I write for a living, Duffy. I'm better at making things up than dealing with what actually exists. You can look around this room and see eighteen things that will give you insight into the woman whose apartment this is. I see a generic bedroom in a generic unit in a generic building. The conclusion I could draw is that it's very clean here."

"Very good," he answered.

Okay, so that was unexpected. "What do you mean, 'very good'? I just told you I can't draw any conclusions about the person who lived here, and you tell me that's a plus?"

Duffy walked in and looked around briefly. "Indeed. And you're wrong. I can't find eighteen things offering information in here. Only four."

That was four more than I'd noticed, but I teed up the question for him anyway. "Which four?" I asked.

"The woman who lived here had very little ego, did not feel fluctuations in temperature, had no friends or family, and kept herself virtually cut off from the rest of the world. Or there is one other possibility."

Having become a straight-line machine, I asked, "What's that?"

"It's more than likely she never lived here at all."

Chapter 16

"So Duffy thinks this apartment was staged to make it look like someone lived there?" Ben Preston sat down at my dining room table and picked up a slice of pizza from the box I'd positioned between us.

We'd decided to stay in and keep it very casual tonight because the last time we'd tried going out to dinner, we'd only been interrupted—by Duffy, of course—and it had felt a little weird. We knew each other a little better now, and besides, I'd had a couple of wearying days following the product of my imagination around on his errands and didn't feel like trying too hard to impress anybody. Ben understood, so he showed up in jeans and a plain, clean blue T-shirt. I'd told him to imagine what he should wear and then dress one step below that. He'd followed orders very well.

"Not exactly," I answered after chewing up and swallowing my bite of the peppers-and-onions half of the pie. Ben had requested and gotten pepperoni, but I'm not a fan. "Duffy says someone definitely was living there, which he decided through some bizarre train of thought that wouldn't make sense to a normal person. But he says that it's meant to seem like Michelle Mosley lived there, but that she never did."

"What makes him think so?" Ben is fascinated by Duffy's methodology, even though he has, theoretically, seen it more often than I have.

"Which part?"

"Both." Ben took a sip of beer from the bottle, which is the way to drink beer. I took a sip of wine from a wineglass, which is the way to drink wine. We were doing everything the way we were supposed to.

"He says someone was living there because there is the proper amount of wear on the furniture and the rugs. He says you can't fake that; either something's been used or it hasn't. And he says even with the obvious cleaning service that comes through periodically, things like light switches and doorknobs show signs of repeated use. Someone at least was living there, and might still be, he thinks. But the doorman said no, there hasn't been anybody in that apartment in years." Even chewing pizza was feeling like too much effort. Oddly, drinking wine was not. I concentrated on that.

"What about the other part, that it was never Damien Mosley's wife?" Ben asked.

"I thought you weren't involved in this case," I reminded him.

"I'm not. It's professional curiosity. Besides, this falls under the 'how was your day, honey?' category." His eyes showed a twinkle of humor. We had not reached the "honey" stage in any form, and Ben knew it.

"Okay, so Duffy says it wasn't Michelle—and we don't know who Michelle actually is, whether they were married or what her original name might be because Duffy hasn't found the records yet—because there is no personalization at all. No photographs. No cosmetics. No idiosyncrasies."

"Couldn't she just be someone who doesn't go in for any of that stuff?" Ben asked. He wasn't comfortable enough in my house to put his foot up on the chair next to him, which I appreciated, but he did seem to blend into the setting well.

"I can see no pictures and no tchotchkes," I said, "but no cosmetics? For a woman in the twenty-first century? That's really unlikely. Besides, Duffy said the second bedroom did show some personality, but it was male. Maybe Damien himself."

"No cosmetics can just be because of the time gone by," Ben suggested. "Someone might have come through the place even a year after whatever happened and cleaned out the personal stuff."

"And left clothing and furniture? A flat-screen TV? A working refrigerator? It's like somebody *wanted* people to think they'd come through and selectively cleaned it out." I am perfectly comfortable in my own house so I did in fact put my feet up on the chair next to me. I wasn't wearing shoes anyway. And everything about this whole situation from the first minute had simply made me tired.

"It doesn't make much sense. Do you want me to see what I can do with this?" Ben put his hand on mine, and it didn't even feel like a false gesture. "I know Duffy wants me to, but he won't ask because he's a stickler for procedure."

I thought about it, but then I shook my head. "No. Duffy's right. The last thing you should be doing is sticking your nose in while you're trying to decide whether to tell your boss that Duffy is a dangerous lunatic. How's that going, by the way?"

Ben half-closed his eyes like he just wanted things to go away. Not me, necessarily, but things. "Not great," he said. "A woman called in with a missing person complaint on her husband, and the only reason the Wallington cops aren't looking into it is that it hasn't been twenty-four hours yet since she last saw him. If it gets to eleven tomorrow morning and the guy doesn't come ambling into the house smelling of beer or perfume, we'll get a call, and Petrosky will want me to call Duffy. Then I'll have to decide."

That could be bad. "Which way are you leaning?" I asked.

But Ben didn't answer. He stood up and walked into the kitchen to get another beer. This was going to be something of a problem since I'd given him the last bottle I'd had in the fridge. I don't drink beer that much and until this afternoon hadn't considered inviting him here for dinner.

"There's no more in there," I warned him. "You want some wine?"

He came back in carrying a glass of water. "I'm driving," he said. "Unless you want me to stay."

Well, there it was. What kind of relationship were Ben and I going to have, and how fast was it going to move? He was an attractive man, and I liked him, certainly. But when I'd been in distress, it was Duffy and not Ben who had come through for me, and I hadn't forgotten that. On the other hand, I might have been rating Ben a little too harshly, and I definitely didn't want *Duffy* asking if he was going to spend the night.

I punted. "Maybe not tonight," I said. That held the option open that another night would be different, didn't it?

Ben didn't look disappointed, and I wasn't sure how to read that. "Okay," he said. "I don't have to leave now, do I?"

I shook my head. He sat back down next to me, reached over, and kissed me, just like that. And I was glad he did. We kept that up for an undisclosed period of time (because I'm not disclosing it) and eventually came up for air. "Living room?" I asked.

"Lead the way." As if he didn't know where it was.

We settled into the nice soft couch, and Ben put his arm around me and held me lightly. That was all. We both just wanted to sit and stop thinking about pretty much anything, I believe.

And oddly, Duffy Madison did not call. I would have almost expected Duffy to sense something was going on with Ben and me and interfere without even knowing why. When we'd dated the one other time, Duffy had seemed unnerved by the idea, as if people from his work should not have relationships that didn't involve finding the missing individual. Then again, Duffy was seeing Emily Needleman now, so maybe his radar had been shut down. So he didn't call.

My father did.

I looked at the caller ID and told Ben it was Dad. He nodded, having met my father, and let go of the hold he'd had on my shoulder. I pushed the talk button and said hello to my father.

"Duffy Madison called," he said. "Something about how a guy got murdered and you're supposed to be able to help him figure out how it happened."

Duffy was telling my dad on me?

"Why is Duffy calling you?" I asked as Ben sat up and looked justifiably startled. "How did he even get your number?"

"From the last time," Dad said. "We exchanged numbers when everybody was looking for you." It was a short period in my life I preferred to block out. Like this guy named Jeff I went out with in college. "What's this all about? Do I need to come down there again?"

"No!" That might have come out a touch more forcefully than I had intended. "There is absolutely no danger to me at all. Nobody's even sure that a guy was murdered. He fell and hit his head on a rock, and I never met him in my life."

"Duffy sounds pretty certain," Dad said.

"Aren't you the one who kept telling me he was crazy and I shouldn't listen to him?"

"I've gotten to know him a little better." My father sounded strangely sheepish. "He came up and visited a month or so ago."

I didn't leap to my feet because this wasn't a movie from 1954, but I did sit up a good deal straighter. Ben gave me a concerned look, and I ignored it because Ben was the one extra thing I couldn't think about right now. "Duffy went up there and visited you?" When in doubt, repeat the other person's words. It doesn't help, but it kills time.

"Yeah," Dad said casually. "He's pretty good company, actually. We talked about baseball a little, and I told him about a photography class I knew about down there because he wanted to know more about the technology available in digital cameras. I understand he met a woman in that class." Dad sounded awfully proud of himself over that one.

My head was starting to ache just a little. "Dad." I blinked a couple of times while Ben wrote, "What?" on a Post-it note I had on the coffee table. You never know when you'll get a usable idea. "Why did Duffy go up there to see you?"

"He needed a place to stay. He said he was looking into a missing guy in Poughkeepsie, and he was going around the area trying to gather information. I'm not that close, but I'm closer than Jersey, so he asked if he could stay here for a couple of days. I said sure. Why? Is that a problem?"

Was there any way in which that was *not* a problem? A guy who thought he was the living embodiment of a fictional character I made up had traveled to Claremont, New York, and stayed with my father while working on finding a missing man I thought was actually his previous identity.

Wait, I'm just getting started. While there, he was traveling back and forth to Poughkeepsie, presumably talking to people involved in the case, probably including those he had then taken me to visit with, not one of whom had so much as blinked in recognition when we walked through their doors.

And the fact that he might very well have been a classmate of some of them in high school, and that Paula (who is one of the most intelligent people I've ever met) believed he had dated one of them and then cruelly ended the relationship, hadn't even completely permeated my brain yet. Okay, so maybe "cruelly" was just implied, but that was the mood I was building.

The levels of deceit and obfuscation were impressive and infuriating at the same time. I clenched my teeth so tightly that I'd probably have to oil the hinges of my jaw later and said, "No. Not a problem. Listen, Dad. I have to get going. There's someone here."

"What?" That jaw-clenching thing had made me pretty much unintelligible. Before I could make more impossible-to-understand noises into the phone, Dad added, "Are you and Duffy having some kind of argument? He said you had refused to help him with this Poughkeepsie thing."

Now Duffy was passive-aggressively trying to get me into his twisted plot by using my father. That was new, and it only made me angrier. So much so that I found I could open my mouth again. But I had enough self-control that I managed not to scream.

I got off the phone with my father as quickly as I could and, again without actually throwing a tantrum or looking up weapons dealers on Google, filled Ben in on the parts of the conversation he couldn't infer on his own.

"I don't see how I can cover for him now," he said finally. "Duffy's gone over the edge."

"There are so many things wrong with this," I agreed. "And I'm not even taking into account the idea that he went out of his way to include my father in whatever goofy plot he's hatching."

"What do you mean? Because he's calling your dad to complain?"

I shook my head, which was definitely calling for some Aleve and wasn't shy about it. "Because he chose to stay with my father, an hour away from the area he was investigating, rather than stay in a hotel in Poughkeepsie. You're telling me a guy who says his investments make it possible for him to go long periods without work was worried about saving the cost of a Holiday Inn?"

Ben leaned forward, thinking. "That is weird. Do you think there's some reason Duffy wants to gather information about your dad?"

"What I'm worried about is that Duffy's using my father to gather information about *me*."

It was a lot to consider. I almost called Dad back to get details, but then I decided that more insights into his sojourn with Duffy would only get me more upset. "Should I call Duffy?" I asked Ben. That's what it had come to; I actually had to ask Ben whether it was a good idea to make a phone call.

"Maybe," he said. "I find it's best to confront the issue head-on. Duffy might have an explanation that's reasonable, and then you'll be able to sleep tonight."

I pondered that while I got some ibuprofen from a cabinet in the kitchen and took it with a glass of water. I'd go back to drinking wine in a minute, but there was something about using alcohol to take pills that seemed a little too 1970s for me.

For some reason, I waited until I was back in the living room with Ben to pull the phone out of my pocket again and push the speed-dial button for the raving lunatic who is using my character's name and personality.

And Duffy, with his unparalleled ability to infuriate me without actually doing much of anything, managed to prolong the suspense by not answering when I called.

There wasn't a whole lot of romantic spark left in the room by then, but Ben and I discussed our Duffy dilemma for another hour without reaching any conclusions about anything before he stood up to leave. He kissed me again just to remind me that this had started out as a date. It was a very satisfactory kiss, which I appreciated for what it was, but the moment ended, and we separated.

He grinned ironically. "You still sure you don't want me to stay?" he asked.

"Not tonight, Ben," I said. "I have a headache."

Chapter 17

I tried calling Duffy twice more the next morning despite a sinus headache that would have killed a normal person. By the time I'd taken a hot shower to steam my respiratory system out and had taken enough ibuprofen to keep Pfizer in business for another day, I'd given up on contacting him and decided he was just a hallucination I'd had who wouldn't answer the phone today. My head cleared up after a couple of hours, and I sat down to work.

Shockingly, writing hadn't gotten any easier while I slept the night before. I read over what I'd written the previous days, spent a half hour or so in despair, went out to Dunkin Donuts for badly needed coffee (it was the kind of morning when making my own seemed too tall an order), and was sitting at my desk again, showered again and dressed for real because that's another way to procrastinate, contemplating cleaning my house.

That's how bad things were. I was thinking of cleaning my house.

It was a day Paula wasn't working, so I could sit and stare at my computer screen for an indefinite period of time if I allowed myself to do so. And that was unquestionably an option, but I had a cornucopia of possible nonwriting things to do, and my desperation level was rising. I decided that in order to maintain the moral high ground in the argument I was having with myself, I would have to take on the task other than writing that I most wanted not to do at this moment.

So I called Louise Refsnyder.

Yep. I really didn't want to write that day.

Just on the off chance that you've never called a woman you've met once to ask whether she was dumped by a guy who might very well be a raving nut case, let me assure you it's not an experience to add to your bucket list. Louise answered the phone (Duffy and I had gotten numbers from everyone we'd interviewed the day we went to Poughkeepsie) already armed with a defensive attitude that was audible simply in her "Hello." Not a question, an obligation.

"Hi, Louise. This is Rachel Goldman. We met the day before yesterday"—good Lord, had it really just been *two days ago?*—"when Duffy Madison and I came up to talk about Damien Mosley." I was an aspiring journalist when I graduated from college and had acquired my telephone interview style the way all aspiring journalists do—by watching *All the President's Men* roughly thirty-six times. Roughly.

"Yeah." Louise was going to be a chatterbox, I could tell. She was probably dredging up negative memories of Duffy standing her up at the prom as we spoke. (I am a world-class assumer, by the way.)

"I just had a few follow-up questions, if you have the time," I went on. Make it sound professional. I was probably being Bob Woodward/Robert Redford because Carl Bernstein/ Dustin Hoffman was going to be more abrasive, and that, at least for me, makes it more difficult to get answers. Because the person you're talking to tends to hang up.

"Yeah." Of course, there's also the possibility she'll do nothing but say "yeah" to you all day, and although that sounds positive, it's usually not terribly helpful. Louise didn't add anything to her incisive comment, so it was clear I'd have to do the bulk of the work here.

"Now, Damien Mosley was a classmate of yours." I pretended I was reading from notes because that made me sound more detached, like this line of questioning wasn't really for my own benefit. I also started with Damien because jumping in with questions about Duffy would have sounded awfully strange.

"Yeah." Writing was starting to look at lot more attractive. The plan was working. Sort of.

"Were you in any clubs with him? Anything like that?" You'll see why I asked that in a minute.

"Clubs?" Louise repeated. Hey, it was a change from "yeah," and that wasn't nothing. It wasn't *something*, either, but you take what you can get.

"Sure," I said. "A look through your high school yearbook shows that you were in the Classics Society and the Honor Society."

Louise sounded like she wanted to talk about high school about as much as she wanted to talk about planning her own funeral. "So what?" she asked. "Do you have a question?"

I had already asked one, but I repeated it for her benefit. "Was Damien Mosley in either of those organizations with you?"

Louise made a noise with her lips. "I don't know," she said. "The Honor Society didn't have meetings or anything. It was just this group for kids who had a grade point average that was high enough. We didn't have the Honor Society dance. We didn't sell Honor Society candy bars as a fundraiser."

"Well, what about the Classics Society?" I said. "That was a group you chose to join, right? Was there anybody of interest in *that* club?" See how clever I was to subtly move the topic off Damien and toward any other people (Duffy) whom Louise might have, you know, known in high school?

"You got that information from my yearbook," she reminded me. "Doesn't it have the names of all the people who were in the club?"

Okay, so she had me there, but Louise was being evasive for reasons that even an especially traumatic breakup wouldn't explain. "Well yes," I said, "but I was wondering if you were especially close to anybody in the Classics Society."

"Close?" Louise asked. "What do you mean by 'close'?"

Cards on the table. "Was Duffy Madison in the Classics Society with you?" I asked.

"Huh?" That had caught Louise off guard. Good. "Duffy Madison?"

"Yeah." I could steal her tactic if I wanted to.

"Wasn't that the guy who was with you when you were here?" she asked.

"Um, yes," I said. "The yearbook lists him as a member of the Classics Society the same year you were in it. Did you know him?"

"No." Louise was back to the one-syllable answers. I'd struck a nerve.

"There were only seven members," I said. "How could you not know somebody who was in that club with you?"

"Look, what has this got to do with Damien Mosley leaving town and not coming back?" Louise was operating under the principle that accusing the accuser—and I wasn't even accusing her of anything—would help her to dodge the question.

It was a decent tactic, considering that I couldn't actually present a connection between the two things unless I were to get into the *Twilight Zone* logic that Duffy used to be Damien and that's why everybody thought they looked alike. Louise had already said they were similar but not *that* similar, so it didn't seem the right road to walk.

"I'm just wondering how that's possible. I mean, if there were six other people in the club, and you did whatever a Classics Society does at the meetings, how could you not remember if the guy was there or not?" I'd chosen to ignore her question entirely because this was *my* interrogation, after all. I got back to being the reporter on the story. Woodward/Redford never let it throw him when the White House guys tried to make *The Washington Post* part of the Watergate story.

Really, you can develop a whole philosophy watching that movie.

"Okay!" Louise shouted. "I give up. You got me, okay? I never went to the Classics Society meetings."

Well, of course she . . . what? But I resisted the urge to repeat her statement back to her in the form of a question. I'm just too professional for that. So it took me a moment to reply. "Why not?" I asked.

The answer took a long time coming, like Louise was trying to bolster her confidence. I heard some liquid swish in the background, and there might have been ice cubes clinking.

It was not yet eleven in the morning.

"I needed a reason to tell my parents why I wasn't coming home," she said finally. There was no slurring of words. Her *s*'s were not sloppy. I was hoping this was the first drink of the day, or that it was ginger ale or orange juice. With ice.

"So you joined the Classics Society?" Maybe that was the least of it, but it was the first thing that struck me.

"Yeah."

I was going to have to do better than that. "Why did you need to put up a smoke screen for your parents?" And as soon as the words were out of my mouth, I realized that was a stupid question.

"So I could be with my boyfriend," Louise said, her tone indicating she too knew I was a bozo. "You know, *be* with him."

It all came flooding toward me at that point. She needed to be with her boyfriend, so she joined the Classics Society. There was no evidence that Duffy had ever gone to a meeting of the Classics Society, either, since none of the other members Paula had contacted remembered him. And then Louise, after taking the SATs, had promptly given up any pretense of applying to colleges. I put it all together in my head, and it spelled out only one solution.

"Louise," I said, my breath coming a little heavier than I intended, "did Duffy Madison get you pregnant?"

"What is it with you and Duffy Madison?" she demanded. "Are you his girlfriend or something?"

It was a much more complicated relationship than that, but I really didn't have the time or the Tylenol to get through it right now. "No," I said. "I'm not his girlfriend. So what happened?"

"I got pregnant, all right, but I don't know anything about your Duffy Madison," Louise said. She was going to drive the point home. "I never met the guy before you came to my house a couple of days ago, okay?"

Okay. Okay. I got it, although I still thought she was lying. Duffy had been going to Poughkeepsie to investigate Damien Mosley's disappearance while he was staying at my father's house a month before.

"So who was the boyfriend?" I asked. I'm not even sure why I cared unless it was Damien Mosley.

"It doesn't matter," Louise said. "I wasn't *really* pregnant."

In my experience, you either are or you're not. "What does that mean?"

"I just thought I was. Turned out about a week later that I wasn't."

A week later? "Then why didn't you go to college?" I asked.

"What's college got to do with it?"

I was beginning to get the idea that maybe I shouldn't make assumptions about people's lives based on my own investigation. Or Paula's. "I thought you didn't go to college because you were pregnant," I said.

"I didn't go to college because I had to go to work," Louise answered. "My dad was almost out of a job, we thought he was going to get laid off, and my mom was only working part-time, and I still don't see what any of this had to do with Damien Mosley."

She had a point, I had to admit. "Were you really involved with Damien right before he vanished?" I asked. What the hell; maybe I could find out *something* with this phone call.

"I don't know if you'd call it *involved*," she said. "He had a wife, but he wasn't living with her. We did what we did, and that was it."

The tone in my ear indicated someone else was trying to call me. I thanked Louise for her trouble—which seemed weird—and clicked through to the other call.

"Is this Ms. Rachel Goldman?" a man asked.

No good phone call ever started that way.

I admitted to being myself. It was one of the few things I was still sure about these days.

"I'm calling about a man named Duffy Madison," the man said. "I'm Sgt. Michael O'Rourke with the North Bergen Police Department."

Alarm bells went off in my head. "What about Duffy Madison?"

A call from the North Bergen police about Duffy? Were they trying to alert me to some new weird breach of protocol my Frankenstein creation had committed? Did they want to know if there *was* such a person as Duffy Madison? If so, how could I answer? But then my mind wandered into darker areas, and all in a flash, I had to wonder if I was Duffy's emergency contact. Had they found his body in the same ditch they'd found Damien Mosley's?

That was the kind of twist I might be looking for at the midpoint of a manuscript. If Duffy was dead, was I responsible?

"Mr. Madison asked us to call you," Sgt. O'Rourke said. I heard myself let out a sigh of relief. Duffy wasn't dead. Or wait—had he asked just before he let out his last agonized gasp? "He said he did not have a lawyer, so we should call you."

A lawyer? "Why does Duffy need a lawyer?" I asked.

"We have him under arrest," O'Rourke answered. "He's being charged with regard to a murder."

Chapter 18

"A murder." Ben Preston sat in the passenger seat of my tiny Prius c, and even though I was mostly watching the road, I stole a glance at him. He looked absolutely bewildered. "A murder," he repeated.

"That's really all I know," I said. "They arrested Duffy, and he said he didn't have a lawyer to represent him, but when they suggested getting someone from the public defender's office, he said they should call me."

Ben shook his head. "Why would they think he killed Damien Mosley?" he said, no doubt thinking out loud. "There's no evidence at all that Duffy ever *met* Damien Mosley."

"They were high school classmates," I reminded him. "Whether Duffy admits to it or not, they might very well have known each other back in the day."

We were taking my car because Ben has one the prosecutor's office lets him use, and since he'd taken half a day off from work to come with me on our Duffy quest, he didn't feel comfortable using his work car. The drive wasn't going to take long, but it felt like hours had passed since O'Rourke had called me.

My first impulse was to call Ben. He's much better steeped in the criminal justice system than I am. I deal strictly in my fictional version, which strives to be accurate but doesn't mind bending the occasional rule in service of a good story. Ben has to work in the real world, which has its drawbacks. It does mean, however, that he knows how this stuff works.

Besides, the last thing I'd wanted to do was go confront Duffy in jail on my own.

"If they're charging him, not just questioning him, that is serious," Ben said. I still wasn't sure whether he was talking to me or to himself. "That means they have sufficient evidence to merit an indictment, or at least they think they do. It's not just speculation."

"What do we do when we get there?" I asked, both to get an answer to the question and to remind Ben that I was in the car with him. He was staring out the side window now, and I was navigating our way to North Bergen. They hadn't had time to transfer Duffy to county lockup yet, in preparation for his arraignment.

It was hard to think of Duffy in those terms.

"First, we need to find him a lawyer," Ben said, snapping out of his reverie and realizing action was required. "Do you know anybody?"

I thought about it. I'd dated a lawyer once, but he was not someone I'd care to call again, even for professional reasons. I had a lawyer who looked over my contracts with my agent

Adam Resnick, and Adam advised me on all the contracts I signed with my publisher. Neither of them was a criminal attorney.

"Not really," I told Ben. "You must know some."

He nodded. "Most of them are prosecutors, but I do know a few good defense attorneys. They're not all crazy about me."

"Hard to believe," I said.

Ben ignored that. "Does Duffy have enough money for this?"

I had no way of knowing anything about Duffy's financial status and told him so. "He seems to have enough to get by even when you guys aren't giving him work," I said. Another wave of insight hit me. "That whole consultant thing is probably out the window for him now anyway, isn't it?"

"It's not good," Ben admitted. "He'll be placed on the inactive list once the paperwork on his arrest hits the database. Petrosky's going to have a lot of questions, and he's not going to be happy with the answers he gets. Even if Duffy is acquitted, it's going to be tough to get a law enforcement agency to put him on their payroll just as a freelancer."

It felt like a page had been turned and there was no going back. We rode (well, Ben rode and I drove) in silence for a couple of minutes. "Poor Duffy," I said, for lack of anything else to say.

Ben ignored that and turned his attention toward me; I could see the shift in his position in my peripheral vision. "Don't tell anybody there I'm with the prosecutor, okay?" he said out of nowhere.

I didn't understand why that was a good idea, but I said I'd do as he asked.

"Good. If I just seem like an interested friend of Duffy's, I might be able to find out more about what made them charge him so quickly. Is there anything you know that would indicate Duffy had a problem with this Mosley guy?"

"Nothing I've heard," I said. "I've told you everything I know."

"Have you?" There was a challenging tone in his voice.

"What's that supposed to mean?" Was I mad at Ben or taking out my growing frustration at the Dodge Ram truck in front of me that was slowing to thirty-five miles per hour in a fifty-five zone? Pennsylvania plates. It figured.

"It means you never told me Duffy believes he's a product of your imagination," Ben said. That tone wasn't challenging, I realized. It was hurt. How could I hold back that information from him?

"I figured that would hurt his employment, and it wasn't my place to tell you," I answered. "I didn't want to cause him trouble."

Ben made a noise in his throat like he was having trouble swallowing something. It was probably my explanation. The Ram slowed to thirty. This wasn't my day.

"Look," I said before he could protest further, "the guy saved my life. He's quirky, but until I got a phone call from the cops a little while ago, I never thought he was dangerous. So there was no reason to tell a guy I'd barely met that Duffy shouldn't be working for you anymore because he was certifiably insane."

Ben grunted. "You realize how that comes across?" he asked. But there was a little more understanding in his tone.

"It sounded better in my head. The question now is, what do we do for Duffy? Is there anything we *can* do?"

"We can find out what his status is and then find him a lawyer. If he's about to be arraigned, we can find out about bail. And maybe we can get a story from your imaginary friend about what actually happened. Usually he's pretty rational about this kind of stuff."

"When it's not about him," I said. I couldn't stand it anymore and passed the Dodge Ram on the right, which you're not supposed to do but is necessary when driving behind a Pennsylvanian. We Jersey girls are not to be messed with when we're on wheels. Or any other time.

"Easy there, Ms. Andretti," Ben said, watching the woman in the Dodge Ram make a rude gesture at us as she faded into memory. "You're not going to help Duffy by smacking us into a highway divider."

"I'm a good driver," I protested, and Ben shut up. For a moment.

Wisely, he chose to change the subject. "I can't imagine what evidence they can have of Duffy being in that park five years ago. I dug all I could, and I didn't find evidence of him being *anywhere* before then."

I told him Paula had found the evidence of someone named Duffy Madison in the Poughkeepsie High School yearbook, and he nodded. "I knew about that, but it's almost like he was there and someone went back and erased him. Any trace there would have been, anything you'd logically assume would be there, is gone."

We arrived at the North Bergen police headquarters, and I parked the car. Ben was out of his door before I managed to kill the engine, and he headed right for the front door. He was more worried about his friend than he wanted to let on, and now he was doing an extremely poor job of hiding it.

There was a cemetery next door to the police building. I didn't take that for a good sign.

I practically had to run to catch up with Ben as he took the steps two at a time. I couldn't remember if I'd locked my car. Of course, it was in front of the police headquarters, but I've heard stories. New Jerseyans have a strong sense of irony.

Despite never having been in the building before, Ben seemed to have a sixth sense about direction. He headed directly to a door marked "Detectives" and noted the desk in front of it. "Probably locked," he said to himself—I no longer seemed to have a function here, having transported Ben to the building—and turned toward the desk.

The dispatcher behind it was an African American woman of about forty who seemed incongruously relaxed in the middle of a police station in a somewhat hectic area. She had large eyes, and they were taking in Ben. "Can I help you?" she asked.

It was a good question, especially the way she asked it, but Ben wasn't in the mood to correct her grammar. "I'm here to find Duffy Madison," he said. "We got a call from a Sgt. O'Rourke that he'd been brought here." Then he seemed to remember that he wasn't going to let anyone know he was a pseudocop, and his voice became more plaintive and uncertain. "Is this the right area?"

She started punching keys on the computer in front of her, then seemed to find what she was looking for. "Duffy Madison?" the woman said slowly. "Is that the guy with the murder from New York?"

"New York?" I said. Ben looked at me a moment as if remembering I was present. Shoot me; I was surprised.

"Yeah, it was the New York State Police put out the BOLO on that guy, I'm pretty sure. He's not in the detective bureau. He's downstairs in holding." She looked at me, then at Ben. "Sorry."

We went downstairs, Ben no longer showing off how he knew everything about law enforcement, and found Sgt. Michael O'Rourke in uniform at a separate desk in the main intake area.

He was a gray-haired man of maybe fifty, thin and naturally skeptical if you believed the look in his eyes. We—Ben—told him who we were, and O'Rourke nodded, not having to refer to a screen. Duffy had no doubt made an impression.

"We got a bulletin from the New York State Police this morning," he said, ushering us to a relatively quiet corner of the large room. "They were looking for someone in connection with a murder. We didn't have to do too much. This Madison guy walks into our house a couple of hours ago asking about a crime scene from five years ago, and somebody has the bulletin from New York open on their computer. They recognize him."

The words were dancing around my head but not entirely penetrating my ears. "I don't understand," I said.

Ben turned and looked at me as if I had broken the Law of Men. He'd asked me to let him do the talking, and there was my voice being completely audible. Again.

I was glad I hadn't let him spend the night. That'd teach him, and he wouldn't even know it.

"I don't understand why you arrested Duffy for a murder that took place in New York State," I said, not reacting to Ben's look. "Damien Mosley died here in North Bergen."

"I don't know about a Damien Mosley," O'Rourke answered. He picked up a tablet computer from a desk that I guessed was his and punched the screen a few times. "This was a shooting in Poughkeepsie, New York. A woman named Michelle Testaverde. Was a cold case; they thought she was homeless, dressed in seventeen coats and whatever. But apparently they took ballistics at the time, and there was a match today. She died five years ago. They think your pal here shot her in the back of the head and then fled here to Jersey."

"Michelle," I murmured to myself. "Damien Mosley's wife."

Chapter 19

"Of course I didn't shoot Michelle Testaverde," Duffy Madison said. "I never even met Michelle Testaverde."

Ben and I, after much discussion during which Ben had been forced to reveal his secret identity as a county investigator, had been allowed into the interrogation room where Duffy, hands shackled to the table, was being held. I was doing my best to hold it together, and Ben looked like his jaw had locked in place and would never unhinge unless Judy Garland came by with an oilcan and lubricated him in the right places.

O'Rourke and whatever detectives were awaiting the transport from the New York State cops to take Duffy to wherever it was he'd be going, but I would bet serious money they were behind the mirror on one wall of the room.

Duffy looked positively stunned. His hair was flopping in front of his eyes, and it was an effort for him to lift his hands high enough to push it back. I don't know if it was the lighting, but his skin looked paler than usual. He was not in a prison orange jumpsuit because he had not been incarcerated in the state of New Jersey, but his usual crisp appearance was ragged. His shirt was untucked. For Duffy Madison, that was the equivalent of appearing naked in public.

I wanted so badly to give him a hug and tell him everything would be all right, but the chains were a problem, and besides, Duffy didn't care much for being touched. Not to mention, I wasn't at all sure *anything* was going to be all right.

"How do they even know Michelle was murdered?" Ben asked. "After five years? What happened?"

Duffy's mouth twitched a little. "I suppose I'm partially to blame for that," he said. For some reason, I was not surprised. "I had been making inquiries into Damien Mosley's disappearance and was asking about his wife, once Rachel and I found out she existed. They went through their files of Jane Does from the time and found one who had been shot in the head. She'd never been identified, but ballistics and dental records now confirmed it was Michelle Testaverde. She had never been reported missing because everyone had been told she was moving to New Jersey to live in Damien's West New York apartment."

"What else?" I knew that tone in his voice; he was holding back.

"I suggested that because she had left no outerwear in the West New York apartment that her heavier clothing had been put on her body to make her appear to be a homeless woman, which would explain why there was no blood or organic material on her coat. Or coats."

That was a lot to take in, so we sat in silence for a few seconds. "Do they think you killed Damien, too?" I asked. Duffy just shrugged.

"They won't tell me *anything*," he complained. "I couldn't see photographs of the crime scene where the body was found. I don't know the first thing about what happened to the woman." From an interrogation room with handcuffs holding him to the table, Duffy Madison was annoyed that he wasn't being considered a consultant on Michelle Testaverde's murder.

"Why do they think you shot Michelle?" Ben asked him. Apparently, his jaw *could* move, but he was trying so hard to be stalwart that he was ignoring the emotion of the moment and was diving in on a professional level. That was probably wise.

"I can't imagine," Duffy said. "I'd never so much as set foot in the city or town of Poughkeepsie before Rachel and I went up yesterday to talk to some of the people who knew Damien Mosley."

The stakes were too high for me to let that go. "That's not true, Duffy," I said. "You have to tell us everything you know now."

Both men turned toward me, but their expressions were a study in contrasts. Ben looked slightly irritated, again leading me to think he didn't care much for when women talked. Duffy appeared terribly puzzled.

"I am telling you the truth," Duffy said.

"No, you're not," I responded, hoping I sounded as gentle as I wanted to sound. "I spoke to my father. I know you spent some time at his house in Claremont so you could go into Poughkeepsie and talk to people involved with Damien Mosley. Did you know Testaverde was his wife's maiden name?"

Duffy shook his head slightly. "I did not drive into Poughkeepsie when I was visiting with your father," he told me. "I led him to believe that's what I was doing, but I had not yet drawn up a list of subjects to interview."

This whole surreal scene just kept getting weirder, and not in a good way. "Why would you go up to my father's house without telling me and then lie to him about why you were there?" I asked Duffy.

Ben looked impatient, like this was a side issue. It wasn't, particularly if Duffy was lying about his presence in Poughkeepsie before he and I had driven there to talk to Walt, Louise, Rod, and the rest of Damien Mosley's bowling team, except Michelle. No wonder Duffy hadn't been able to find her.

Had he only been putting on a show about trying?

"I wanted to get to know your dad better," Duffy explained. Not that the explanation was all that illuminating. "I thought that if I could research your history better, I might have a clearer picture of where I had come from."

I took a sideways glance at the mirror wall. "You know where you came from, Duffy. And there's evidence to indicate that you came from—"

Ben jumped in before I could implicate Duffy any further. "Did the cops tell you anything about why you're a suspect in this homicide?" he asked.

"They're just holding me until the New York authorities can get here and take possession," Duffy said. His speech when he talked to Ben, much as when he talked to Lt. Antonio in my books, tended to sound coarser and more cop-like. "The North Bergen officers don't know why I'm a suspect, and if they did, they wouldn't tell me. This isn't their case."

No doubt O'Rourke and his colleagues were nodding on the other side of the wall. Indeed, it wasn't their case, and I was betting they were glad.

"Have you been arraigned?" Ben asked. "I can't imagine they'll do that here."

Duffy looked away. That means he has to say something he thinks will upset the person he's talking to and either doesn't want to say it or doesn't want to see the other person's reaction. I knew he wouldn't lie, but I knew what was coming would not make me any happier.

"I have not been arraigned," he said through a slit between his lips. "I doubt I will be arraigned when I am taken back to Dutchess County."

Under normal circumstances (which I remembered from the time before I'd met this version of Duffy), that would have sufficed. But I knew his face, and I knew what his expression meant. Ben probably did as well, but I got there quicker.

"Have they charged you, Duffy?" I asked. O'Rourke had said on the phone that Duffy had been charged in the murder, but now that we knew the crime had taken place in another state, that didn't make any sense. The North Bergen cops weren't going to file charges in a murder that took place in Poughkeepsie.

Duffy continued to stare at the wall as if it held some odd fascination. "No," he said finally.

Ben's eyes narrowed. He'd trusted Duffy without question up until, basically, yesterday. His trust had been seriously rocked by the revelation that Duffy was probably stricken with some mental illness and now was unraveling faster. Could he believe what his consultant said now? I knew he could, but it wasn't going to be a pleasant experience.

"Why did the sergeant call Rachel and tell her you'd been charged?" he asked.

Duffy mumbled something, which I had never heard him do before. I'd only written him mumbling once, and that was a really bad moment for him. If you want to find out what, buy a copy of *Olly Olly Oxen Free*. And get a new one. Used book stores don't pay royalties.

"What?" Ben said.

"I asked him to say that," Duffy said. He took a breath and looked Ben in the eye without defiance but with dignity. "I wasn't sure Rachel would come if he didn't."

My brain was firing, I was sure, but no coherent thoughts were being transmitted to my mouth. He didn't think I'd come if he hadn't been charged with a murder? Just being held for questioning in a murder wasn't enough. I had a strong urge to commit a violent act of my own but managed to suppress it even if I couldn't actually scrape together speaking. It was a lucky thing Ben was there.

"What exactly is your status right now?" Ben said. His voice had a tiny edge of stress in it. Well, maybe *tiny* isn't exactly the word.

"I am being held for questioning by the Poughkeepsie police in connection with the apparent shooting of Michelle Testaverde," Duffy answered. "I imagine they will hold me for a while, perhaps a day or two, until they have to let me go for lack of evidence."

Ben squinted in the direction of the table between us. "They're cuffing you to the desk until they can give you to the cops from New York?" he said. "Did you hit somebody or something? Resist arrest?" Forget that Duffy hadn't actually been arrested. Not yet, at least. The handcuffs did make Duffy's story a little harder to swallow.

There was the look away again. He was like a five-year-old caught doing something he shouldn't. "I asked the sergeant to do that," he said. "I thought it would make me look more . . . sympathetic."

I saw the muscles in Ben's upper arms spasm a little.

"What else haven't you told us?" I asked Duffy. It was possible Ben was having the same problem now as I'd been experiencing a minute earlier in forming a cohesive sentence. It seemed to be going around in this room.

"I think that's it," Duffy said. "I apologize if this was an inconvenience, and I did not want to deceive you, but I did not expect this to happen when I walked into the building today. I don't know any criminal defense attorneys to call, and I thought you might be the best person to help me find one, Rachel."

Yes, because crime fiction novelists are definitely the people you want to ask about your defense, particularly when you work regularly with lawyers in the prosecutor's office and you have an investigator at your disposal.

"Why?" I asked.

"You made me the way I am," Duffy answered. "I assumed you would know."

O'Rourke opened the door before I could scream at him to get a grip and remember his past life. I still sort of regret that; it would have been cathartic even if it wasn't productive. "That's enough time," the sergeant said.

Ben stood, and I followed his lead. We started out of the room as a uniformed officer came in to unshackle Duffy from the desk. "You shouldn't have bothered," I told her. "It didn't make him more sympathetic."

"Huh?" she said.

"Forget it."

We waited outside until the New York State troopers came to escort Duffy to Poughkeepsie, where he would be held for questioning. Ben had tried to get someone from the Dutchess County Prosecutor's Office on the phone to confer sort-of-cop-to-sort-of-cop but had been stopped by a wall of automated answering that was undoubtedly sold at the time as being more efficient to the caller. He left a message for someone there and then turned to me.

"We have to find him a lawyer," he said. "I don't want that man opening his mouth in a roomful of cops without someone there to tell him to shut up. Do you know anybody?"

I shook my head. "If he needs a book agent, I know somebody," I said. "To get him through questioning on a murder? Not a soul. And it should be a New York lawyer, not one from here. The rules are different."

"I have a cousin who's a cop on Long Island," Ben said. "Maybe he'll know of somebody." He dug his phone out of his jacket pocket and began pressing buttons.

The situation was out of my control, and I never respond well to that. I got up and walked to the desk, where a sergeant who was not O'Rourke was sitting, doing something on his computer that seemed to occupy none of his attention.

"Any idea when the New York troopers will get here?" I asked. I thought I had a pleasant tone to my voice.

Apparently, the sergeant, whose nametag read "Carter," did not agree. "You already know everything I do," he snarled. Which was interesting, because I don't know the first thing about being a desk sergeant, so that threw some shade on his assumed job skills.

"Is this typical?" I asked, desperate to get some actual information so I could show Ben I was useful. "For you to hand off prisoners to another state just for questioning?"

Carter stopped looking at his computer screen, which was irritating him, to look at me, who was irritating him more. "Lady," he said, "most of the time we get simple assaults, complaints about barking dogs, break-ins, and the occasional shooting. We don't extradite people to Portugal." Today, for him, was a day like all days. For me it was a day in which a guy I might or might not have caused to be alive was in deep trouble, and I wanted to help. So I pushed on.

"Yeah, but this is just New York," I said, trying to prove to the guy that the situation in which I was involved was much more relevant than he thought. "Does that happen a lot?"

Carter was no longer looking at me; he was treating me as I was now assuming he treated his wife, so I could dislike him faster. "New York happens every day," he said. "Go east. You can't miss it." Everybody's a comedian.

I gave up on my mission to rehabilitate Carter and sat back down on the uncomfortable molded plastic chair that seems to have been mandated for every police station in the world. I assumed there was a company somewhere that made them and was keeping an entire community of salt-of-the-earth Americans employed. Hey, you do what you do to sleep at night, and I'll do what I do.

Ben had already ended his call and was putting his phone back in his pocket. He did not ask me what I'd found out, which was both irritating in that it inferred that I couldn't have discovered anything and helpful in that I didn't have to tell him I hadn't.

"Did you find a lawyer for Duffy?" I asked him.

He made a face like I'd asked him if he'd built that log cabin yet. "Did I—?" He shook his head. "Oh, that's what you thought I was doing on the phone. No. I'll call my cousin once we know what Duffy's actual status is, because if a lawyer has to go to Dutchess County to hear Duffy being questioned, there's no point in telling him we're in North Bergen. And cops often don't listen to other cops. O'Rourke might have gotten the situation wrong."

"So what were you doing?" I asked.

"I was calling Petrosky," Ben said. "I'm taking a few days of vacation time. How long will it take you to pack a bag?"

This seemed a weird time to hop on a plane to Aruba and see if Ben and I had a future. "Why?"

"I think we should go to Poughkeepsie and try to figure out what happened to Michelle Testaverde," Ben said.

Chapter 20

In the end, it was Paula who found Duffy a criminal defense attorney. That's because it turned out Ben's cousin the cop didn't trust any attorneys and made some joke about sharks that wasn't funny, and also because Duffy was not charged but was being held overnight for questioning, so he needed a lawyer fast. I called Paula because that's what I always do when something needs to happen fast. And as she always does, she made no drama out of the situation and just solved the problem. I want to be like Paula when I grow up. Make that *if* I grow up.

I was having trouble with the thought of Duffy spending the night in a holding cell, but Ben said there was nothing that could be done about it. He wasn't charged, he hadn't been arraigned, and therefore there was no bail posted. The lawyer, a guy named Nelson Sanders who operated out of Poughkeepsie, said the accommodations wouldn't be as bad as we thought, and he would report back as soon as he'd met with Duffy and heard what the cops thought they had to tie him to Michelle Testaverde's killing.

Ben and I decided not to get in the car and drive immediately to Poughkeepsie. This was largely because the cops
certainly weren't going to let us listen in on his questioning,
and Sanders, who believed we were paying Duffy's legal bills
(we'd have to talk to Duffy about that), was sure to give us a
detailed report.

Instead, we planned on going up there the next day. I called
my father first to let him know I'd be an hour away instead of
the usual four hours. It seemed like the thing to do, and Dad
offered his house as a place for Ben and me to stay while we
were in the area. I would have loved to see my father, but an
hour commute back and forth was unreasonable when there
were perfectly good hotels nearby. If Duffy had actually been
investigating and hadn't been playing mind games, he'd have
opted for a hotel nearer the site of Damien Mosley's disappearance, too.

Ben booked us a room with two double beds in a hotel
in the center of town. I'd thought about calling Walt Kendig
for recommendations on both the hotel and the lawyer, but
Ben said not to let anyone involved know where we were
staying.

I waited for the phone to ring all that evening to hear
from Nelson Sanders and didn't get the call until eight. I
conferenced in Ben from his cell phone, and once we were
assembled, Sanders gave us the news as he saw it.

"That guy is a pip," he said as soon as Duffy's name was
mentioned. "He's already shown the cops two different ways
to better secure him in his cell. Said he could have escaped if

he'd wanted to but that it would just set off a manhunt and would be inconvenient to his investigation." He chuckled. "Inconvenient."

"What's his legal situation?" Ben asked. He sounded tired and maybe like he'd had a scotch. Or three.

"At the moment, he doesn't have one," Sanders said. "He's not charged, like I told you. They want to hold him for questioning, but they've already questioned him, so I'm wondering what else they have up their sleeve. Duffy's been anything but quiet. They can barely get their questions in before he's rattling off answers that can take twenty minutes to finish. A pip, that guy." I was getting the message that Duffy was a pip. It wasn't the word I'd have chosen at that moment, but I did have to remind myself I owed my life (and, if you believed him, my livelihood) to the guy.

"Are they going to question him more tonight?" Ben was being professional even if he was just a touch impaired. I'm sure Sanders didn't notice it, and if I hadn't known Ben for a little while, I probably wouldn't have, either.

"No," said the attorney. "They know better than to ask him anything without me there, and I'm not there."

"Where are you?" Ben asked. It wasn't the first question I would have asked, but he was an investigator, and I write for a living. The thousand words for today were looming in my office as soon as I cleaned up the mac and cheese I'd made myself. They don't call it comfort food for nothing.

"I'm at home having dinner with my wife." Sanders sounded a trifle put off by the question, as if it was odd that

Ben would ask and was criticizing him for not being with his client. I'd had roughly the same thought, since it was plausible that Duffy wouldn't have to spend the night in jail if the questioning ended sooner. "It's a courtesy that I'm calling you tonight. I could have waited until tomorrow morning and given you a more complete report."

"What's going to happen in the morning?" I said. There was no point in getting these two guys to butt heads over the phone tonight. Women were not put on this planet to be buffers between men. It's a side service we sometimes offer while we plot our takeover of the world. Go ahead. Assume I'm kidding.

"According to the cop I spoke to, they have some additional concerns that will take overnight to confirm. Right now, I've gotta tell you, they don't have much of anything on Duffy." He was already calling the guy Duffy. It had taken me three days to come up with that name, and now people were using it within five minutes of meeting him. I wasn't clear on whether to be flattered or annoyed.

"What *do* they have?" Ben sort of demanded. "Why did they bring him in to begin with? They think he killed this woman Michelle Terranova?"

"Testaverde," Sanders corrected him. Maybe he *was* beginning to notice that Ben had visited the bar in his home tonight. "And I don't know whether they actually think Duffy shot her. What they have is circumstantial. They were supposedly in the high school here at the same time, although nobody can find Duffy's records. He was here asking questions about her husband who disappeared right about the same time Michelle got shot. It was a five-year-old cold case, and he was poking around in it."

"That makes him suspicious?" I said. "On what planet does asking about a disappearance make you a suspect in a murder?"

"It's the fact that it was such an old case." It was Ben, not Sanders, who answered me. "Some guys want to be the genius, you know, solve the case the cops couldn't solve so they're seen as a hero. They commit the crime and then wait for it to be solved. Sometimes it doesn't get solved, and they get tired of waiting."

"That's the theory this Dougherty guy was using," Sanders said. "But I think they're grasping at straws. They want to look like they finally solved something, and that's the way—"

"Wait," I said. "Sgt. Dougherty is the cop who brought in Duffy? Sgt. Phillip Dougherty?"

"Yeah," Sanders answered. "How'd you know that?"

"He was the cop Duffy and I were talking to when we first got to Poughkeepsie," I told him. "It's a wonder they didn't come and arrest me, too."

"Well, they have one more thing on Duffy," Sanders said. "Apparently, he knew where the gun was hidden."

I heard Ben draw breath sharply. "The murder weapon?" he asked.

"Yeah. The pistol that killed Michelle Testaverde. He said he knew where it was, and after five years of looking, his guess was right on the money."

"Where was it?" Ben asked.

But I already knew. "It was in a small compartment in the ceiling of the apartment where Damien Mosley used to live," I said. "All you would have to do is open a little box in the ceiling, and you'd find the gun."

There was silence on both their phones. "You'd better not tell that to the cops up here," Sanders advised. "Then they actually *might* come down there and arrest you, too."

"How did you know that?" Ben asked me.

"I'll tell you later." Then I said to Sanders, "It's not because I shot Michelle. Because I didn't."

"Imagine my relief." He went on to say something about his wife holding dinner, promised to call us in the morning, and hung up, leaving Ben and me on the phone by ourselves.

We both let out a sigh at the same time. "Your friend Duffy has us both in knots," Ben said. His *s* wasn't slurred, but he wasn't fooling anybody.

"*My* friend? The guy showed up at my door and practically said I was his mommy." There was a silence. Neither of us wanted to hang up and be alone with our thoughts, I guessed.

"So what about that gun?" Ben asked. "How did you know it was up in some ceiling?"

"Duffy wanted to look in that little notch when we were looking at Damien Mosley's old apartment," I told him. "I said the woman who was living there now had been gracious enough in letting us into the place and we should leave her alone. She agreed with me, and eventually I got Duffy to leave."

Another long pause. "I'm going to go ahead and say it," Ben said.

But I knew what "it" was. "Honestly, I have no idea," I said.

"No idea of what?"

"Whether or not Duffy actually killed Michelle Testaverde," I told him. "Was that the trauma, the event that made him become Duffy Madison? Is the guy at the bottom of the ditch somebody else, and the man we know as Duffy used to be Damien Mosley? Did he kill Duffy Madison, the one that was in the Poughkeepsie High School yearbook? I really don't know."

There was another long, pregnant pause. "Do you want to go up there right now?" Ben asked.

"I'll pack a bag and come pick you up," I told him. There was no way I was letting him drive.

Chapter 21

It wasn't a huge surprise that the hotel where Ben had booked us a room had a similar one available a night early. Poughkeepsie is a nice town, but it was the middle of the week and not exactly a tourist hotspot at the moment.

We checked in and unpacked. I like to unpack in a hotel room even if I'm just going to be there for one night. I don't want to have to rummage through my suitcase every time I need something, and I get to hang some stuff up.

Because I'd driven all the way up (Ben was fairly sober, but I wasn't taking any chances), I had not been able to take out my laptop and log the thousand words for the day, so that was my first order of business after putting everything I'd brought into one of the hotel's drawers. Ben was basically living out of his case, which was smaller than mine and probably contained nothing more than socks and briefs. Or boxers. I didn't find out.

We were on a mission. The problem was, we didn't know what the mission required us to do.

Did we want to save Duffy? Normally, that would be the priority when two people came to deal with the possible imprisonment of a mutual friend. But the trip from Adamstown had clarified one thing for both of us: We didn't know enough about Duffy Madison to definitively say he was not the killer of Michelle Testaverde (Mosley?) and possibly the guy at the bottom of the ditch in North Bergen.

"I've worked more than ten cases with Duffy," Ben had said earlier from the passenger seat. I could have dictated the thousand words to him to type into my laptop, but I hate dictating. I don't like hearing my words read aloud even when I'm making them up. Three of the Duffy books are available on audio (MP3 or disc, audiobook fans!), and I barely got through the first chapter of the first one. The actor performing the work was wonderful, capturing each character and giving each one a specific voice. It was my words that I couldn't stand hearing. I put on a Circe Link/Christian Nesmith CD and never turned back. "I don't know anything more about him than what happened in those cases," Ben continued. "The guy never opens up about anything. Before you said he believes you made him up, I had no idea just how crazy Duffy is."

"Maybe he's not crazy," I said. Before Ben could be skeptical out loud, I added, "Maybe he's just so traumatized by something that his logical nature—and we've both seen that he has a logical nature—decided he needed to be someone else to deal with the horror of it. Maybe he stumbled across one of my books, and that's how he got to be Duffy Madison."

"Explain the Duffy Madison in the Poughkeepsie year-book," Ben said. He sat back and closed his eyes. I understood the impulse.

"If I could explain any of this stuff, we'd have only half the problems we have right now," I told him. I wasn't sure I knew what I was talking about, but it sounded good. Some-times that's all dialogue does, I've discovered, and sometimes that's enough. "I don't know why that name is in the year-book. Nobody, and I mean nobody, from that class remem-bers anything about a Duffy Madison being there." I told him about Louise Refsnyder, who had aggressively not dated Duffy in high school.

"We'll figure it out when we get there," Ben said, and thirty seconds later, he was snoring lightly. I turned the volume down on Circe and Christian. A little.

Now in the hotel room, which luckily had a desk, I set up my laptop while Ben, having changed into sweats in the bathroom, stretched out on one of the beds. "Do you mind if I put on the TV?" he asked, pointing with the remote, which seemed to limit my options for answering.

"Nah, it's okay." I got a pair of earbuds out of my coat and plugged them into the laptop. It's instrumental music when I'm writing so no words can catch in my head. So I opened the iTunes playlist I have marked "Classical" and set the controls to shuffle. Ben turned on the TV to a basketball game, and I turned my attention to my computer screen. This time I chose only to read the last paragraph I had written the day before sim-ply because I didn't think I could bear to go back any further.

About 237 words in—give or take—I was still struggling for plot, but the characters who weren't Duffy seemed to be coming along all right. He was offscreen in this particular scene, and that made it easier for me to write. With flesh-and-blood Duffy sitting in a cell for the night, I preferred not to think about him and concentrated instead on Lt. Antonio and her boss, Captain Reynolds, discussing a clue that Duffy had unearthed at the scene of the crime.

It wasn't easy—it never is—but I was engrossed enough that I almost didn't notice when my cell phone, sitting next to the laptop on my desk, buzzed with a text message. Ben actually had to point over and say fairly loudly, "Your phone." I picked it up and looked at it.

The message was from Walt Kendig, and it read, *Damien's wife Michelle murdered 5 yrs ago. I hear suspect in custody.* Some people write text messages like complex rubrics of symbols that need to be deciphered. Others write them like telegrams. Walt fell into the latter category.

I felt a quick pang of guilt for not letting Walt know Ben and I were in town, but I just didn't have the energy for him *and* 763 more words all in one night. I texted back, *I know. Will call you tomorrow.* I figured it would satisfy Walt that the famous author was still interested in talking to him (sort of) and indicate it was late and I was tired and he should, you know, leave me alone until the next day.

I had written only another thirty-six words (only 727 to go) when it became clear Walt was not going to take a hint. *Don't know who suspect is yet*, he sent.

I chose not to tell him that I did know and decided to ignore the text. Let Walt assume I had gone to bed. Ben looked a little irritated, but maybe his team was losing. It was hard to tell. I know Ben well enough to share a hotel room with two beds in it but not well enough to know which teams he might root for. Which I suppose is an odd sort of relationship, but one that could go in a number of directions, very few of which had anything to do with basketball.

But Walt was apparently not endowed with the taking-a-hint gene, and he kept going. *Michelle shot when Damien left. He shot too?* Was Walt asking whether Damien had shot Michelle or if Damien had been shot at the same time as Michelle?

There comes a time when an exchange of text messages is just a really slow phone conversation. And if I was in fact going get my thousand words added to the manuscript tonight—and I was—I had to get Walt off my back gently but quickly.

I picked up the phone and called him. "I didn't want to disturb you," Walt said. "So I didn't call, but I'm glad you did. Will this be in your next book?" People never get tired of asking a writer what's going into her next book. If we knew, writing the novel would be so much easier.

"I don't think so, Walt." I had told Ben about Walt, so he didn't look incredibly surprised, but he was looking at me and not the TV screen. "How did you find out about the arrest for Michelle's murder?"

Ben sat up.

Walt decided to be coy, which is virtually never a good idea. "Oh, I have my sources," he said.

"That's not good enough, Walt. This is serious. Do you have a friend on the police force?"

Ben shook his head, indicating you should never give the person you're asking for information an answer they can simply accept and parrot back to you. In short, don't give them an easy out.

"Yes, but I didn't hear it there," Walt said, which was a little refreshing. I hadn't given the store away. "But the city attorney comes to us to do his taxes. I'm not saying he told me anything, but . . ." That was exactly what he was saying.

"Okay, here's the thing, Walt," I said, looking at my screen, which oddly had not accumulated any additional words while I hadn't been looking. I needed to get back to work before I literally fell asleep on my keyboard. "I knew about the arrest, and I'm working on it. But since you are going to find out anyway, the suspect in custody—just for questioning, not an arrest—is Duffy Madison."

Ben's face showed thought, then approval. Fine. Tell him that much and see what happens.

"Duffy Madison?" It wasn't a question, not like Walt couldn't remember who that person might be. It was a challenge, as if to say that it wasn't possible Duffy could be a suspect, which I probably would have agreed with. Yesterday. "Aren't you with Duffy Madison?"

Did Walt think Duffy and I were an item because I wrote a character he assumed simply had the same name? "No," I said. "I'm not with Duffy. He's spending the night in police custody, but I have every reason to think he'll be released tomorrow morning."

But the moment I'd said I wasn't with Duffy, Ben sprang up from the bed and hustled to the window. He pulled back the drape on one side very carefully and looked out.

"I'm just . . . surprised, is all," Walt said. "It never occurred to me that—I mean, I never even met the guy before a couple of days ago. Why would he have wanted to kill Michelle five years ago?"

It was good covering, but it was covering. I could practically hear Walt sweating through the phone. I didn't walk over to the window because I thought two people looking out would be much more conspicuous than one, and besides, Ben would tell me what he was seeing. My job, as Ben gestured to me with a rolling hand motion, seemed to be to keep Walt talking on the phone.

"I really couldn't say," I told him. "We haven't met with the police yet. How well did you know Michelle?"

"Oh, not very well." I was trying to hear any noise that might have been in the background on Walt's end of the call, but he was keeping his phone close to his face apparently. There wasn't much to go on. "She was on the bowling team, and that's mostly how I knew her. I didn't hang out with that crowd in high school. I was two years ahead of them." He had said that much before, but it had been more convincing then.

Ben watched out through the window and seemed to be focusing directly ahead. It wasn't like he was looking around to see if there was something there. He was looking to a certain spot because there *was* something there, and it was probably Walt.

But if there was no noise around him, Walt wasn't standing out in the hotel parking lot. How had he even found us? How long had he been watching?

Had he asked if I was with Duffy meaning that he thought I really was with Duffy at that moment? Indicating that he'd watched Ben and me walk into the hotel? If that was the case, he'd been on the trail for a while.

That wasn't a very comforting thought.

Ben didn't repeat his hand gesture, so I guessed he had seen everything he could, but then he got his cell phone from his pants pocket and pushed a few buttons. Then he pointed the phone toward the window, and I wondered if he was taking a photograph.

"Can you think of a reason anyone would want her dead?" I asked.

"Nothing comes to mind," he answered. "But then I didn't really know her very well."

One of the curses of being a crime fiction writer is that it's very difficult to stop thinking like a crime fiction writer. So when Walt said he didn't know Michelle Testaverde well, my first thought was, *That's what the killer would say.*

"Who did know her well?" I asked. "Besides Damien."

"Oh, I don't know," Walt said. He sounded nervous, like he was talking faster than he intended to. "Everybody I told you about before. Lou, Rod. Barry, the guy from Rapscallion's."

He'd said Barry had left for California a year ago, at least the third destination someone had mentioned for him. Late enough that he easily could have been around to shoot Michelle. "Do you remember Barry's last name?" I asked. "Was he in your high school class?"

"I don't know. There were a lot of people in our class." Walt coughed once, and I thought I heard a car go by not far from his phone. "His last name? I really don't know. You could check with Lou."

Yeah, because talking to Louise Refsnyder was definitely on my list of things not to avoid when traveling to Poughkeepsie.

Ben made a hang-up gesture with his hand, indicating I should end the call. "Thanks for the help, Walt," I said.

"Wait!" he called back. "If you're not with Duffy Madison, who are you with?"

I hung up on Walt. I've never done that to a fan before. I hope never to do it again.

A few seconds went by while I breathed heavily and not for a good reason. Ben watched, then turned his head to watch some more and let the curtain drop. He looked at me.

"Your pal Walt was watching the hotel from his car," he said. "That's assuming he drives a ridiculously old MG with duct tape holding the front right fender on."

I blinked. "I saw that car in front of his office when Duffy and I went there," I said.

"As soon as you hung up, he started it up and drove away."

Chapter 22

Suffice it to say I did not have a lot of confidence in the rest of the words I wrote that night. I had plenty of time to write them, though, because I certainly couldn't sleep after all that had gone on that day.

Ben slept well, I took it, if the snoring was any indicator. He didn't keep me awake, because everything else did until about three in the morning when actual fatigue finally smacked me between the eyes, and my neuroses could no longer hold their own in the battle. So I'd had about four hours of rest when Ben nudged me gently to get up and go begin the process of getting Duffy out of jail. If such a thing was possible.

We began with breakfast in the hotel lobby, which had been advertised as "continental" and "free." That second part was true if you didn't factor into your calculation the idea that the hotel had included the breakfast in your room rate. So not eating it would have been silly. I got a cheese omelet, home fries, an English muffin, and a large coffee, which I had every intention of refilling at least twice before leaving.

"What's the game plan for today?" I asked Ben as he hunkered down into his choice, a bran muffin and coffee. The man had a lot to learn about the word *free* and how to take advantage of it.

"Well, the first order of business is obviously to get over to the cop shop and find out what Duffy's status is after they question him further," Ben said. I could see the rest of the day would be easier for me if I could find a quick app for my phone that would translate from cop speak into English. "After that I think our top priorities should be finding out who Barry is—and whether he has a last name—and locating him."

I chewed a bite of English muffin. Would it actually kill these places to pay for Thomas's? This was a piece of puffy white bread with a second-rate publicist. "I'll call Paula and see what she can do," I said. "Just because our peeping buddy Walt says Barry wasn't in high school with the gang doesn't mean it's true. What do you make of old Walt, anyway?" I asked Ben.

"He seems unnaturally interested in you and who you might be with at any given moment," Ben said. "I think it's a good thing we're together on this so I can look out for him."

"Don't pull your punches, Ben. Tell me what you really think." Having met Walt, it was difficult to be unnerved by the thought of him, but if Ben kept talking like that, I was sure I could scrape some fear together. I'd leave it open as an option.

"I'm not saying the guy is Hannibal Lecter." Ben held up his hands in a defensive posture. "It's just that he followed us to the hotel last night. How could he have known we were going to be there?"

"He didn't know we were going to be there," I reminded him. "He knew *I* was going to be there. He doesn't know who you are yet."

"That's interesting all by itself, and maybe it'll come in handy. Did you say anything on any of your social media accounts about coming up here last night?"

I shook my head. "It would never occur to me to broadcast my movements to a lot of people I don't know," I said. "Most of my readers—probably all of them—are lovely people, but I'm not going to be sending them an itinerary of which hotel I'm staying in on a given night."

"So how could Walt have found out?" Ben wasn't asking me so much as he was opening the subject to discussion.

"I'm thinking he knows somebody in the police department, and when he found out Duffy was being held, he staked out the most likely hotel in town because he knew I'd be coming." Which was a real feat, since even I hadn't known I was going to make the trip to Poughkeepsie again.

"Except he *didn't* know Duffy had been held. He only knew Michelle was listed as a murder victim and someone was in custody. He thought Duffy was with you." Ben finished his coffee and looked at me. I only had a few home fries left and was feeling, you know, how you feel after you've gorged yourself on free food. Walking was going to be a challenge.

"Maybe that's it," I countered. "He heard there was a suspect in custody and figured Duffy Madison would be riding up here to solve the case all by himself, like he does in the books. And since Duffy and I were together when Walt met us, he assumed I would just naturally appear by his side, chronicling his every movement for my readers in *The Strand Magazine*."

"The what?"

I gulped down my coffee. "Let's go see a guy about a guy," I said. That was like cop speak, right?

Ben just grinned and stood up. "Let's," he said.

*   *   *

We drove to the police station and parked a block away. There's parking near the headquarters, but Ben said it was a nice day and we should walk. He probably was concerned Walt was watching the building with binoculars. Our lack of a car didn't seem like a huge advantage.

So perhaps you can imagine our surprise when we arrived at the main entrance of the Poughkeepsie Police Department headquarters and found Duffy Madison standing just outside the front door, grinning.

He clearly enjoyed the moment he had as we approached, no doubt with both our mouths hanging open in shock. It was Ben who actually recovered first.

"This is your idea of being grilled by the cops?"

Then a thought occurred to me. "You didn't actually escape that cell, did you?" I asked.

Duffy, possibly for the first time since I'd met this version of him, laughed. "No, although it was certainly plausible. The configuration of the hinges in the cell doors—"

Ben held up his hand. "Not now, Duffy. Why are you standing out here when they were holding you on suspicion of a five-year-old murder?"

"Because the police didn't have enough evidence to charge him, and they knew it." The voice was familiar from the phone, but of course neither Ben nor I had ever met Nelson Sanders before.

He was a short, stocky (not fat) man in a dark suit who was currently walking through the front door of the police headquarters with a briefcase in one hand and an iPad in the other. He stuck the tablet computer under his left arm to shake hands with Ben, then me. "Nelson Sanders," he said.

"You got him out," I said, indicating Duffy. Just in case Sanders wasn't aware of what he had just managed to accomplish.

"We let them question your friend last night, and over my objections they held him until this morning, but ten minutes into the questioning, we were getting nothing but repetition, and I made it clear that they either had to charge my client or let him go. They opted for the latter, and I'm fairly sure they'll have somebody watching him until he gets himself back over the state border into New Jersey." He turned toward Duffy and looked him sternly in the face. "Which is the very next thing you're going to do, Madison."

Duffy did not seem intimidated in the least. In fact, he was still smiling from ear to ear. There's nothing he likes better than cops, and he'd gotten to spend the night with some, in a perfectly professional way of course. "I think I can be of more use here," he told Sanders.

"I don't care where you can be of more *use*," the lawyer said. "I care about where you're least likely to look even more guilty." He turned to face me. "See what you can do with this guy, would you? He's a pip." Like I needed to be told.

Wait, me? How did this get to be my responsibility? "Mr. Sanders is right, Duffy," I tried. "The top priority right now is to make sure that we can keep you from getting charged in Michelle Testaverde's murder." I figured I'd better keep talking before Duffy could come up with seventeen reasons he should stay, so I quickly added, "Why do they think you were involved, anyway?"

Sanders picked up the question, probably because he wanted it answered in legal terms and not whatever it is Duffy speaks. "They say his knowledge of the murder weapon's whereabouts indicates he's the one that put it there. The fact that he was poking around in Damien Mosley's disappearance is not enough for the detective here; to him it's Duffy trying to set himself up as a hero and not him actually trying to solve the crime." Looking at Duffy, he added, "Why *were* you trying to solve that one, anyway?"

Knowing Duffy was going to be honest, the last thing we needed if Sanders was going to remain even a little convinced that his client wasn't crazy, I said, "It was something

I asked him to do," which wasn't technically true but came close enough since I had been the impetus. "It's for something I'm writing." That part was true; I had been convinced, sort of, that Duffy solving Damien Mosley's disappearance would help me get past the difficulties with the new book. I'd *wanted* to believe it, anyway.

Duffy looked at me but did not offer a protest, which I appreciated.

But he was not as happy when I finished by saying, "And you're right, Mr. Sanders. We'll get Duffy back to New Jersey as soon as possible."

"But this aspect of the case opens so many more avenues of questioning!" Duffy protested. "We can go back to each of the people we questioned before and talk about Michelle's murder. I'll bet they know quite a bit." I had no idea what made him think that, but there was no use arguing with him.

Ben, I think, was trying to reason with Duffy, but in a manly and professional way (men think that way), when he said, "You're coming home because you'll just muddy the waters here, Duffy. Come back to the hotel with Rachel and me, and we'll pack our bags. We're all driving home today."

"But—" Duffy said no more. He knew when he was beaten.

We said our thank-yous to Sanders, who said he would be calling in a day or two to help devise a strategy going forward. He also said to call "if anything else happens," which meant he'd gotten a really strong sense of who Duffy Madison actually was and wanted to be ready.

Duffy got into the back seat of my Prius c, which is not as small as you might expect, and immediately began trying to convince Ben—not me—that we should stay the morning at least and interview one or two suspects. What could it hurt?

Ben countered by trying to distract Duffy, telling him about Walt's vigil at the hotel and his suggestion we look for Barry, but noted we did not even know Barry's last name.

"It's Barry Spader," he said.

I stole a glance at Ben as I drove. He looked at me with a "what?" expression. "How do you know that?" he finally demanded of Duffy.

"He was not just a bartender, but the owner of Rapscallion's, the bar where Louise and Damien were working," he said plainly. "We'd been told he was a waiter, but the fact was he owned it and only served tables on occasion. A quick check of the business records showed that. He moved out of Poughkeepsie a little over two years ago after selling the business for a decent, but hardly astonishing, sum."

"So he could have been around when Michelle and possibly Damien died," I said.

"*Possibly* Damien?" Duffy echoed back.

"Well, there hasn't been a positive identification yet," I reminded him.

"The body at the bottom of the ditch is Damien Mosley's," Duffy insisted. "There is no question in my mind. And he was murdered, certainly. It's possible the same person was behind both killings, but I tend to doubt it."

That took a moment to sink in. "You think we're dealing with *two* killers?" Ben said as I pulled the car into the hotel lot and parked as near to a door as I could. We didn't have much luggage, but I like to keep the trip to the car short when I can.

"It seems likely," Duffy answered. We all got out of the car, and he looked around as if sizing up the surroundings. It was a hotel parking lot. The end. No sign of our pal Walt sitting in his car with a pair of binoculars and . . . I don't like to think about it. "The method is the same in that both victims were shot, but Michelle's body, the Jane Doe the police discovered, was in an alley across the city. Damien's was in a public park. And I'm not sure the gunshot was the plan in Damien's murder; I think the killer might have been trying to frighten him into falling over the edge. It wasn't until he or she realized Damien wouldn't comply that the gun was fired, and even then the first shot was not at the victim but into the woods."

"You think he was trying to get Damien to flinch?" Ben asked.

We walked in through the main lobby and headed toward the elevators. "That would be my first guess, but the crime scene was five years old. Rachel and I saw photographs but not the scene from every angle. There was evidence of some ritual or intimidation. Damien was wearing no shoes when he was shot."

I saw two older ladies at the other bank of elevators widen their eyes and walk away in the direction of the coffee shop. They'd wait until we were out of the way.

The elevator came at that moment, and the three of us got on. Ben pushed the button, and the doors closed. "What significance do you think the shoes had?" he asked Duffy.

Duffy shrugged. "It's possible it was just a way of ensuring that Damien couldn't run away. The path is rugged, and it would be uncomfortable at least to try to escape with nothing to protect his feet. It could have been more complicated than that, but there's no way of knowing until we have more information about the killer."

The elevator doors opened, and we got out. I let Ben lead the way toward our room because I wanted to see the venue as Duffy saw it. He has a way of sizing up an area that is infuriatingly accurate when you ask him about it. The man's memory is astonishing as long as you don't go back more than five years.

"What about Michelle's shooting?" Ben asked. "How did you know the gun would be in . . ."

"In Rosalind Woo's ceiling," I finished for him. "Just because there was a compartment, it had to hold the weapon?"

"I didn't know," Duffy said. "As it turned out, the gun was hidden even inside the compartment. Another panel had to be removed to find it. Ms. Woo did not even know it was there."

"Then why was she so adamant about not letting anybody look there?" I asked.

"It was where she was keeping her stash of marijuana," Duffy answered.

We got to the room, and Ben keyed us in. This was where Duffy's observational abilities would be especially interesting to me. I wanted to see what information he got and what he was looking for.

I was not disappointed. Duffy looked around the room in sections of thirty degrees at a time. He turned his head a little at a time as if taking a snapshot of the room to store in his head, then turned some more. It was such a gradual process, you almost didn't notice him moving his feet to keep turning all the way around for a 360-degree look, in sections.

He spent the most time looking at the two beds, both of which had clearly been slept in. I wondered why that was a priority for him.

"Did the cops bust Rosalind?" I asked him. "I'd hate to be the cause of trouble for her."

The question didn't stop his circular momentum. "They gave her a quick glance when they found it, but Ms. Woo was clever and asked them what that was in the bag. They looked at each other and considered, but once they found the gun, the cannabis was not really a high priority for them."

Ben started throwing his things into his tiny traveling bag, so I took the cue and went into the bathroom for some of my stuff. "How do you think we'll be able to find Barry Spader?" I asked Duffy.

There was no immediate answer. I looked out through the bathroom door and saw Ben facing the window, putting his socks from the day before in his bag. I wouldn't qualify the action as endearing, but it was cute.

I walked out of the bathroom looking at Ben but asking Duffy the question again because he obviously hadn't heard me the first time.

When I got to the bedroom, I looked around and asked Ben, "Where's Duffy?"

Ben stiffened and turned around to look. "Uh-oh," he said.

Duffy Madison had taken the opportunity when both of us had our backs turned (Ben literally) to bolt from the hotel room.

Ben sighed and started unpacking.

Chapter 23

"Look, I haven't seen anybody at all since you were here the last time," Rod Wilkerson said to me.

I know. You're wondering why Ben and I didn't run directly through the hotel room door and try to catch Duffy before he could get away and, in his zest to solve Michelle Testaverde's murder, manage to incriminate himself even further. Certainly it would have seemed an option at the very least.

But Duffy being Duffy, he would have found the least obtrusive, least obvious way to make his way out of the building. Yes, I have thought Duffy's thoughts for him many times, but under duress I couldn't be sure my Duffy and his Duffy would definitely do the same thing.

Besides, Ben had wanted to talk to the witnesses we'd already met and try to track down Barry Spader. "We'll use this as an excuse to stay and see what we can find out," he said when I was wildly gesticulating at him only moments later. "We know Duffy wants to keep investigating. If we go back and talk to each witness, we might get lucky and find him in one of their houses."

Since my suggestion was going to be calling the police and getting Duffy arrested again, and since there were no charges upon which to arrest him at the moment, I had to agree. So we'd decided to start with Rod first, mostly because Duffy was on foot and Rod's house was closest to the hotel.

But Duffy must have figured that was what we would do because he was not at Rod's place, and Rod had quickly confirmed that Duffy had not visited since the time he and I had dropped in a few days earlier.

"Nobody?" Ben asked him now. "You have a financial consulting business and a real estate license. It's been days. You haven't seen anybody?"

"Everything is run out of the house," Rod said, settling back into a comfortable-looking easy chair in his small, neat, sterile living room. "I haven't had to show a house to anybody for a week or so, and the rest of my work is on the computer or the phone. Since my divorce, I've gone weeks without seeing another human being sometimes."

I reminded myself not to get divorced unless it was absolutely necessary. I'd have to actually start dating again to get that process rolling, but it was worth noting.

"You lied to Duffy and me about knowing Louise, and you never mentioned you were on the bowling team," I told Rod. I was getting kind of sick of Rod. "Why should we believe you now?"

Rod looked away, suddenly finding a very bland painting on his wall fascinating. Either he was lying—again—or he was embarrassed. "I had a thing with Lou, right before I got married, and I didn't want to talk about it," he said. "I didn't think the bowling team was important. Why bring it up if it had nothing to do with Damien? He was the one you were asking about."

Ben shook his head, realizing he was not discussing the subject he wanted to cover. Previous recriminations were not relevant to him. "Okay, so Duffy hasn't been here. If I were you, I'd expect him to knock on the door sometime today, possibly very soon. Make sure he knows he should call me or Rachel as soon as he shows up, okay?"

Rod made an indifferent face and shrugged. "Whatever."

"Do you have any idea how to get in touch with Barry Spader?" I asked. Might as well cover the ground we had left. Unless Duffy solved the whole plot by sunset—which was hardly out of the question—we'd probably be spending another night in Poughkeepsie, and I was mentally counting the pairs of underwear I'd packed. I could make it through today and tomorrow, and then things would get interesting, or I'd get shopping in a hurry. The hotel probably had a laundry room. So, shopping.

"Barry? From Rapscallion's?" Rod actually perked up at the mention of the name. It was the most interested I'd seen him. Of course I knew the guy less well than I know Phil, the man who reads my gas meter once a month, but I thought the change in mood was significant.

213

"And from your *bowling team*," I reminded him. Again.

"That's the one," Ben said. "Any idea where we can find him?"

Ben was in full cop mode now and had a little growl to his voice I had not heard before that was actually kind of interesting. I'm so easy.

"Okay, fine. I knew the guy. I wasn't an especially close friend of his or anything," Rod said, but his face was still sort of lit up. "I heard about him from Damien and saw him once in a while. But I know when the club closed up, he decided he'd had enough of cold winters and took off for someplace warm. New Orleans, I think." Yet another in a series of destinations we'd heard for Barry. Paula had not yet found him in West Virginia, Phoenix, Peoria, or California, but New Orleans could be fun this time of year. Or any other time of year.

"Are you in touch with him?" Ben asked. "Phone number, e-mail address, anything like that?"

Rod leaned forward in the chair and probably didn't even realize he'd done so. "Why? Do you think he had something to do with Damien disappearing?"

Wow. Rod was at least one murder behind. "Rod, the police had discovered that a murder victim they couldn't identify five years ago is actually Michelle Testaverde," I told him. I saw Ben watch closely for the reaction.

Rod laughed.

"You're kidding!" he barked. "Really? Michelle got killed?" I'd seen ten-year-olds with better senses of propriety. "Who did it?"

"We don't know," I told him. "We thought Barry might be able to answer some questions for us. You obviously didn't know anything about Michelle's murder."

Ben frowned, but Rod's face was still incredulous and amused. "No!" Rod said. "That really caught me off guard. Wow. You must really think I'm awful. It's just, you know how there are certain people that you know are headed for something, but you don't know exactly what? And then when you hear something like that, it just doesn't surprise you very much. How'd she get killed?"

I looked at Ben to see if that was classified information and let him answer. "She was shot in the back of the head," he said. "Now, about Barry Spader's contact information . . ."

Rod got up and walked to a small desk in a corner of the room where a laptop computer was sitting. He opened it and began typing. "I'll see if I have anything," he said. "I keep records. You never know if someone's going to want to move back home and buy a house or something." It's all about contacts.

He clicked and keyed for a while and then looked up. "Aha!" he said. No doubt Sir Isaac Newton was not as eloquent when the apple (or plum) fell on his head (or nearby—accounts differ). "Here he is. Barry Spader. I was wrong; he didn't go to New Orleans. He's in Arlington, Virginia." I get those two mixed up all the time, too.

"Four-hour drive," Ben muttered to himself, although he was calculating from New Jersey, not Poughkeepsie. From here it would probably take about six hours to get to Arlington. "Can you send the information to Rachel's phone?" Great. So now Rod would have my cell phone number. Oh, wait. I gave it to him the last time I was here. Never mind.

"Sure," Rod said and did the requisite moves with his mouse and his keyboard. "Now what can you tell me about Michelle getting shot?"

"What can we tell *you*?" I was not in my most tactful of moods. "We thought you would be able to tell *us* something. Why would anybody want Michelle dead?"

He walked back to the easy chair and sat down slowly, letting himself relax into the cushions. Rod, for reasons I wouldn't dare to question, seemed to be enjoying this inquiry.

"Well, I can't say I was in the inner circle, but there were rumors going around at the time." He couldn't adequately hide the grin that wanted to break out on his face. Honestly, I've had conversations with fourth graders that were more nuanced.

"What kind of rumors?" Ben asked.

"I don't like to gossip," Rod answered him.

Ben had clearly had enough. "Yes, you do," he told Rod. "You like nothing better than to gossip. And we're very happy to hear it, but let's give up on the fiction that you actually don't want to dish the dirt here. Rachel and I are on very short time, and we don't have the luxury of being able to wait for you to play coy with us for hours. So please just tell us what you know, and we will acknowledge that you didn't gossip but were very helpful in an ongoing investigation. How's that?"

It clearly wasn't what Rod had expected, and he was choosing from a smorgasbord of reactions but didn't know which would be most effective. He went for submissive, which was a relief to us all. His shoulders slumped in the chair, and he hung his head a little.

"Like I said, I wasn't the closest with that whole bunch, at least not after I got married," he began. "But I do know that she was not exactly the most faithful of wives, and Damien knew it."

So if we were to believe what Louise Refsnyder had told Duffy and me—and I saw no reason we should—both partners in the marriage were cheating on each other. My first thought was that it must have been exhausting. "Who was she seeing?" I asked. Somehow I knew it would be someone we had already met.

"From what I hear, half the young male population of Dutchess County," Rod said, gaining back some of his bravado (but not much). "I heard there were at least three guys."

"Under normal circumstances, the husband would be the first suspect in her death," Ben suggested, perhaps to himself. "But Damien Mosley was already missing when Michelle was killed." Then he looked at me. "Right?"

"Actually, we never really got a specific date when Damien left," I said. "There was never a police report filed. Michelle had supposedly already left for West New York and wasn't around to file one. Nobody else lived with Damien, as far as we know."

"I don't remember," Rod said, as if someone had asked him. "I mean, I never knew Michelle had been shot. I remember everybody saying she had moved into Damien's place in Jersey that summer." When people from anywhere else say *Jersey* like that, it drives us natives up the wall. Do we ever say you're from *York*?

(We get to say *Jersey* whenever we want, though, because we live in it.)

"There's one person who can tell us if it's possible that Damien was the one who killed his wife," I said, reaching for my phone.

Ben's forehead wrinkled. "Who?"

"Duffy Madison."

* * *

It took almost no effort to get Duffy to come out of hiding, which in his case turned out to be at Oakwood, the bar that had evolved from Rapscallion's. I texted him and told him to stay where he was once he admitted being there.

All I'd had to do to roust him was to say that Ben and I had new information on Michelle Testaverde's murder and that it might connect to Damien Mosley's disappearance. Duffy, investigative maniac that he is, couldn't resist. We thanked Rod for all he believed he had done for us, and I drove the two of us to the address my GPS found for Oakwood.

It was exactly what you'd expect from the name: an oak-paneled restaurant and bar catering less to hipsters—there was no irony on the walls here—and more to the hipsters' parents. I'm not nearly old enough to have parented someone with a man bun and ironic facial hair, but I still appreciated the calm, welcoming atmosphere at Oakwood.

Turned out the atmosphere was welcoming as long as you'd brought your American Express card with you, because the prices here were not exactly attuned to the budget of the average (or, some say, above average) crime fiction writer. Luckily, I was with two chivalrous men, at least one of whom believed I had created him. They owed me.

Ben and I found Duffy at the bar, which I would not have expected. He doesn't drink alcohol very often and almost never in public. But when we entered the place, there was Duffy on a barstool, deep in conversation with a man in a blue pinstripe suit who apparently hadn't heard the eighties were over. The man was knocking back a double Chivas as we approached and already signaling the bartender, a comely brunette no doubt working her way through Vassar or the Culinary Institute of America (CIA) in nearby Hyde Park, for another.

Duffy waved us over. "Ben! Rachel!" People always do that because apparently they think you don't know your own name. "Come meet Mr. Polanski."

Ben and I managed not to give each other incredulous looks as we approached. It also became clear, the nearer we got, that Duffy had a glass of ginger ale in front of him, while Mr. Polanski—whoever he was—was already working on his new scotch. Duffy was smiling oddly, like a person who really doesn't want to get his picture taken but is forced by his family to say *cheese*. This was Duffy pretending with all his might to be ingratiating.

"Mr. Polanski has been telling me a very interesting story," Duffy said after introductions had been made. Mr. Polanski's first name appeared to be "Mr."

I had to figure this had something to do with Michelle Testaverde's murder, but the idea that Duffy had just wandered into a bar and found a witness was, to say the least, unlikely.

"What kind of story?" Ben asked. Ben knows how to deliver a straight line when necessary.

"Mr. Polanski"—who still had not spoken other than to say hello—"is the owner of this establishment," Duffy said. "He bought the building and the liquor license from Barry Spader, then did extensive renovations on the facility and the business plan."

"It used to be a strip club," Mr. Polanski said, more proudly than you might expect and with a definite slurring of his *s*. "I made it a classy restaurant." I was willing to take him at his word, but it reminded me that we hadn't actually eaten since the free breakfast at the hotel, which seemed like quite some time ago. Maybe Duffy could talk his new friend into giving us a discount.

"Yes, it's very nice," Ben said, reinforcing the subject's point of view in order to provoke more conversation. I had looked up certain interrogation techniques for the second Duffy book, *Little Boy Lost*, available at your local bookstore, if you're lucky enough to have one, and online. "So why was Barry selling his business?" Because let's face it, we weren't the least bit interested in Mr. Polanski, and we were interested in Barry Spader, who might very well have shot Michelle or Damien or both and then fled to Arlington, Virginia, which I'm assuming has an extradition treaty with the United States.

"He wanted to leave town," Polanski said. "Said he'd had enough of the cold and the snow." To each his own. I'm not a huge fan of winter, but Poughkeepsie isn't the arctic. I'd miss the change of seasons if I moved to, say, San Diego. Not that I wouldn't like to test this theory, but perhaps my mind was straying just a bit.

"The interesting part," Duffy said, "was the price of the transaction. Don't you think so, Mr. Polanski?"

Clearly, Duffy was leading his new buddy into a certain piece of information he'd mentioned before, perhaps even while still sober (if Duffy had gotten here early enough for that).

Polanski finished his drink and signaled for another. Not surprisingly, the bartender knew her boss and placed it in front of him immediately even as she took the empty glass away. This, and she wouldn't even get a tip, except maybe from Duffy.

"Damn right." Polanski's speech was definitely becoming a problem for him now, and it wasn't exactly a walk in the park for those of us trying to understand what he was trying to say. "I stole this place from old Barry." He took a significant swig of his current drink, and I saw the bartender move the bottle of Chivas closer to where she was working so she could be ready when he needed another. That wouldn't be long. "Took him for all he was worth. And I wasn't even trying to do that."

Duffy, who had not so much as touched the glass in front of him since we'd entered, patted Polanski on the shoulder in what I'm sure he thought was the appropriate gesture of support. Polanski was too drunk to decide if it was appropriate or not and didn't seem to notice Duffy's hand at all.

"No one thinks you cheated Mr. Spader," Duffy said. "But he really did sell the business to you at a major discount, didn't he?"

Polanski now seemed to remember that he was an important businessman, at least the most important within earshot. He stood up straighter and gestured toward Duffy with his right hand, which was holding the drink. A little of the scotch dribbled onto the bar, but Polanski didn't seem to notice. "You're damn right," he reiterated. "A business like this, with a liquor license and a kitchen, should have gone for three times what I paid."

Ben's mouth twitched; something had clicked in his mind. He looked at Duffy. "So Barry might have been more desperate to get out of town than he let on," he said.

Duffy's smile became more genuine and broader. "Exactly."

"Sure," Polanski agreed, swaying just a touch. "You don't give up that kind of money just because you hate the snow."

I hadn't said, well, anything up until now because I didn't know what the point of the conversation might be until this moment. "But Barry left years after Michelle Testaverde supposedly left to live in the West New York apartment with her husband. Why was he in such a hurry all of a sudden?"

Ben and Duffy must have suddenly realized I was still in the room because they both turned toward me with identical expressions of mild surprise. They both nodded. Polanski just looked mystified.

"Who are you again?" he asked me. "And who is Michelle Testamonte?"

We all ignored him, and Duffy's mouth flattened out a little. "There is a theory," he said. "Suppose Barry Spader was involved with the murders but wasn't the person who pulled the trigger. He knows what happened but can't tell anyone about it because he has some implication. It is possible that living here and working in this building with all its memories of the people who were gone built up inside him. He couldn't abide with all the thoughts, so he decided to get out. That could be why the price was irrelevant. He just needed to leave."

"That's not a theory," Ben said. "That's a guess."

Duffy smiled. "Tomato, tomahto," he said.

"I need food," I announced to no one in particular. "Should we go somewhere else? This place looks a little pricey." It was a calculated gamble.

And it paid off. "You're not going anywhere!" Polanski shouted. "Lunch is on the house!" He gestured to the room in general, and a hostess who was possibly even more attractive than the bartender—I was sensing a pattern—appeared at his side and ushered us, minus the pickled restaurateur, to a table.

Once drink and appetizer orders (hey, it was on the house) were taken, I asked Duffy, "What happened when you tried to contact Barry Spader?" It followed that once he knew there was such a person, Duffy certainly would have followed up on the lead.

"I left two messages on his voice mail but hadn't heard back until just before I came here," he answered.

"Yeah, about that whole running out on us in the hotel thing . . ." Ben began.

Duffy looked up at him, all innocence. "Yes?"

There was a medium-sized pause. "Forget it." Ben waved a hand. He had nice hands, I noticed.

"So you heard from Barry when you were fleeing us and making your way to the site of the former Rapscallion's?" I said. I can get the conversation back on topic when I want to.

"Yes. He called and sounded somewhat bewildered, like he couldn't understand why someone would ask him about something as obscure as the murder of a person he knew." Duffy shook his head in astonishment. "Almost as if I were being rude to interrupt his day."

I looked at Ben. "Imagine," I said.

Duffy did not respond to that, but as is his habit, he plowed on through. "I finally managed to engage him in conversation about Michelle Testaverde, and he said she had been, and I'm quoting, 'a singular soul filled with love and joy.' The fact that she married Damien Mosley had apparently come as some surprise, as Damien was known as something of a darker personality, a little more brooding and pessimistic."

"Do you think Barry had a thing for Michelle?" Ben asked.

Duffy took a moment as if translating in his head. "It did occur to me, but I didn't have time to ask. Barry said he was late for a meeting and would call me back in two hours. That was about forty minutes ago."

"So we have time to eat," I said. The server, whose name was Maureen (for some reason, it has become important that we know the names of our servers although they don't know ours—not sure how I feel about that), had brought our drinks and said the appetizers would be on their way momentarily.

"You said you had news for me," Duffy reminded me.

We filled him in on the conversation we'd had with Rod Wilkerson about Michelle's murder and our suspicions, if they were even that developed, that Damien himself might have become jealous of his wife's affairs and gone the instant-divorce route.

"It comes down to a question of timing," Ben finished up. He turned to Duffy. "Do you remember the date that the body you think is Damien Mosley's was discovered?"

Not so much as a blink. "September twenty-third, five years ago."

"Rod said it was going around that Michelle had moved to West New York that summer," Ben reminded us. "So if he's right, and if Michelle was shot instead of moving, it's chronologically possible Damien did shoot his wife. Assuming that was Damien at the bottom of the cliff."

"It was," Duffy said again. It is best not to argue.

Ben leaned back in his chair as a platter of soft tortillas and fillings for fajitas was placed in front of us. "It looks like we're driving to Arlington, Virginia," he said.

I was halfway to filling a tortilla, but I stopped to look at him. "Don't be silly," I said. "We're not driving six hours to talk to one guy."

"We're not?"

"No. That's why Skype was invented."

Chapter 24

Since we had not actually checked out of the hotel, the room Ben and I had booked was the natural place for us to videoconference with Barry Spader, former Poughkeepsie tavern keeper turned Virginia . . . entrepreneur? I really wasn't sure what business Barry was in now.

The room had been cleaned and neatened by the housekeeping staff, which was nice, although Duffy had seen it in its natural state and drawn whatever conclusions he'd drawn. Why did I care what a fictional character thought about my hotel room? It was a question most writers don't get to ask themselves, and I envy them.

Once Barry had indeed called Duffy back on his cell, it had been suggested that we amble (in my car) back to the hotel following our lunch at Oakwood and meet with Barry face-to-pixel, which was the second best thing and saved us a very long car trip. Six hours in a vehicle with Duffy Madison . . . It was difficult enough spending a thousand words a day with the guy.

Barry, it turned out on my laptop, was a very average-looking guy with unremarkable brown hair sitting, as far as I could tell, at an uninspiring desk in a typical room. The leaves on the trees outside his window were starting to change color, and that was the most interesting thing about looking at the screen right now. I'd say more about him, but I'd have to get out a thesaurus for more words meaning *regular*.

"The thing is, I bought the club from my father," he was saying now. His voice was . . . well, you know. "He was the guy who loved running a strip club. I didn't like it. I didn't like hiring girls to dance, and I didn't like having to watch every guy who walked in to see if he was going to start trouble. I didn't need to hang around in a bar. I don't even drink. But it was the family business, and he was retiring, so . . ."

"What made you decide you'd had enough last year?" Ben, sitting in the hotel-issued desk chair to my right, was trying to conduct a dignified interview. Having three adult humans maneuvering around a laptop screen thirteen inches wide was lending the whole thing a slight air of farce, but Ben was in there pitching. "Why hadn't you left years earlier?"

"I had a mortgage on a house and a mortgage on the bar," Barry answered. "My father had taken out equity loans and listed the business as collateral. As soon as I could pay that off, I was out of there. The weather wasn't keeping me in New York, either."

"If the cold was a factor, you could have moved to Florida or Arizona," Duffy piped up. I practically had to dive off the side chair so he could be seen. Barry was definitely looking from face to face on his end, and I figured we looked like we were being held prisoner on the back of a vinyl album cover. "There are many warmer climates than in Arlington, Virginia."

Barry seemed to find Duffy odd. Imagine. That too was a disappointment. None of these Poughkeepsie High graduates recognized the guy who was supposed to have been in their graduating class! Didn't Barry *want* to help me prove Duffy was crazy?

Barry narrowed his eyes and watched as my brain dropping situated himself in an area he thought was between Ben and me and I thought would come across as his disembodied head floating over us.

"I just got in the car and started driving south," Barry told him. "When I got here, I looked around for jobs in sales because that's what I was good at. I got one working for a company that makes cardboard boxes, and I stayed for a while. It's been about a year and a half now."

"Why did you stay?" I asked. I figured I had to get in on the conversation somehow; it was my computer.

"I got married," he answered. "Met a girl I liked, and every time I thought I'd move on to a new place, I asked her to come with me, but she wouldn't. So I stayed here instead. We're married a little over six months now."

Duffy coughed theatrically, indicating he believed we were getting too far off topic. Normally, on an investigation (or at least the only one I'd ever seen them work together),

Duffy would defer to Ben, who was, after all, his boss. But without the need to report to the Bergen County prosecutor on this matter, Duffy was almost gleeful in his ability to do things exactly in the manner he wanted to do them.

"Getting back to your time in Poughkeepsie," he said, "I am curious about your involvement with a few people you knew from your high school class, your business, and your bowling team."

"I was wondering what this was really about," Barry said. "You'd texted me about Michelle Testaverde and Damien Mosley. What's going on? They both sort of vanished out of Poughkeepsie around the same time, years before I left. Are they back?"

"No, and they won't be coming back," Duffy said. He was being more gruff and blunt than I was used to. It's a tactic I write in for him very rarely, only when he believes a witness is not telling the truth. I wondered what Barry was lying about. "Both of them are deceased, and each of them was murdered."

Ben's eyes were riveted to the screen as Barry reacted. On the computer screen, there is always a slight lag in time, and you can hear your own voice echoing in the other person's computer, so there was a pause right away. But then Barry heard what Duffy had said, and his head snapped back in his chair. His eyes grew wide.

"Deceased," he said. "They're dead?" There seemed to be no point in explaining that the two words mean the same thing; we all knew he was processing the information. If the news wasn't a surprise to Barry, he was a very good actor and was wasting himself in a sales job in Virginia. "Somebody killed them? Who? Why?"

"Two excellent questions, Mr. Spader," Duffy countered. His tone still indicated some impatience with the guy on the other end of the . . . Internet feed, or something. Hey, if I ever need to find out for a book, I'll research it (Paula will research it). "What can you tell us about the time when both Damien Mosley and Michelle Testaverde were leaving Poughkeepsie?"

"Wait. Let me think about this. You mean you think it happened around then? It must be six years ago."

"Five," Duffy told him.

"Okay, five years ago." Barry was shaking his head slightly with each word now. "That's when they got killed? How come nobody knew about it then?"

"Again, something I really wish I could answer," Duffy told him. "What can you tell us that might help with all these questions? What was going on within the group, the bowling team, at that time?" Duffy did not ask if Barry remembered; that would be giving him too convenient a way out of answering. He assumed Barry remembered everything and could summon it at will. It's Duffy's way of thinking, and it simplifies my process enormously.

"Well, was that around the time Damien asked Michelle to marry him?" Barry asked. He was now, as Duffy had probably hoped, trying to be the good student in class who could help the teacher so he wouldn't be mad anymore. I considered that an optimistic viewpoint, but I knew Duffy better than Barry.

"I am not certain when the proposal was made, but from what we have been able to determine, Damien and Michelle were married by the time they both were murdered," Duffy said.

"Married?" Barry asked. It seemed an odd question. Wasn't that what was *supposed* to happen after an engagement?

"Yes," Duffy said. "So the time line would seem to indicate that the proposal took place sometime before either of them disappeared from the area."

But Barry was shaking his head. "No," he told Duffy. "That's not what happened."

"I don't understand." Ben had decided to cut through the etiquette and hopefully move the conversation along. "What do you mean, that's not what happened? Did Damien and Michelle stay here in Poughkeepsie after they were married?"

The headshaking was more emphatic. "No. You're missing the point. It's not the time line that's the problem. You're saying Michelle and Damien were married, and I'm saying they weren't."

The three of us on Barry's computer screen looked at each other with what I'm sure looked like complete and utter puzzlement, because that's what it was.

"Damien asked Michelle to marry him. I was there," Barry said. "But they never got married. She said no."

Chapter 25

"This explains a great many things," Duffy Madison said.

I stared at him. Of all the things Duffy had ever said to me—and there had been some doozies—this was among the most baffling. I looked over at Ben, who seemed to have disengaged from our conversation, his eyes staring straight ahead like he was waiting for Dracula to walk in through the door of the hotel room.

We had finished up our questioning of Barry Spader after another ten or fifteen minutes, most of which was engaged in the three of us trying to wrap our heads around what he had been saying. Damien Mosley had gotten down on one knee at the bowling alley where the team's league met, produced a ring from the pocket of his jeans, and asked Michelle Testaverde to marry him.

According to Barry, she had looked absolutely stunned by the question, which is not entirely unusual. But he said she also looked terrified, and that was not the kind of reaction a guy might hope to get to a marriage proposal.

"I'm not saying she was afraid of Damien himself," Barry had said, "but the idea of being married to him, or maybe to anyone, seemed to horrify her. She actually took a step back, away from him, and set off the foul line buzzer on the lane. Damien didn't understand right away, and he asked again. Michelle had to say no in front of everybody. It was not a fabulous night. Pretty sure we didn't go back to the bar for a drink afterward."

"What was their relationship like after that?" I asked. "It must have been kind of awkward to hang around with both of them."

"I don't think I ever saw them together in the same room after that night," Barry said. "The bowling team kind of broke up. Michelle left first, and before they could find a replacement for her on the bowling team, Damien called to say he was quitting. We couldn't find two more bowlers in time for the end of the season, so we just dropped out. I think everybody pretty much understood."

He said Michelle and Damien were seen only separately after the proposal, and that once Michelle left the team, she was hardly seen by anyone at all. Like Damien's supposed exit from Poughkeepsie, Michelle's was noticed in the long term rather than the short. After a while, Barry said, people just realized they hadn't seen either of the two for some time.

We thanked him for his help, which I thought just made everything more difficult to understand, and disconnected the computer connection so Barry could go back to his wife and his job in Arlington. Now Duffy was saying what he'd told us had helped to clear up a number of issues, and I was staring at him blankly, I'm sure.

"You know, just because I made you up doesn't mean I understand you all the time," I told him. Hey, I can use his delusion just as effectively as he can. "What do you mean it clears things up?"

"Well, consider it," Duffy said. I groaned inwardly; it was going to be one of those Duffy lectures where I was supposed to figure it out for myself and therefore be taught a valuable lesson and gain self-esteem. I'd hated this when I was in second grade, and the technique had not risen in my estimation in the ensuing years. "If Michelle Testaverde declined Damien Mosley's marriage proposal, we have solved a number of smaller questions that had arisen in this case."

He waited for me to offer a guess. I didn't. Ben continued to stew in his own juices, which wasn't helping me much. I'd never really considered sharing a hotel room with two men, but if I had, I was sure I'd anticipated more fun than this.

Duffy realized I wasn't going to answer and went to Plan B, which was just telling us—or me, since I wasn't sure Ben was listening—stuff. "If they were never married, we can understand why it was impossible to find any recording of a marriage certificate in the area," he began. "If they were never married, the fact that Michelle never seems to have lived in the West New York apartment makes more sense. As for the murders, again a time line is the biggest stumbling block, since no one so far has managed to pinpoint the date of the rejected proposal versus the time both Michelle and then Damien were murdered."

Ben didn't stop staring, but his mouth moved, and words came out, which I considered something of a relief. I'd been worried this situation had dropped him into some kind of investigator coma from which only clues could cause him to awaken.

"Did Michelle die first?" he asked. "Are we certain her murder came before Damien's, if Damien really is the body at the bottom of the cliff?"

Duffy didn't sigh; he wouldn't show that kind of impatience with Ben. But he did take a moment before answering, and his voice had the slightest edge of frustration at our inability to see the obvious. I really shouldn't have modeled him on Sherlock Holmes; I see that now. Encyclopedia Brown was so much more affable.

"Damien Mosley died from a gunshot wound to the head and then fell down a hill onto a poorly placed rock," he said carefully. "The trauma to his head, indicated in the medical examiner's report, did not include a bullet wound because of the damage done, but I am expecting a call from the North Bergen Police Department at any moment that will confirm or disprove my findings."

"That doesn't answer my question," Ben noted. "Are we sure of the order in which the two people died?"

"We are not," Duffy admitted. "It's critical that we pinpoint the date of the marriage proposal from Damien to Michelle, which Barry Spader claims was rejected."

"Claims?" I asked. "Do we have some indication that Barry is lying, or mistaken?"

"There is the fact that everyone else we have spoken to believed Michelle and Damien to be a married couple," Duffy said. "When one witness says something happened, and no one else corroborates that information, it might not be suspicious, but it is certainly questionable."

"Then we should go back to our sources," Ben said. "Find out whether anybody actually attended the wedding, if there was one."

"I'll call Walt Kendig," I said. "He's probably watching us with binoculars now anyway."

Walt was more than pleased to meet with us, particularly Ben, whom he had not yet met. I absolutely refused to let him anywhere near our hotel room whether there were two other men present or not, and Ben agreed that would be a poor maneuver. So we met at the same hipster diner near Walt's office despite having had a fairly extensive lunch not long before.

Walt had not yet eaten, so he ordered a turkey club with sweet potato fries and a coke while Ben and I ordered coffee, and Duffy sufficed with a diet soda. I thought of the diet sodas at that Plaza Diner in Adamstown and was pleased to stick with the coffee. I didn't really want either, but I hate to make a waitress work for nothing.

The corn muffin I ordered with it was an impulse. It was organic, too.

"I wasn't at Michelle and Damien's wedding," he said while we were waiting for our orders to show up. Walt was watching Ben carefully. Ben doesn't appear in any of the Duffy Madison books because he's a real person, so Walt was least familiar with him out of the three of us. But the way he kept looking from Ben to me was a little unsettling. I was starting to think Walt might be an author groupie.

I'm told—and believe me, I'd never seen it in practice— that some readers become so attached to the stories they're told in books that they latch onto the authors and believe they have a personal relationship with the person who provides those stories. I sort of understand it; when a book really gets to me, it can feel like the author is writing specifically to my brain. But I don't think I've ever so much as written a fan e-mail to an author. Some of my writing friends have told me (and the stories are always about people they know, and not them personally) that some readers get so caught up in the attachment that they actually start to contact the author, try to ingratiate themselves and become a part of the writer's life. It's touching in its own way, but when it reaches the point of stalking, it can be seriously disturbing.

I'm told.

Now Walt was watching my hotel room from his car and glancing from Ben—the man sharing that room, whose circumstances Walt knew nothing about—to me. I couldn't read his expression. For all I knew, Walt was a cop groupie and had designs on Ben, but I didn't think so.

"But you're sure they were married?" Ben asked, and Walt's eyes turned to him and held on his face.

He shrugged. "That was what I heard, and I had no reason to think it wasn't true. Why?"

"From whom did you hear that Michelle and Damien were married?" Duffy asked. He wasn't going to answer Walt's question, which was wise. Duffy is, if I might say so myself, a really intelligent investigator.

Walt waited while our drinks were distributed at the table and asked about his turkey club, which the waitress assured him would be just a minute in arriving. Then he looked at Duffy. "I think Damien told me, but I don't really remember," he said. "Why?"

"Were you present when Damien proposed marriage to Michelle?" Duffy asked. Again Walt's question was going unacknowledged, but he showed no amount of upset about it.

"Well, sort of," Walt replied, and he looked at Duffy with an expression that practically begged for a straight line.

But Duffy didn't pick up on it, so I decided to move the conversation along. "What do you mean, sort of?" I asked.

"There was this one time Damien actually proposed to Michelle at the bowling alley, and she said no," Walt answered, now fixing his gaze squarely on me. "But I think that was kind of a joke, you know? Like a way to show her he was serious, but not a real proposal. I mean, who proposes when he's sitting on a one/seven split?"

"So if Michelle said no in front of you, why are you so sure they were really married?" Ben asked.

Walt looked surprised by the question, as if the answer was obvious. "Damien told me," he said.

Okay, that was something. I didn't know what, but it was something. I hoped Ben and Duffy had better thoughts than that.

Ben leaned in and lowered his voice, maybe for effect. "Damien Mosley told you that he and Michelle Testaverde were married?" he asked.

Again, Walt seemed puzzled that the question had even been asked. "Yeah. Maybe two weeks after that bowling alley thing. He said they'd gotten blood tests and gotten married in Connecticut or someplace. Not here in town, I know that. And he said Michelle wanted to leave town and was going to his apartment in Jersey. Said he'd follow her there. They quit the bowling team, so I had no reason to see them after that, and it took a while before I realized anybody thought they were missing." He caught himself and gestured with his right hand in a "well, sort of" movement. "Actually, that anybody thought Damien had left or vanished or something. The idea was that Michelle had moved already."

That sounded wrong to me. "She just left? She didn't say good-bye to anybody? Just one day here and one day there?"

Walt nodded as the waitress brought his sandwich, overwhelmed on the plate by sweet potato fries. You could tell sweet potatoes and cooking oil were cheap, whereas turkey, bacon, and tomatoes might have been a little pricier. The club sandwich was pretty thin. The Plaza Diner at home did a much better job.

I'd only been gone since yesterday, and I was getting homesick for Adamstown.

As soon as the waitress left, Walt took a bite and then gestured with one of his fries in his right hand. "I don't know if she told any of her other friends," he said. "I don't know if she *had* any other friends. I just know that nobody on the bowling team or at Rapscallion's ever heard from her. Word was she thought she was better than us and didn't have to mingle with the riffraff anymore."

But Duffy had other concerns; he was already thinking ahead to verifying Walt's statements. "Do you know where in Connecticut they were married?" he asked. A license and a marriage certificate would make him feel so much more comfortable. I've known people like that.

Walt shrugged. "I'm not even sure it *was* Connecticut," he said. "It was five years ago. Might have been Maryland. Isn't that where people used to go to get married? I know it wasn't Vegas."

"What time of year was it?" Ben asked. No doubt he was thinking it would be easier to search marriage records for the year if we had a general time period to limit the inquiry.

"Fall," Walt said after he'd swallowed his latest bite. "I remember that. It was just starting to get cold out at night, you know, like now."

He didn't seem to have any more useful knowledge to share on the two dead people. But since the conversation was winding down and I didn't see any reason for pretense, I looked Walt dead in the face.

"How come you were watching the window of my hotel room last night?" I asked.

Walt was so stunned, he stopped eating. Ben and Duffy stared at me, I assume because they were appalled that I had breached the protocol of talking to Walt only about the two murders. But call me crazy, I don't like it when some guy spends his evenings watching where I sleep unless I invite him to do so.

"I don't know what you're talking about," he attempted.

"Yes, you do," I said. "If you want us to believe one word of what you've told us so far in the past few days, you'd better make sure you tell the truth now. Otherwise I'm going to assume you just like telling people lies and having the spotlight whether you deserve it or not. So spill. Now. Why were you outside the hotel watching my room?"

Duffy's mouth opened and closed a couple of times. But I think Ben looked at me with a different kind of respect than I'd seen from him before. When we first met, I was a potential victim in need of protection. I was making a step away from that role and into that of a formidable colleague.

Hey, I make up stuff for a living. I can assume things with a guy I'm sort of dating.

Walt actually put down the quarter of the sandwich he'd been working on and seemed to think the situation over carefully. After a moment of contemplation, he shook his head slowly.

"I honestly have no idea what you're talking about."

That didn't answer my question. "We saw you," I said.

"No you didn't, because I wasn't there. I don't even have a car at the moment. Mine was stolen."

I looked at Ben, who shrugged and started pushing buttons on his phone.

"What kind of car?" I asked Walt.

"A 1972 MG. I can't imagine why somebody would want to steal it; the thing is falling apart. I mean, it's wicked cool, but I can't afford to keep it up. I parked it in the lot next to my apartment last night when I got home from work yesterday, and when I came out this morning, it was gone, and no, I didn't report it to my insurance company, but I did call the cops. What's my insurance company going to do? The car's not worth more than what they could get for scrap metal."

"But you called me last night right when I got to my hotel," I said, trying to convince Walt it would be better to own up to his infraction. "You were trying to figure out what I was doing in the hotel."

"I heard from a friend in the police department that they had a suspect in Michelle's murder, and I hadn't even known Michelle had been murdered," Walt said, staring at his food not because he was desperate for another bite but because he wanted to avoid eye contact. "I figured that meant you and Duffy were coming back, and I wanted to be ready to help you. Honest."

"How'd you find my car to follow me?" I said.

Now Walt did look up and meet my gaze, in surprise. "I didn't," he said. "I don't know who was following you, but if you saw my car, it was whoever stole it."

"Why were you asking about who was in the room with me?" I asked.

"It's embarrassing."

For him or me? I wasn't sure I wanted to find out, but Ben pressed on. "That's not really the priority right now," he said.

Walt, still looking down, nodded. "Okay. I wanted to see if you were in the room alone, and if not, whether Duffy was there with you. I wanted to see if you two were a thing." Walt had devolved into a fourteen-year-old girl in front of my eyes. It was actually a sad thing to see.

So he'd been right. It was embarrassing. For all of us.

There was a sort of stunned silence, which was actually a blessing because in my writer's ear, I heard Duffy saying in a huff, "No, we are not a *thing*." But he didn't. Instead, I spoke to Walt as I would to a child who liked to watch people in hotel rooms through binoculars. Because I wasn't sure I believed him about that.

"You can't do that anymore," I told him. "That's not okay. I get that you really enjoy my books, and I'm very honored, but my private life is, you know, private. You understand?"

Walt broke his gaze and looked down as he nodded guilt-ily. "Yeah. I do. It felt weird when I was asking, even, but for some reason, it was really important for me to know that. I'm very sorry, and I hope you'll forgive me."

It was important to make a strong impression about how serious an infraction Walt had committed, so I decided not to let him off the hook immediately. "I'll think about it, but I need to see that you really do get what I'm saying, Walt. For now, let's leave it at the point where I'm grateful for you enjoy-ing the books, and that's as far as we go, okay?"

I didn't glance at Ben, but peripherally I saw his head nod. Duffy was to Walt's left in the booth, so I could see him even when fixing my focus on Walt. Duffy didn't move. He was probably trying to decide whether his own interest in the hotel room Ben had rented for us had violated some trust. Duffy is mostly an introvert. Except when he's not.

"Okay, Ms. Goldman," Walt said, taking us back to the beginning of our relationship. He was the dedicated fan, and I was the revered (by him) author. I'd let him dangle for a while and then indicate he was forgiven, assuming there was no one outside my hotel room window tonight. "I really am sorry."

So that said, we concluded our business. Walt had the remainder of his sandwich packed to take home, and Ben, Duffy, and I paid our part of the tab and got up to leave. I realized I'd never even gotten my muffin, which was just as well.

On the way to the door, Ben said, "I checked with the Poughkeepsie police website. It's a matter of public record. Walt did not report a stolen car."

Then we went outside, and the police arrested Duffy.

Chapter 26

"This is bogus," said Nelson Sanders. "They get one piece of physical evidence that's been sitting around for five years, and they think they can make a case with that? Something else is going on, and it's not pretty."

I could agree that what was happening here was not an attractive thing to see. Duffy had been handcuffed and placed in the back of a police cruiser, while a uniformed officer named Crawford (according to his nameplate) recited his Miranda rights. (Just as an aside: As a writer, I find the Miranda rights much less wordy and difficult to understand than any other legal document I can recall. It's not great, catchy writing, but the key is be easily comprehended, and the words accomplish that. End of rant.)

"I don't get it," Ben said. "They told you they have the murder weapon, that it's that gun they dug out of Damien Mosley's ceiling, and that ties Michelle's shooting to Duffy? How does *that* work?"

Duffy, off being further "processed" like a slice of Kraft American cheese, was nowhere to be seen. We were standing in a waiting area in the police station outside the bullpen, and our conversation was being conducted at a low volume. Because maybe someone would hear us and . . . I'm not actually sure why we were being so quiet.

"They say the gun has Duffy's fingerprints on it," Sanders added. "Which makes pretty much no sense at all. Nobody on this planet can put him in Dutchess County on the night Michelle died. We're not even sure if the two of them ever met. The idea that this weapon has been sitting around for more than a whole presidential term and they find his prints on there, clear enough to be positively identified after all that time, is pretty suspicious."

And that was just the beginning. "What happens now?" I asked.

"Now we wait for him to be arraigned, which should happen today because it's early enough," Sanders told us. "The judge will set bail, and we'll have to see how high that's going to be. If Duffy can pay it, there won't be a problem. Do you know anything about his finances?"

Ben and I glanced at each other. "Not really," Ben said.

"I'll talk to Duffy about it when we get to court," Sanders said. "I can't imagine they'll see him as a flight risk, but you never know in cases when the defendant is from out of state. Look, there's nothing you two can do here until the arraignment. I'll call you as soon as I know when that's going to be." He nodded at us and headed back toward the desk to pester the sergeant some more. The man was worth every penny Duffy was paying him. However he was doing that.

"What do you think?" Ben said after Sanders left.

"I think my stomach is tied up in knots, and I feel utterly powerless. How about you?"

"I want to go talk to Louise Refsnyder," he exhaled.

I figured the day couldn't go a whole lot worse, so I agreed, although the idea that "worse" might actually be a possibility was a sobering thought. I called Paula through my Prius c's Bluetooth while I was driving to Louise's place, which I actually could find without GPS now.

After getting her up to speed on the events of the day, which began with seeing Duffy out of jail and led to seeing Duffy back in jail, Paula filled me in on what she'd been able to find out from Adamstown, a place for which I was becoming ever more nostalgic by the minute.

"I still don't know if there was a Duffy Madison at Poughkeepsie High School during the years we need," she reported. "There's a space for him in the yearbook, but school records don't show him as registered. Now there are some areas I can't look because I'm not in the system, so it's possible he was homeschooled and registered in the high school for clerical reasons. It's possible he had some kind of disability and couldn't attend. It's also possible there is no such person as Duffy Madison, and the two of us are being played for fools." This was the most hysterical I'd ever heard Paula sound, which corresponded neatly to my most calm and rational moment.

"What about other Madisons?" I asked. "Siblings? Cousins? Dolleys?"

"That's interesting," Paula answered, ignoring my feeble first lady/ice cream maker joke. "There was a Susannah Madison two years before Duffy's supposed graduation date. She is currently living in Lake Tahoe under the married name Susannah Hong. I've left a message but haven't heard back yet."

Ben looked at me somewhat askance. He still wasn't used to the idea of digging into Duffy's past to discover whether he was real. To Ben, Duffy was still that guy he'd been working with.

"That's good," I told Paula. "Keep on that as it comes, but for the moment, our priority is finding a way to get Duffy out of jail. Have you come up with anything new on Louise or the others we've met up here?"

"I looked into that Walt Kendig you were telling me about," Paula answered. "His story is not exactly thrill-packed. He's never been out of Poughkeepsie for more than a week at a time, unmarried, no children. Works as a CPA for a firm that prepares taxes for locals and some walk-ins. Bought himself a condo, an apartment in a converted school building, and pays his mortgage on time. Spends most of his money on books and birding as far as I can tell."

At least he didn't have any incredibly expensive high-tech surveillance equipment, I thought. "What about Louise and Rob?" I asked.

"We already knew much of Louise's past," Paula said. I could hear her flipping through a notebook she keeps on her desk; Paula is skittish about leaving her research strictly on a computer or in the cloud. She lives under the assumption that the whole Internet is constantly on the brink of collapse, and the only reason she cares is that her work would be lost. "Right now she's working as a supervisor at a FedEx plant from five in the afternoon to one in the morning. You've seen her house, so you could tell me more about it than I can tell you."

"I doubt that," I said.

I could hear the smile on Paula's face. "Thank you. But the fact is, since the time of her pregnancy and divorce, Louise has lived a fairly mundane life. She does have a thing for men, though. From what I can tell, she's had a lot of boyfriends. They don't seem to last very long, but Facebook and other sources would indicate she stays friendly with a number of them."

"Any married ones?" Ben asked.

Paula took a moment. I'd told her Ben was in the car with me, but that was the first time he'd spoken since we'd started the call. She recovered quickly. "It's hard to tell because those would usually not be broadcast all over social media," she said. "It's possible, but I don't know that I can say certainly it's happened."

Paula hates it when she doesn't have a definitive answer.

"That's fine," I told her. "We're going to see Louise right now. What do you think we should ask her?" Paula has great insight in such matters, and I'll often ask her advice when I'm stuck on a plot point but never a character moment. Those are all mine.

"From what you've told me, I'd ask her about the Poughkeepsie Police Department," she answered. "If there's a gun with Duffy's fingerprints on it, somebody planted it there. Who in the department would want to do that, and why? A local like Louise, especially one whose social media shows she has definitely dated a cop or two, might have some idea."

Ben nodded. I wasn't looking directly at him because we were pulling up in front of Louise's house, but I was willing to bet he looked impressed with Paula and sheepish that he hadn't thought of that himself.

"You're a gem," I told Paula.

"Awww . . ."

We disconnected the call just as I was parking three houses down from Louise Refsnyder. Ben and I got out of the car and started back toward Louise's front door.

"Paula would make a good detective," Ben said.

"Don't tell her that. I could never replace her."

Louise opened the door wearing an impatient expression that changed when she saw Ben standing to my right. The look she gave him paired with the idea that Ben and I might be dating and were at least sharing a hotel room at the moment roused some competitive feelings in me, which I pushed back down where they belonged. This was business.

But Ben was noticing Louise. I'd never been on this kind of visit with him before, so I wondered whether he gave that look to every woman he might want to get information from. Another feeling to ignore for the moment.

"What is it this time?" That was Louise, directed to me. "You want to know about the time I got put in the corner in first grade?"

"I'm here to ask about Michelle Testaverde's murder," I said. "I didn't know if you were aware of that."

By now I'd learned to watch for the reaction, and Louise presented us with a whopper. Her face paled, and her mouth dropped open; she actually took a step backward that seemed instinctual and not planned. Her hand let go of the doorknob, and she made some noises that weren't exactly meant to be coherent, in my opinion. It took her a good long moment to compose herself.

"Michelle was murdered?" Louise said. More gargling noises. "When?"

That seemed an odd first question, but what's the logical one? "About five years ago," Ben told her. "Right around the time she and Damien Mosley supposedly moved into his apartment in New Jersey." Then he gestured toward the doorway. "Can we come in?"

I was grateful when Louise nodded and opened the door wider, so I didn't even mention to Ben that the question should have been, "*May* we come in?" It seemed a secondary issue at the time.

We sat in her kitchen again, Michelle pouring herself a gin and offering us nothing. I didn't care, and Ben didn't say anything about it. "What happened?" Louise finally managed.

Ben told her what we knew, leaving out the part where Duffy was arrested and awaiting arraignment, probably because that might prejudice her take on the subject but also because neither Ben nor I wanted to consider that reality at the moment. When he had finished with his recap, Louise refilled her glass and took a healthy swig.

"Who would have done that?" she rasped.

"That's kind of what we're trying to figure out," I said. "We started off knowing that Damien had vanished from town, and that led us to Michelle, and the next thing we know, Michelle was shot and there's a good chance Damien was, too, at the bottom of a ridge in a park in New Jersey. It doesn't seem to make any sense."

Ben didn't want to wallow in that idea. He was used to the idea of moving forward on an investigation, and he wasn't going to stop now. "We're told that before they both disappeared, Damien sort of proposed to Michelle at the bowling alley during a league match, and she turned him down," he said. "Were you there?"

She wiped her mouth with the back of her hand and nodded. "Yeah, but they ended up getting married anyway," she said.

"Were you at the wedding?" I asked.

Louise laughed without any joy. "Me? No. I didn't get invited."

Ben's eyes got more intense. "Do you know anybody who was?" he asked.

Louise sat forward looking annoyed, like her word was being challenged. "Sure!" Her eyes went up and to the right— her left—indicating she was trying to remember something. "Um . . ." She didn't add to that.

"What's wrong?" Ben asked. It was his good-cop voice, oozing kindness and understanding. Now I knew he was just playing it up to get Louise to talk.

Louise looked at him as if surprised he'd spoken. "Fact is, I can't remember anybody telling me they went to the wedding," she said. "I just heard they were married, from Walt, maybe. But it never came up. I didn't expect to get invited to their wedding; I mean, we weren't tight friends or anything, so when they got married and I didn't go, that didn't seem strange at all. But now that you ask, I don't know anybody who went to that wedding."

I tried to duplicate Ben's tone, but it was difficult for me because I'd decided I didn't like Louise, and covering up my feelings is not a strong suit. Assume the effort was there. "The last time I was here, you said you and Damien had been having . . . a relationship before he disappeared. And there was some talk that Michelle was cheating, too. Do you know how they reacted to that? Did either of them find out about the other?"

Louise looked away, and I knew what that meant. "Yeah, see, here's the thing about that," she said. "I was lying."

"About which part?" The fake kindness was probably out of my voice.

"About me and Damien. I didn't like the way you were looking at me, and I figured maybe you were an old friend or a girlfriend of his or something, so I made up that story about me and him. That never actually happened."

I opened my mouth, but Ben wisely beat me to the punch. "You never slept with Damien Mosley," he said calmly.

"No. As far as I know, Damien was with Michelle and only Michelle."

"What about the other part, where Michelle was supposedly having at least one affair behind Damien's back?" Ben asked.

Louise resumed eye contact. With Ben. "As far as I know, that part is true."

"Who was she cheating with?" I asked. It probably should have been, "With whom was she cheating?" but who says that, really?

"I don't know," Louise said. "There was talk at the time, but I wasn't really seeing them. Damien was still working at the club once in a while, but he never complained about Michelle. I don't know if he heard anything about what she was doing."

Every time we learned something new, it made the whole situation more confusing.

I remembered what Paula had said and decided there was no reason not to go all in with Louise. "Do you know anybody in the police department?" I asked her.

Immediately, her expression showed suspicion. "Why?"

"There's some evidence in the case of Michelle's murder that is questionable," Ben said, moving Louise's focus away from me, which was probably wise. "One of the things we're trying to determine is how it might have gotten into the evidence room if it wasn't real."

"So you figure that hey, Louise gets around, she must have been with somebody in the department?" She wasn't even cutting Ben any slack now. "You figure I just have a thing with every guy in town?"

To be fair, that was kind of what I had been thinking, but Ben had been involved in these things before and knew how to handle them. It would be very instructive for a future Duffy book.

"That's not what we're saying," he said soothingly. "We figure you know this town a lot better than either of us, and you might have some insight into the police department. You might have heard things about cops who might not be completely perfect on the job. You know, like a guy who used to give a nice-looking girl a break on a speeding ticket and now maybe is a detective or has access to high-profile cases. Something like that. We were just relying on your knowledge because we don't have the insight we need here."

It was so convincing, I made a mental note never to believe anything Ben said to me again. But it did seem to work on Louise, who tilted her head to one side as she was listening and nodded a little.

"I actually did date a cop for a little while about a year ago," she said. "I'm not giving you his name because maybe he'll call me again sometime, but he did talk about some of the other guys in the department, the ones who were standing in his way of being promoted, you know? And it's possible there is someone there who cuts the occasional corner. I don't know anything about evidence or anything, but I know he said not to let this guy decide you were a problem because he'd find a way to get rid of you. Legal, you know? Or at least it would look legal. And he wouldn't shoot you or anything—there was no violence I knew about. Just a little rule-bending."

"Thank you," Ben said. "That's very helpful." *It was?* "What was his name?"

Louise blinked. "I told you I wasn't going to say his name. I might want to see him again, and I can't be seen as a snitch."

"The crooked cop," I jumped in. "Not the one you were dating."

"Oh!" Louise waved a hand. "Sorry. All I remember is that my cop, the one I was seeing, told me to watch out for the sergeant they called Phil."

It took a moment. My brain sifted through its invisible Rolodex, and then my head must have snapped straight up. I stared a little.

"What?" Ben asked.

"Dougherty. Sgt. Phillip Dougherty." Duffy and I had met him at our first stop in Poughkeepsie. He had met us and found Duffy annoying. Would that be enough to have him falsify evidence against Duffy in Michelle's murder?

"Yeah, that's it," Louise said. "Phil Dougherty. That's the guy."

Chapter 27

Ben and I sat in my car, but I hadn't turned on the engine yet. Not that you could necessarily tell; hybrid cars in the electric battery mode are pretty much silent. But before we went anywhere else—especially back to the municipal building to see Duffy get arraigned, because Sanders had texted that would happen within the hour—I needed to get straight what we'd do if we ran into Sgt. Phillip Dougherty.

"He put fingerprints on the gun five years after it was used?" I said. "He got hold of Duffy's prints when we went to see him, and he found a way to move them to the gun, right?"

"It's actually not all that possible to do that, no matter what you've seen in the movies," Ben said. "Fingerprints are way too fragile. Doing it with Scotch tape or something would probably smear them to the point that they would no longer be usable."

"So how did the prints get on the gun?" I asked. "Do you think Duffy really shot Michelle Testaverde and left the gun in the ceiling five years ago?"

"No. I'm coming around to the idea that there was no Duffy before five years ago." I gave him a look. "I'm kidding. But there's no reason to think Duffy and Michelle ever met each other. Nobody else on the bowling team or anywhere else up here seems to have seen Duffy before. What motivation would he have to randomly shoot a stranger in the back of the head? And does that mean he shot Damien Mosley in North Bergen later on? It doesn't make sense."

"So how do we explain the fingerprints on the gun?"

"We don't. I need better information." Ben pointed at the ignition button. "Let's go. Duffy's getting arraigned in ten minutes, and we need to be there. If someone has to speak on his behalf, I want it to be you or me. Preferably me."

I turned the car on and started making a K-turn to get us in the proper direction for the municipal building. "Oh yeah? What makes you better to testify than me?"

"If it's you, they're going to ask how you know Duffy, and you're going to have to say you're the author of a series of books that aren't about him but are and that he thinks you created him on your computer. That's what."

"Okay, you have a decent point. What do I do if we run into Phil Dougherty?"

Ben considered a moment. "Walk the other way," he said.

"That doesn't help."

He shrugged. "*I* never met the guy."

We walked into the building, which houses both the police headquarters and the municipal court and offices. Sanders had alerted us to be in the courtroom and not to seek out him or Duffy on the police side because they wouldn't be accessible. In fact, his text to me had been clear: *Just sit and watch.*

I could do that.

We waited through three other pieces of court business, a speeding ticket and two eviction notices, before Duffy was led in. He was not wearing prison orange but the clothes he'd been in when he was brought from North Bergen to Poughkeepsie. His wrists and ankles were not chained. He strode in behind Nelson Sanders looking around the room with intense interest, filing away every detail of the place in the event anything that happened to him here—like being charged with murder—might become important. He didn't even notice Ben and me when he came in. I mean, it's not like I expected a happy wave or anything, but he was so engrossed in the surroundings that we might as well not have been there.

I never should have written the guy to be that observant. In fact, I never should have written him. That was the lesson to take away from this. From now on, I'd stick to science fiction and only write about people who lived on Jupiter or something. By the time they got to my front door to confront me, I'd have been dead for a couple of centuries. Win-win, if you choose to look at it that way.

Sanders nodded in our direction, anyway.

Duffy sat next to Sanders at the table to the judge's right and our left. I felt impelled to move to that side, as if I were supporting the groom at a wedding, but Ben didn't seem to think that was important, so I figured it might be a faux pas and stayed where I was.

As soon as the shuffling cleared and the prosecutor (with his assistant) was seated at the opposite table, the judge, a woman of Hispanic descent in her midfifties by my estimate, got right to business. The court clerk read the case number and announced loudly that the matter would be the people of the state of New York versus Duffy Madison. That seemed a pretty serious mismatch. New York has almost twenty million people. I wasn't even sure Duffy counted as one.

Not that he seemed the least bit daunted by the odds. He was sitting with his usual great posture, spine straight, head moving from side to side as if he'd never seen a courtroom before. The man had surely testified at trials related to cases he'd investigated. But I guess being the center of attention had its novelty. *He* knew he hadn't killed Michelle Testaverde, so what could possibly go wrong?

"This is a case relating to a murder committed five years ago." The judge, whose nameplate identified her as Julia Menendez, was reading documents in front of her using half-glasses. She looked over the top at the prosecutor. "Is that correct, Mr. Reilly?"

"Yes, Your Honor." Reilly was also reading and didn't look up, which I thought should mean Duffy would be set free immediately. No such luck.

Sanders stood up. "Judge, the defense moves for immediate dismissal of these charges given the almost total lack of evidence compiled by the prosecution and the amount of time that has elapsed since the crime."

"There is no statute of limitations on murder in this state," the judge reminded him.

"We are aware of that, Your Honor, but even if this crime had been committed yesterday, the prosecution has no witness, nothing placing my client at the scene, and no motive for the murder. I believe this to be a desperation play by the prosecutor to close a cold case using the one shred of evidence he has in his possession, which I will argue has been tainted by five years spent isolated in a place where any number of people could have tampered with it. Honestly, Judge, there is absolutely nothing here that justifies charging my client at this time."

Judge Menendez turned her attention to the opposite side of the room. "Mr. Reilly?" she said.

"Your Honor, we have more than enough evidence to convict Mr. Madison of this crime." Reilly actually stood up and faced the judge, but even so, he looked tired. His shoulders drooped. His expression was one of incredible fatigue. How many murders did they get around here that this guy could be so blasé about it? "We have the murder weapon with his fingerprints clearly on it, and we have his recent behavior, which prompted our reopening this case to begin with."

"Once again, Judge, the defense questions any piece of physical evidence that has been sitting out of the control of the police for that long. This is not enough to even consider sending a man to prison for life."

Duffy seemed fascinated by the proceedings and didn't even flinch at the idea of a life sentence without parole, which can be given in New York. Maybe he wasn't really absorbing the fact that he was the defendant.

"It is pretty thin, Mr. Reilly," Judge Menendez said.

"We are not asking the court to decide the case today," the prosecutor said. "We're simply making the charges in preparation for the trial. We believe the defendant is a flight risk and ask the court to take that into consideration."

"A flight risk?" Sanders replied, still on his feet. "What leads to that conclusion?"

"A good question, Mr. Reilly," the judge said, once again consulting the file before her. "Mr. Madison is a consultant in law enforcement and has been living at the same address for five years."

"Precisely the amount of time since the murder," Reilly pointed out. "And in another state."

The judge looked down at Sanders. "I'll grant you it's circumstantial, Mr. Sanders, but the coincidence is compelling."

"But it is just that, Judge—a coincidence. Will the prosecution also charge everyone else who moved out of Poughkeepsie five years ago?"

Judge Menendez's eyes took on an annoyed gleam, which I did not think was a good sign for Duffy. "How many of them will have fingerprints on the murder weapon, Counselor?" she asked.

Sanders didn't look all that perturbed by the judge's tone. "There's no way for us to know, Your Honor. I suspect it will be as many as the prosecutor's office wants there to be."

"Objection," Reilly said. Sure, insult me, but I'm not going to get mad. I'll just object.

"Sustained. Careful, Mr. Sanders, or you could be getting too close to contempt for me to ignore." Judge Menendez pointed a finger warningly at Sanders, who still did not appear worried. I'd have fallen to my knees and begged for forgiveness, which is why I never went to law school.

"My apologies, Your Honor."

Judge Menendez sat back. "All right. I think there is enough evidence present to deny your motion for dismissal, Mr. Sanders. So let's proceed. The defendant will rise."

I thought Sanders was going to raise another objection, but he saw the look in the judge's eyes and instead turned his gaze to Duffy, who was looking positively entranced. Sanders gestured for him to stand, and Duffy nodded, remembering that he was indeed the defendant here.

"How do you plead?" the judge asked.

Sanders nodded toward Duffy, who seemed to be thinking about it. "Oh. Um, not guilty, Your Honor," he said. He grinned when he said it as if pleased with himself for getting his lines right.

Judge Menendez looked at him for a moment after that and then drew a deep breath. "Okay. I'll set this case for trial. Are there any arguments regarding bail?"

"The state opposes bail for the reasons we stated before," Reilly said. "We believe the defendant to be a flight risk."

"There is no chance Mr. Madison is going anywhere but home to New Jersey, where he is easily located," Sanders argued. "He will be available for any proceedings the court deems necessary. We feel bail should be set and should be set low, Judge."

The woman on the bench regarded Duffy carefully. "Mr. Madison," she said, "do you plan on trying to avoid your trial?"

"I would not miss it for the world," Duffy said sincerely. "I am looking forward to it."

"Uh-huh." Judge Menendez looked at him a while longer. "Is there someone here who can vouch for Mr. Madison, Counselor?"

Sanders stood up again. "Yes, Your Honor. Mr. Preston of the Bergen County Prosecutor's Office, who supervises Mr. Madison, is present in the courtroom." He looked toward Ben, who stood up.

"Mr. Preston, how long have you known Mr. Madison?" the judge asked.

"About five years," Ben told her.

Judge Menendez sighed softly. "That number again." She looked at Ben. "Do you consider him to be reliable?"

"Almost to a fault," Ben said. "He gets to work before I do. He sometimes stays after I leave. If I ask him to show up somewhere in a half hour, he's there in fifteen minutes. And he keeps his word, Judge. If Duffy says he'll do something, he will do it, and you don't even have to think about it again."

The judge seemed to take that into account. "All right," she said. "Mr. Reilly, I'm going to grant bail and set it at one hundred thousand dollars."

I gasped. Ben, sitting back down next to me, said, "He can pay a ten percent cash bond."

Ten thousand dollars? Cash?

Reilly looked irritated but said nothing and sat in his chair at the prosecutor's table fiddling with a pen. He seemed anxious for the proceedings to conclude, perhaps so he could get in a round of golf before it got dark.

"This case is remanded for hearing at a date to be set," Judge Menendez said and actually hit her gavel on the pad in front of her. The bailiff shouted, "All rise!" and everybody stood as the judge left the courtroom. I thought she was shaking her head in disbelief as she went, but that could be my writer's mind embellishing. It does that on occasion.

As soon as we could, Ben and I made it to the defense table, where Duffy was still looking around like a four-year-old seeing the Magic Kingdom for the first time, and Sanders was filing documents away in his briefcase. The law did not appear to have heard of electronic data.

Another officer of the court, one with a gun strapped to his hip, approached just as we made it to the table. He reached out a hand to Duffy.

"Are you okay?" I asked Duffy as he stood to go with the trooper. "Is there anything I can bring you?"

"That won't be necessary," Duffy said. "I'll be with you shortly."

Huh? He was being led off to jail. "You will?"

"Certainly. As soon as I can get to my wallet, I will pay the bail, and I'll meet you outside." Duffy pointed toward the front of the courthouse as if I didn't know where outside was.

"Ten thousand dollars?" I said in disbelief.

Duffy stopped for a moment, making the trooper turn and look at him. "The judge said one hundred thousand," he said, correcting me.

The trooper took his arm. "It's ten percent bond for cash," he told Duffy.

"Oh, very well then," Duffy told us. "As soon as I can get to my ATM card, I will be right with you."

Ben and I looked at each other. What was he saying?

"It's ten thousand dollars," I told Duffy. Maybe he was so overwhelmed that he wasn't going the math in his head.

"Yes," he said as they made it to the door. "That should not be a problem." And he left right behind the trooper. He might have been on the absolute best middle school field trip ever.

I looked at Ben. "It should not be a problem?" I echoed.

He looked straight ahead and watched Duffy disappear through the door. "I'm going to start asking him for investment advice."

We met Duffy outside the municipal building twenty minutes later.

He was, as before, almost completely unperturbed, treating his arraignment like an amazingly interesting piece of theater that had been arranged strictly for his edification. I mean, the man was *whistling* when he walked out through the front door.

"It's getting late," he said by way of greeting. Not *thanks for coming and showing support* or *oh my god, do you think I'll go to jail for life*? No. "Perhaps we should make dinner plans, and I should book a room at the hotel near you."

"You're buying that one," Ben said. "Maybe both. Where'd you get all this money?"

"It's not *that* much," Duffy said, as if that answered the question. "Besides, I will get it back when I am exonerated. Shall we?"

So we did. We went back to the hotel and booked Duffy a room after some anxiety—the desk clerk was claiming they were booked up and offered to put a rollaway bed in the room with Ben and me until he saw the look on my face. He had no luggage, of course, so a visit to a clothing store was going to be in order, but Duffy suggested dinner first and said that since Ben and I had come to Poughkeepsie on his behalf, he would indeed pay the tab at the restaurant.

Unfortunately, I did not have the wherewithal to ask the hotel concierge what the most expensive place in town might be.

We ended up at a soul food place with a very extensive bar and live jazz music. Duffy, a vegetarian, had a little trouble finding an entrée but managed with a large salad and vegetarian gumbo. Ben went with the baby back ribs, and I asked for some fried chicken and waffles because that's what you do. If I exploded from all the food, I wouldn't have to write a thousand words when I got back to the hotel room, which seemed like incentive enough that evening.

Ben dove right in as soon as the orders were placed. "You seem awfully calm for a guy who's facing a lifetime in prison," he told Duffy.

"Certainly, because I expect not to spend any time in jail at all," Duffy said. "There is no evidence against me that will stand up in court for more than ten seconds. The clumsy attempt to make me seem like the culprit is really not worthy of our attention, to be blunt."

"How can you be that sure?" I asked. "The judge wasn't convinced."

"The judge would have to be overwhelmed to dismiss the charges without any hearing at all," Duffy said. "She was skeptical enough, and besides, she would not be hearing the case if it was brought to trial anyway. Her job was to see to the arraignment, and that is what she did. I thought she was quite fair."

Ben shook his head, perhaps to clear it a little. "Duffy, how could your fingerprints have gotten on that gun? Were you here in Poughkeepsie five years ago at the time Damien and Michelle were shot?"

"Of course not."

"You can't be sure of that," I told him. "You honestly don't know where you were five years ago; you have no memories that go back before that."

"Because I did not yet exist," Duffy said as if it made perfect sense. "You had not written me into existence yet."

"Do you understand how that's going to sound on the witness stand?" I asked him.

"I doubt it will come up."

Luckily, our drinks had been ordered and delivered, because I think Ben needed the scotch he was taking in. "You're always driven by science and fact," he told Duffy. "How can you think that you just rose out of the dust by yourself? Certainly you have to have a theory at least on the physics of what you think happened."

"I have nothing on which to base my research," Duffy admitted. "There are no verifiable cases I know of in which characters from fiction suddenly appeared in physical form. So I can't make any claims based on science now. But I can speculate on how those fingerprints might have shown up on the gun that shot Michelle Testaverde."

Aha. "How?" I asked.

"They didn't. There is no reliable way to transfer fingerprints from one object to another that clearly intact." Duffy took a sip of the diet cola he'd ordered, because in addition to being a vegetarian, he is a killjoy. "The only reasonable explanation is that the records of the fingerprints were falsified."

"So the reports of the detectives and the forensics lab were changed to make it look like your fingerprints were on the gun?" Ben said. Now he was a cop working a case.

"That is my theory," Duffy said. "Although I must admit I have no basis for speculation on the motive someone in the police department might have had to make those alterations in the reports."

Our meals arrived just then, and we dug in. Even Duffy, whose day had included being let out of police custody and then being put back into police custody only to be let out on bail, a twelve-hour cycle that would exhaust an actual human being, seemed enthusiastic about the plant-based repast in front of him. So there wasn't much shop talk for a few minutes.

Finally, Ben took a break from his pig-based dinner and stopped to wipe his chin, which was fortunate. "Louise Refsnyder told us that if you want something fixed in the Poughkeepsie PD, you have to see Phillip Dougherty," he told Duffy. "Why would the sergeant have a grudge against you?"

"He might not." I intercepted the question because I'd already been giving it some thought. "But someone who does have a grudge, or at least wants to be scratched off the suspect list, might have gotten to Dougherty and *encouraged* him to make some changes in the evidence records."

"You think Dougherty took a bribe to falsify records?" Ben seemed stunned, and I wasn't sure if it was because I was pouring maple syrup on fried chicken. "He could go to jail for that in any number of ways."

"It seems the most logical explanation," Duffy agreed, chewing. "And it opens a number of possibilities."

"What kind of possibilities?" Ben asked.

"One can always trace the money back to the source, and that is the way to determine which of our suspects might be the one interested in diverting attention now that the crime has resurfaced," Duffy told him. "If we can determine whose bank account might have suffered a significant deduction lately, we might have some idea of a direction."

The sun was just starting to go down, but I knew Paula and I knew how she operated, or more to the point, how dedicated she was to working. Her actual methods were probably better left unexamined, at least closely.

I texted her quickly: *Check bank records on following names. Look for big deductions*. She responded within seconds after I sent a second text with the names in question.

"What are you doing?" Ben asked.

"You don't want to know, necessarily."

But Duffy was in full Sherlock mode, to the point that I half expected him to don a deerstalker and start smoking a pipe. He did neither.

"If we can trace the money . . . but we'll have to know how much was involved. What do we know about this Sgt. Dougherty?"

"Nothing specific," Ben said. "Louise said a cop she dated, who she would not name, had said if you wanted something fixed in town, you went to Phil Dougherty."

"But what was interesting," I said, thinking out loud, "was that both Rod Wilkerson and Walt Kendig mentioned having a friend on the police force we could call if we needed help. They both seemed eager to use their influence, like we would be impressed with them for being so well connected."

"So Wilkerson, Kendig, *and* Refsnyder all had a contact on the police force?" Duffy seemed fascinated. He stopped spearing bits of salad.

"It's not that small a town," Ben said, although he kept eating. Being a vegetarian is very noble, but fun? I didn't have enough data to make a determination, Duffy would say. "It's not Mayberry. Everybody doesn't know the sheriff."

Duffy chewed over the information, not the lettuce. "It is something of a coincidence that all three mentioned a police connection, even if they have all lived here for quite some time. Do you think there was some diversion involved? Were they trying to draw your attention away—"

He stopped talking, and a look of complete understanding came over his face.

"What?" Ben had no doubt seen this happen before. "What do you know?"

"The money wasn't paid to get me arrested and convicted," Duffy said. "Whoever is behind this—and it could be one or all of the suspects we've discussed—knows the evidence against me won't hold up. Nobody believes I killed Michelle Testaverde, and no one thinks I'm going to jail for doing so."

"So why go through all the trouble and expense of framing you?" I asked.

Duffy regarded me with a look. "If you were writing this story, what would the motivation be?"

A lesson? *Now*? There was no point in fighting it. I gave the question some thought. "The idea wasn't to get you arrested," I said. "It was to get you out of the way."

"Precisely," Duffy said. "And doing so had the added benefit of getting Ben and you distracted enough to be where the killer would want you to be. At the police station and not where something else was going on."

"What?" I asked. There'd be no lesson on this one.

"We can't say yet," Duffy answered. "The point was to get us all away from someone's activities today."

"We were at Louise's house while you were in the cell," Ben pointed out. "So Louise is still in play."

It was an unfortunate turn of phrase, but I let it go. "So where does that leave us?" I asked.

"Something else might be happening," Duffy answered. "I would advise that neither of you ask for a dessert menu. We have work to do."

Chapter 28

Paula texted me back when I was standing in the bushes on the corner of a property across the street from Rod Wilkerson's house. I had the phone on vibrate so there was no loud sound, but I still started a little violently at the shock of the sudden movement and the slight buzzing. Not that I thought anyone could hear it from across the street.

Duffy, Ben, and I had split up the three Poughkeepsie contacts we had for a kind of stakeout. It had been—of course—Duffy's idea.

"After all the activity of the day and the obvious pains someone is taking to cover up the death of Michelle Testaverde, it is not an enormous leap to suspect one or more of these people could be involved in the crime," he'd begun in the parking lot of the barbecue place we'd left hastily. "There are three people in town whom we know had some contact with the victims in these murders, and each of them has behaved suspiciously in some way when we questioned them. It might also have been worthwhile to watch Barry Spader and Sgt. Dougherty, but Barry is in

275

Virginia, and the sergeant is working the night shift at the police station. That makes the surveillance simpler since there are three of us and three of them."

Simpler. The man thought that was simpler.

It led to us splitting up nonetheless. Duffy and Ben were trailing Walt and Louise, respectively. That was largely due to the fact that those two Poughkeepsie residents lived within two blocks of each other while Rod lived on the other side of town, and that meant the person with the car (that's me) would be better utilized at his house. I wasn't crazy about Ben watching Louise in her house at night, but I do admit to some sense of payback that Walt was under surveillance when he didn't know it. Karma is a crime fiction writer.

I don't know about the two guys, but I was standing in the bushes as the temperature started to drop just a little and wondering what I was doing there. For one thing, I really had no sense of what it was I should be looking for. The shades were drawn in all of Rod's windows, and there were lights in both front rooms. Contrary to the 1950s song, there were no silhouettes on the shades.

I was watching a house. They don't tend to do much.

So when Paula texted, alarming though it was for a moment, I felt a little bit of relief from the tedium. Watching a house is not all that dissimilar to watching grass grow, except that the grass is actually doing something, so if you are crazy enough to watch for days, you'll see a difference. Houses will deteriorate on their own, but it'll take years.

I got my phone out of my pocket as it buzzed and looked at the message, which read, *No huge withdrawals but am on to something and will get back to you.* Paula is an information tease. If she said she was looking into something and implying it might get interesting, you (or at least I) could count on significant data coming soon. It gave me a ray of light to hope for while the sun went down over Rod Wilkerson's house.

Rod had a driveway with a four-year-old Honda Accord in it. It seemed odd because he made at least part of his living selling real estate, and realtors tend to have larger cars, SUVs, and the like to accommodate people shopping for houses more comfortably. Maybe Rod was a bad real estate agent. Somebody had to be.

Ben, Duffy, and I had established a text group before we'd split up so we could all communicate easily. Duffy had objected to the idea of our breaking radio silence, but Ben said we needed to be alerted immediately when something happened at any of the locations under watch, and Duffy, even in this unofficial investigation, deferred to Ben.

Rod's house sat there. It's what houses do.

Then my worst nightmare came true.

A woman walked out of the house on the corner, the one whose shrubbery was serving as my cover, and looked over in my direction. "What are you doing there?" she called fairly loudly. "Who are you?"

I remember when people would see a stranger nearby and ask if there was anything they could do to help. Those days are gone. It's possible I was imagining them.

"I'm not doing anything," I said in a stage whisper. "I'm just standing here."

"Is this drugs?" the woman bleated. "Are you buying drugs?"

"No, ma'am. There's no one else here. I'm just standing outside on a nice night." I looked over at Rod's house. It was maintaining its insistence on embodying the opposite of activity. For once I was grateful for that.

"Well, stand outside somewhere else!" she shouted. "This is private property! Get out of here, or I'll call the police!"

Thanks, lady.

I gave up my position just to get the volume level on the street to subside. I didn't see any neighbors looking through windows or opening doors, which was helpful. I just nodded at the woman and walked off her property and toward my car, which I'd parked a block away. Normally, I would have surveilled Rod's house from the Prius c, but his street allowed parking only on the side on which his house stood, and it was parked up. Putting my car in his driveway seemed just a little obvious for the task at hand.

The woman watched me as I walked away, then shook her head with derision and stomped back into her house.

I didn't go all the way back to the car, though. I figured if Rod's house was just going to sit there, I didn't necessarily need a prime vantage point. There were trees on the street that might obstruct my view from certain angles, but if I leaned next to one of the trees on my side of the street, Rod would only see me if he knew he was being watched. And if he knew that, my effort had already failed.

The phone buzzed again, and I looked at it. The text was from Ben. *Louise staying in the house but moving around a lot.* Movement in the house. I wondered what that looked like.

I texted back, *Rod's house is a house.* I figured that was an evocative summation of my experience so far. I didn't get into the whole writing biz for nothing, you know.

Duffy texted nothing, undoubtedly to prove to us that he was disciplined and we were not. For a guy who based his life on fact and deduction, he could be as petty as a twelve-year-old girl when he felt like it.

So Ben pushed his buttons and texted, *Duffy check in.*

Seconds later came, *Roger.* I'm sure Duffy would have preferred something even more terse, like *Rog,* but he went with convention and acknowledged Ben's request. Lord, the man could be a pain sometimes. I wondered why I'd created him in the first place.

Then one of the lights went out in Rod's bedroom, or at least the front room on the second floor. I walked a couple of trees closer. I checked my phone for another text from Duffy, but nothing more came in. I texted back: *Anything happening?*

There was no answer. I tried to do the right thing and just wait, assuming Duffy was in the middle of something and didn't want his phone to make a noise right now. I waited for much longer than I wanted to, which was probably about five minutes. Then I waited a little bit more, but each minute felt like an hour.

Nothing happened. Then everything happened at once.

My phone buzzed with a new text from Ben: *Louise on the move. Getting in her car. Heading south.*

And then I heard a gunshot reverberate through Rod's house.

I hadn't seen a flash of light, but I had been looking down at my phone and not at the house when the shot rang out. I texted to the group: *Shots fired at Rod's house.* Technically, it had been one shot, but you never hear cops say that in the movies: "Shot fired!" It didn't have the same dramatic *oomph* that way.

When my phone buzzed after that, it was a call, not a text, from Ben. "Gunshots?" he said. "Are you okay?"

"Yeah. It was actually one gunshot. I'm across the street. I just heard it; I didn't see it. I can get closer."

"No!" Ben sounded like he wanted to jump through the phone. "Don't go near the house. Do you hear anything else? People yelling? More shots? Anything like that?"

"No, outside of that, it's been quiet," I said. That sounded stupid. "A couple of people have stuck their heads out of their front doors to look, but they don't seem especially worried. Maybe Rod takes target practice in his house every night."

"Call the PDP," Ben said. "Report the shots. I'm going to head that way right now."

It took me a moment, I'll confess, to realize the PDP was the Poughkeepsie Police Department. I write for a living; don't judge. "You're on foot," I told Ben, although I could be relatively sure he knew he wasn't in a motor vehicle at the moment. "It'll take you a while."

"Well, I can't do much good here," he answered. "Louise took off in her car, and I don't run *that* fast. Now call the cops and wait for me. Don't move, Rachel." And he hung up before I could argue, which was just as well because I had no intention of contesting his point. I did wish he'd said it in a slightly less condescending *let-the-men-handle-it-little-lady* way, but you can't have everything. He was right that I should stay there and call the police. I could have suggested he get an Uber, but he'd probably think of that anyway.

I was about to dial the cops when I realized Duffy had not responded to my text about the gunshot. That was very odd; it was the kind of thing Duffy would usually leap at. He loved solving crimes, and there was little doubt he'd find the idea of a discharged firearm in the home of one of our suspects irresistible.

And yet he'd resisted. My stomach clenched a little, and I noticed the damp chill in the air all of a sudden. I didn't like it.

If there was nothing wrong, Duffy would be annoyed with me for calling, I mused. But we'd been texting, and that didn't seem to bother him too much. I decided to try that again and sent: *Duffy? Respond please.*

A minute went by. Two. I know because I kept checking my watch, and it was moving much slower than usual, it seemed. Time passed, and no reply from Duffy.

That guy was going to drive me crazy. Maybe I already *was* crazy, and everything that had happened to me since he called my house the first time was a hallucination. There was something strangely comforting in the thought.

I called his cell phone and got sent directly to voice mail. That wasn't good. It was very, very not good.

Maybe I should call Ben. I texted him: *Duffy's not answering.*

No immediate answer from Ben. What was I supposed to be doing? Right. Calling the cops.

But it was weird that there had been one gunshot and then nothing. You'd—or at least I'd—expect other noises from the place. I definitely wasn't going into Rod's house, but I could certainly get closer. Just to hear.

I had taken exactly two steps when the phone buzzed. Ben: *Probably turned off his phone.* That was sensible. Ben was on his way. I'd just cross the street to see if there was anything else to hear and report back to him when he got here. And I'd call the cops as soon as I knew if there were moans or other scary sounds.

This was not something I'd refrain from having a character do; I was not taking an unnecessary chance. I could see the house, so I'd know if anyone came out. I wouldn't get close, not even inside the front walk. I'd learned my lesson about venturing where I shouldn't.

See, I have this policy about not looking for trouble. Even when I was trying to help Ben and Duffy catch a serial killer, I did my very best to avoid danger. The fact that it ended up with me coming very close to being the killer's next victim was irrelevant. In that argument. Clearly, I would have preferred not to have been in that situation.

Maybe that wasn't a good example.

Anyway, I approached the house very carefully and slowly. I had my phone up next to my ear despite not actually being on a call. Years of spending evenings in New York City had taught me how to be a less attractive target for people who might be looking for targets. I didn't say anything into the phone, but I did nod now and again to give the impression I was listening to someone.

I thought about calling my father, but the explanation alone would have lasted until after Ben got to me. It might have lasted until the sun came back up the next morning.

Nothing seemed to be going on in the house. There was no sound coming from the windows, and the front ones were open. There was no visible movement. Lights stayed on where they were on and off where they were off. It was almost like nobody was home, but I'd heard the gunshot. Unless it was part of a suicide attempt on Rod's part, there had to be someone inside, and alive.

The cops. Right. I wasn't going inside, so I wasn't going to learn anything else. It was time to summon the people whose job it was to figure this stuff out, or at least to haul the body away.

Crime writers. We're like everyone else, only we constantly think there's a dead body, or should be, in every location.

Just to cover myself for the unseen, nonexistent audience I was imagining, I said, "Okay, talk to you later," into my phone and then brought it down away from my ear. I pulled up the keypad and had punched the "9" of "9-1-1" when I heard a sound behind me.

I wasn't sure what it was, but when I started to turn my head, I heard a voice I only vaguely recognized say, "Don't turn around."

That's never good.

But that was no reason to think things couldn't get worse. Not a moment later, I felt a pressure in the left side of my lower back, the side away from the street, where it was less likely to be seen by any neighbor still curious enough to be watching through the front door or the living room window. A hard, round pressure right around the location of my kidney.

The barrel of a pistol.

Chapter 29

The semifamiliar voice, which was not Rod's, was speaking in low tones, so it was more difficult to get a read on the speaker. "That's good. Just keep looking forward and give me your phone."

Give him my *phone*? This guy wasn't just a dangerous person with a gun in his hand; he was completely insane. Asking a Jersey girl to hand over her phone is tantamount to asking a Texan to stop wearing a large belt buckle or a Canadian to admit that baseball is a better game than hockey. It's just not going to happen.

"No," I said in a conversational, bland tone. "You can shoot me in the street, but I'm keeping my phone. What if I get a text on the way to the hospital?"

"If I shoot you, you're not going to make it to the hospital," the man said, just as casually and just as calmly. That made it scarier somehow. "Now give me your phone."

Okay, so I'd give him my phone. After I pressed "1-1," something I was hoping I had done without looking at the touch screen.

Apparently my aim was off because the phone made a rude noise, and the guy snatched it out of my hand with his right. He was holding the gun in his left hand. I wondered if that was significant.

Mostly I was pissed off at myself. I hadn't done anything wrong, no too-stupid-to-live move that I'd have avoided at all costs in one of my books. Yeah, I could have called the cops earlier, but would they be here by now? Probably not. What if Sgt. Phil Dougherty was leading the charge? That wouldn't have helped.

No, I'd played it smart, and I still had a gun in my back. Life ain't fair.

"Feel better?" the guy behind me asked. "You didn't have to give me the phone; I just took it."

"Yeah, I hope that makes it into my obituary." Maybe I shouldn't have given him any ideas, but I doubted the pistol in my back meant he just wanted to get to know me better as a person. My snarky side comes out whenever my life is threatened. "So you can sneak up on a girl on a dark street. Is this how you shot Michelle Testaverde?" Guns, Poughkeepsie . . . it seemed a pretty decent bet I was dealing with Michelle's killer. If I was a gambler, I would have bet heavily on that assumption.

"I didn't shoot Michelle," the guy said. "I loved Michelle." Now you know why I'm not a gambler.

"So who did?" I asked. If I was going to get shot, the least the guy could do was answer my questions.

"Walk toward the house," he said. Apparently he didn't want to do the least he could do. The cad.

"Why? So you can shoot me there? I don't think I want to help you."

"Do it, because if you don't, I'm going to shoot you here, and if you do, maybe I won't shoot you at all."

Finally, a reasonable argument. I started walking toward the house.

"Slowly," said the guy with the gun. He didn't want the pistol visible. That left it open to me to decide whether I wanted to obey his command and probably get shot in the house or take a chance and almost certainly get shot on the street.

This was not like deciding whether Duffy Madison the character should be driving a Honda or a Hyundai, and that choice took me three days to make. (He ended up driving a Prius c because that was the car I knew best.)

In the end, I just walked to the damn house. It wasn't even really a conscious decision so much as it was a reaction to my primal fear of getting shot. If I could put it off even for a minute, that was worth doing.

"Nice and slow," the guy said. It wasn't a warning, just a reminder. But the way he said it made me want to bolt for the door at top speed just to thwart his wishes.

I was getting a little irritated, in case you hadn't caught that bit of subtlety just yet.

We got to the front door of Rod Wilkerson's house about an hour later, it felt like. Once at the threshold, however, we stopped, and the guy behind me didn't say anything. I wondered whether I should knock. I mean, who wants to barge in on somebody and get shot in the back at the same time?

"What?" the guy finally said.

"What do you mean, what?" I wasn't giving him any ideas. If he wanted to turn back now and forget the whole thing, it would certainly be all right with me. You grab on to somewhat unlikely scenarios when you're desperate.

"Open the door." Like it was obvious that was what I should do.

I figured that meant I didn't need to ring the doorbell, so I reached for the doorknob and turned it. The door swung open into the house. I really didn't want to look, having heard that gunshot only a few minutes before. (Really? That wasn't three days ago?)

But all that was inside the house was furniture. The same furniture I'd seen when we'd interviewed Rod twice before, once with Duffy and once with Ben. No bloodstains on the rug. No corpse on the couch. The TV wasn't even on.

"Where's Rod?" I asked.

"Go in." I didn't see how that was helpful.

Inside, without the ambient noise of the street, the gun guy's voice was just a bit more familiar. I knew I'd heard it recently but couldn't place it exactly. Did it have something to do with these two murders? That seemed fairly obvious. But it definitely wasn't Rod, and it certainly wasn't Walt Kendig. I'd spoken to Sgt. Dougherty only briefly a couple of days ago, but somehow the back of my brain was telling me that wasn't his voice. Should I turn around and look?

I followed his instructions and walked into the room, then sort of felt the movement of his right foot pushing the door closed behind us. The gun never left that spot on my back.

Now I was exactly where I wouldn't want a character to be, inside and out of sight of the street with a ruthless killer (or maybe a ruthful killer; what did I know?) holding a deadly weapon to my back. I think it was the unfairness of it all that overwhelmed me. If I was going to get killed, at the very least I was going to know who killed me. It was small comfort, but you set the bar pretty low under such circumstances.

I took two steps into the room at a faster pace than I'd been using, which meant I actually broke physical contact with the barrel of the gun. Then I spun around to face my assailant.

And found myself looking into Barry Spader's eyes.

Honest to goodness, I actually said, "What the—" and stared.

"That wasn't smart," Barry snarled at me. "You've seen my face."

I managed to regain the power of speech. "Yeah, like you weren't going to shoot me anyway. But you're in Arlington, Virginia! How'd you get here so fast?"

"Take three steps back," he said, gesturing with the pistol.

That didn't sound good. "Why?" I asked. My voice wasn't nearly as defiant as I'd hoped it would be.

"Because I'm not going to shoot you right now unless you make me, and I want you in the center of the room where I know there won't be any surprises." Okay, that was fair. I took the three steps back and avoided a side table by inches. It was the part about not shooting me now that made me feel better about being compliant.

"Arlington, Virginia," I reminded Barry.

His mouth flattened into an expression of utter contempt. "I was never in Arlington," he said. "I was never in any of those places they thought I'd gone. I left this town, and I lived in the city for a few years."

The city. "Manhattan?" I said. If I could keep him talking for just a few minutes, Ben would get here, figure out I was in the house, and possibly even prevent me from getting shot. That would be good.

Barry nodded. "I had a nice place on the Upper East Side," he said. "Selling the bar gave me enough for a big down payment, and the mortgage wasn't too bad. It's the co-op fees that really get you."

Maybe that was why he'd come to Rod Wilkerson's house—to discuss real estate. "I know," I agreed. "Prices in the city are out of control." Why not? If I could find common ground, agree with Barry on a thing or two, the whole shooting thing could become less certain. It was hard to think of much else, especially since the pistol was still pointed at my midsection.

"But I saw you in Arlington on my laptop only a few hours ago," I said.

"You saw me at a friend's place in New Rochelle. I could have told you I was anywhere." He was enjoying the idea of fooling us, reveling in the idea that it was so easy to have convinced Ben, Duffy, and me he'd been in Virginia. I decided to start detesting Barry Spader right now.

"If you didn't shoot Michelle Testaverde, what's all the cloak and dagger?" I demanded. Well, asked. "What's the whole point of manufacturing evidence and framing Duffy if you didn't do anything wrong?" And before it was out of my mouth, I knew what it was all about, at least up to a point.

Sure, Barry hadn't shot Michelle. He loved Michelle. Know who else loved Michelle?

Damien Mosley.

I didn't say it. I wasn't stupid enough to say, *You shot Damien!* But Barry probably saw the look on my face and determined exactly what I was thinking. I make up stuff for a living, but I'm not the best liar you ever met in your life, and I'm not great at hiding the thoughts and feelings running through my brain. So it was a decent bet I was showing a certain growing understanding of the situation in front of me.

"I never said I didn't shoot *anyone*," Barry said.

But it didn't add up: If Barry had killed Damien Mosley, he did that in North Bergen, New Jersey. If he hadn't shot Michelle Testaverde, there was no crime to cover up in Poughkeepsie, New York. So what was the missing piece I wasn't thinking of right at the moment?

I'd never seen the door open when I was outside. I was looking at the house from an angle from which the front and side doors were visible. If there was a back door and Barry had used it, I should have seen him walking around the house to come up behind me. So that meant Barry hadn't been in the house before he'd ambushed me in the street; he'd been coming from somewhere else. I might not have been part of the plan at all.

That left me with a bad feeling that wasn't alleviated when Barry motioned me to a chair with the pistol.

"I have to go outside for just a minute," he said. "And I wouldn't want you taking the opportunity to leave before the party's over." Why do people with guns always talk like that? I thought it was just a movie thing, but apparently Barry really did want to sound like an evil genius. Or he'd just seen the same movies and figured that was what he was *supposed* to say.

I didn't move, but he pulled back the hammer on the gun, and I realized he didn't actually need me alive.

"Sit," he said. So I sat.

He continued to aim the gun in my direction while reaching into a side table drawer and pulling out some duct tape with his left hand. It wasn't the kind of table you'd expect to house home maintenance supplies, and this wasn't Barry's house—as far as I knew—so that led to the conclusion that he'd planned to tape someone into a chair tonight. But he hadn't been expecting me.

At least he didn't put tape over my mouth. If nobody in the neighborhood had called the police when there was a gunshot, there was no reason to think my shouting was going to be interpreted as anything but a TV show being played far too loudly.

Barry finished encasing me in the tufted chair and then put the tape down on the table and put the gun in his jacket pocket. Then, whistling (I swear!), he walked out the back door and disappeared.

Was this somehow an opportunity? I couldn't get out of the chair, certainly, and it did seem useless to scream, but could I crab-walk the chair through the front door? Suppose Barry had been lying about coming back. That would be a positive in that he wasn't actually shooting me, but it would leave me in a very difficult position and would not help Ben and Duffy find me.

None of that mattered because it was clear in seconds that Barry would be back, and soon. I heard a car door open in the driveway near the back of the house, then I heard a grunt, and the car door slammed again. There was some more grunting, someone exerting himself, and after a short time, the back door opened again.

Barry walked back into the living room with something slung over his left shoulder. Something large and heavy, based on the noises he made walking into the room. I couldn't see him until he was entirely back in the living room, and then I saw him unload his burden and lay it on the carpeted floor.

It was Duffy Madison. And he wasn't moving.

Chapter 30

All in all, this had been a pretty horrible day, and it wasn't getting any better.

Barry caught his breath after spreading Duffy out on the rug. He actually put his hands on his thighs and took a few moments to breathe in and out, recovering from the effort. Duffy isn't a huge man, but he's not small, and as—I hate to use the expression—dead weight, he certainly wasn't easy to lift or carry any distance. Barry was stronger than he'd first looked, which also wasn't exactly good news.

"What did you do to him?" I said after I had recovered from the sight. I didn't have to do any heavy breathing, but it was still a shock.

"Did you people really think I didn't know you were watching everyone?" Barry sneered. He referred to himself alone. No one helping him. Worth filing away. I was thinking like Duffy. "I knew you'd be watching Walt's place and Lou's house. I went by there and caught your pal here by surprise the same way I did with you, firing a gun into not much of anything and letting him think something was going down. He bought it, and he dashed into the house to be the knight in shining armor. I hit him with a fireplace poker."

Duffy did indeed have a nasty-looking lump on the side of his head reaching down to his left eye. He showed no signs of consciousness, but his chest was rising and falling, so he was breathing. That was something, although it was questionable how long it would continue.

Now I was concerned about Ben too. He should have been here by now, or had I lost a sense of time? It was certain I couldn't reach into my pocket for my phone (because it wasn't there) to look at the time. Even if I wore a wristwatch, it would be out of my sight range now. "What time is it?" I asked Barry.

"What do you care?"

That wasn't encouraging.

Okay, let's come down on the side of optimism and say Ben simply hasn't had time to walk here from Louise's house yet. It couldn't be much longer, could it? I mean, it has to be only a five- or six-minute drive. How many minutes is that in walking? Or running? Had Ben called the police? Why would he, when he thought I'd called them?

I honestly didn't want to ask Barry about his dastardly plan. I know in the movies, it's impossible for the bad guy to dispatch the good guy (they never do) without first explaining everything he plans to do, giving said good guy a chance to figure out the cleverest, least predictable way (if the screenwriter is as good as a crime fiction novelist) to avoid the planned fate. But the truth was, I didn't want to know what Barry had planned for Duffy and me. Mostly me. But also Duffy. If he never wanted to tell me, that would be fine in my book.

My book! How was I going to get a thousand words written *today*? There were only a few hours left, and I was in no position get to a keyboard.

Writers are nuts.

Still, it wouldn't hurt to keep Barry talking. Not that I would find out anything particularly interesting, but it would give Ben time to pick up the pace and come rescue us, which was obviously his role in our little melodrama. I get the whole strong-woman-character thing, but at the moment, I was duct-taped to a chair, and that cuts down on a girl's physical options. Talking was what I did best anyway.

"Where's Rod?" I asked him. "What did you do with him to get the house?"

Barry waved a hand. "He's fine. I called and told him I was moving back into town and needed a line on a new condo. He's sitting at the bar in Oakwood right now waiting for me." He made a sputtery noise with his lips. "Dope."

"You're a swell guy, Barry," I said.

He didn't answer. He was looking around the room as if deciding how to redecorate and paying most of his attention to the floor. Whatever he was thinking, I wanted him to stop thinking it.

"So you didn't shoot Michelle, but you shot Damien," I said. "How does that make sense?"

"How much do you weigh?" Barry asked me, and that was the moment I decided to see him rot in a jail cell for the rest of his natural life.

Rest easy; there was no chance in heaven or on earth I was going to answer that question. I plunged ahead. "You loved Michelle. Did you kill Damien because he was stealing her away from you?"

That got his attention. He stopped what he was doing, which was stretching Duffy out on the rug flat, and glared at me. "He didn't steal her away—he *killed* her because she loved me!" Barry took two steps toward me, his fury reaching the boiling point.

Perhaps this whole getting-him-to-talk idea had been ill-conceived.

But once Barry had moved past Duffy to advance toward me, Duffy turned his head slightly and opened his eyes. Well, one of them, anyway.

He smiled a little and winked at me.

It was a form of encouragement and reassurance, so I took it. "Damien Mosley killed Michelle Testaverde?" I asked. Largely because it was news to me.

"That's right." Barry was still snarling, but the edge of violence in his demeanor from a moment ago seemed to dissipate. "He thought she loved him, but she kept telling him to scram. He even asked her to marry him—at a *bowling alley*—and she said no! What more did the guy need?"

It occurred to me that some people needed to be hit over the head, but since that had already happened to Duffy, who had closed his eyes again should Barry look in that direction, I refrained from suggesting it.

"So he shot her?" I said.

I noticed Duffy nod just a little on the floor. He'd known this already. Of course. Even lying with an indentation in his skull, the guy had to show off about what a great deducer he was.

"Yeah, but I didn't find out until much later. He said Michelle was moving into his apartment in Jersey, and a van showed up to take all her stuff there. I couldn't find her, and she wasn't answering her phone. I knew she didn't want to marry him, but she wouldn't answer me. It never occurred to me she was dead."

"So what happened?" *Where the hell are you, Ben?*

"I went to the place in Jersey to try to talk some sense into her. I mean, if Michelle was marrying Damien just because she thought he had more money than me, I could sell the bar and really get out of here. That's what I should have done. Then. I should have done it then." Barry shook his head, reproaching himself. I took note of it. The killer who regretted not acting sooner. It could be poignant even while being menacing. Hey. Everything's fodder for the work.

"And when you got there, Michelle wasn't there, right?" I needed to move the narrative along, which was risky but might give me something to use in my defense against whatever this maudlin nutcase might have in store for me.

"No. Her clothes, some of them, were there. Damien let me in, but he didn't want me to look around. I did anyway, and I yelled at him to show me where Michelle was. He said she was shopping. It was September, and all her light jackets were in the closet. She wasn't out shopping."

The clothing was used to make Michelle's corpse look like a homeless woman. Duffy, prone though he was, had been right. This was getting tiresome.

"So you went straight from no jacket to he must have killed her?" I said.

Barry moved back to where Duffy was lying, ensuring he would not be able to move again. I didn't know if I was sorry or not. "No, of course not." He walked to the edge of the rug and started to roll it up, then shook his head and let it go. "Too big," he said.

"Okay, how did you figure it out?" I asked. Now I was worried. Ben could have walked here backward by now. Were Rod or Louise in on the plot? Sgt. Dougherty? Did that make sense? The guy was a semicrooked cop, but killing people or helping to kill people? Seemed a stretch.

"I didn't," Barry said, sizing up Duffy one more time. He seemed to be trying to figure out how to move the prone body, which led me to wonder why he'd hauled Duffy into the house to begin with. "Damien was so guilty, he practically blurted it out at me. I mean, I had to push him up against a wall first and maybe hurt him a little, but he admitted it finally." He pulled a box cutter out of his other jacket pocket, which did not make me feel a whole lot better. Then he walked over to me.

"Come on. I just got an idea," he said and started cutting the duct tape away from my wrists and ankles. Maybe he'd decided to undo this whole evening.

At that moment, I would have signed up for that plan in a heartbeat.

Then Barry said, "Help me carry him."

It occurred to me to refuse, believe me. It occurred to me a number of times in a nanosecond. If Barry didn't think he could get Duffy out of the room without my help, I saw no reason to offer it.

Except there was that box cutter in his hand. That was a reason. A pretty good reason. The gun in his pocket. Another good reason.

"Why'd you bring him in here if you want to take him out again?" I asked rather than agree to anything right away.

"I just decided what I'm going to do with him," Barry said. "You take the feet." He pointed, in case I didn't know Duffy's feet from his head.

"What *are* you going to do with him?" I wasn't sure I wanted to know, but I was asking on Duffy's behalf. This kind of thing would absolutely entrance him.

Barry looked me in the eye. "I'm not going to do anything," he said with a fearsome chill in his voice. "*You're* going to kill him."

Duffy didn't move a muscle, but my stomach moved around inside me.

"I'm not that mad at him," I said. "I'm getting used to the guy."

"Shut up." The quick wit in the room was overwhelming. "Now get his feet."

Box cutter be damned. "No," I said.

Barry looked up from his study of Duffy with astonishment in his eyes. "What do you mean, no?"

"Is there a letter in the word you don't understand?" It's a variation on a theme. There's only so much one has to work with.

Barry reached into his pocket again, and I thought I was about to see the box cutter. But no, it got worse. Out came the small snub-nosed pistol. He was playing his hole card. "I think maybe *you* don't understand," he said. "Get the feet."

I got the feet.

We dragged Duffy, who I personally knew could get up and walk anytime he wanted, to the car, where Barry unceremoniously dumped him into the back seat. I had been betting on the trunk, but my batting average for assumptions tonight was pretty low, so it wasn't a huge surprise that I was wrong.

"Get in front," Barry ordered. I thought running off into the dark was a better option, but the street, even back here, was awfully well lit, and I knew this guy had a history of shooting people in the dark. He walked over to the passenger door of his SUV and opened it, then gestured me in. Idiot that I am, I sat down and put on the safety harness. Wouldn't want to get killed in a car crash on the way to my own execution, after all.

He drove in silence. I didn't know Poughkeepsie very well after only a few days, so for all I knew, we were going to Niagara Falls or Woodstock. I thought of asking if we could stop off at my father's house on the way so I could say good-bye, but as it turned out, we were only in the car for about ten minutes.

Barry stopped the car at what appeared to be a random spot next to a bridge. He got out of the car and ordered me out when he got to the passenger side. I didn't see any point to staying the in car, so I followed his instructions. He looked up.

The Walkway over the Hudson is a bridge that was completed in 1889 as a railroad bridge and was converted to the world's longest footbridge and pedestrian walkway on October 3, 2009. It stands 212 feet above the Hudson River from Poughkeepsie on one side to Highland, New York, on the other. It has become a major tourist attraction and spans 6,768 feet in total.

Those are all true facts. You can look them up. I just did. You didn't think I knew all that stuff off the top of my head, did you? I sure didn't know them that night.

One thing I can tell you from personal experience is that you have to climb up a whole bunch of stairs to get to the walkway. Another thing: 212 feet is really high.

I looked at the stairs, then I looked at Duffy, then I looked at Barry. "There's no chance I'm getting the feet for that climb," I told him.

"You won't need to," he said ominously. Then he walked to the back door and opened it. He pointed the gun. At me. It was inside his jacket pocket, but I got the point. "Come on, Duffy," he said. "You're awake, and everybody knows it. Get out of the car, or I'll shoot your girlfriend."

Duffy opened his eyes and maneuvered himself out of the SUV as if he'd awakened from a refreshing nap. He said nothing. He'd tried what he could, but it hadn't worked, so now he'd move on to the next thing. It's how I write him. He wouldn't even protest the use of the word *girlfriend*, although I knew it was bugging him. I wasn't crazy for it myself.

He tripped getting out of the car and fell forward toward Barry, who instinctively put up his hands to catch the falling man. Duffy seemed a little unsteady on his feet and held onto Barry for a long moment, steadying himself. Then he straightened his posture and held up his hands, palms out, to show he was all right. "You can't get away like that," Barry told him. "Or any other way."

Barry had clearly learned how to speak by watching James Bond movies and paying attention only to the villains. I was shocked he didn't have a British accent.

His right hand went back into his pocket, and he extended it just enough to remind us there was a lethal weapon in there. He gestured to the stairs.

"Climb," he said.

It was not a short climb. Duffy went first, then me, then Barry. We'd tried to get him to go ahead of us, but Barry, however melodramatic, was not stupid. About a third of the way up, Duffy asked why Barry was operating out of Rod Wilkerson's house.

"Convenience," the confessed killer (wait—*had* he confessed?) answered. "Rod sold my old house for me, and I needed a place to bring the two of you. I called him and asked him to meet me across town at Oakwood. He's probably still there waiting for me to tell him about the great business opportunity I told him I had." He laughed derisively at the thought of his old friend (?) being stood up and used badly.

Duffy, who had ostensibly been unconscious when Barry and I were discussing Michelle's murder, decided to use that to clarify the situation. "You shot Damien Mosley, didn't you?" he asked. "Why did you take him to the park in North Bergen? You could have shot him in his apartment."

Barry made a noise to indicate Duffy was less brilliant than he might have imagined, which was probably true but beside the point. "I didn't have the gun with me when I went to the Jersey apartment," he said. "I figured I knew where it was because Damien always kept his stash of weed in that little crevice in his Poughkeepsie ceiling. I needed proof he shot Michelle, and I found it right there. So I took it and went back to Jersey and used it on him just like he deserved."

Duffy clearly didn't feel comfortable with having led Barry to admitting the crime. In his mind, the confession has to come willingly, unforced. Barry could—I could hear it in Duffy's thought process, which let's face it, I made up—have been bragging to impress us and never have shot Damien at all. Duffy coughed as we approached the upper level of the bridge walkway.

"What?" Barry said. He seemed quite annoyed at having to deal with these pesky questions.

"The footprints at the scene of Damien's murder seem to indicate his killer was a woman," Duffy lied. "I've seen the photographs, and the shoes from the second set of footprints were not your size."

"You're wrong," Barry said. We walked out onto the bridge. There was no one around; the place closes down at dusk, and we were easily past that. Barry gestured with the gun pocket that we should start walking out away from Poughkeepsie and across the Hudson. "There was only one set of footprints. I made Damien take his shoes off. I doubt his bare feet were leaving much of a mark."

That had puzzled me from the time Duffy had shown me the pictures. "Why did you do that?" I asked.

"I was hoping there would be sharp rocks or glass on the ground," Barry answered with a very unpleasant tone in his voice. "I wanted his last steps to be painful."

I didn't ask any more questions after that. But Duffy, whose readings of people's feelings is actually quite sensitive except when it gets in the way of his investigations, wasn't thinking about Damien Mosley's feet.

"Damien's car was parked near the scene of the shooting," he said. "It stayed there after he was dead. How did you get away?"

"I took the bus. I was standing far enough from Damien that I didn't have any blood or anything on me, so there was nothing to notice. I had exact change ready. It wasn't a problem. Okay, stop here."

We were almost at the exact center of the span across the river. I was starting to get a really queasy feeling about how Barry was planning on the next few minutes to take shape.

He looked right and left again to ensure no witnesses were present on the bridge. Certainly there would be police patrols at regular intervals, but probably not very often. He knew this wasn't going to take a lot of time. He took the gun out of his pocket.

"This looks like a good spot," Barry said.

"I'm not crazy about it," I told him. "I mean, it's right in the middle of the bridge. It looks staged. Too perfect. No, I think we should keep walking, don't you?" I took two steps before he shouted.

"No! Stop right there and don't move, get it?" He'd segued from Auric Goldfinger to Edward G. Robinson. Stress makes men less genteel.

"There is no reason to harm us," Duffy attempted. "We didn't witness you killing Damien Mosley. We don't pose a threat to you at all." That was a stretch, and he knew it.

Barry grunted. "You know what happened to Damien Mosley. Five years later, and you had to stick your nose in it. Even when I got you arrested, you wouldn't stop. What did I ever do to you, anyway?"

Duffy and I looked at each other because we had no answer to the question. Finally, Duffy said to him, "Why did you need me out of the way this afternoon? I assume that's what the subterfuge with the fingerprints was about."

"It was just a delaying tactic. After you got in touch and we had our lovely Skype chat, I needed time to get here and figure out what to do with you and get ready. It was easy enough to keep you off the trail for a few hours. I would have preferred them keeping you overnight, but it didn't work out that way."

"But Ben and I kept asking questions," I said weakly. There was no answer. That's how significant Ben and I were.

Barry smiled, which did not make me feel better. "I'm not going to harm you," he said to me, ignoring my protest. You'd think that would be good news, but the look on his face indicated otherwise. He pointed the gun at me. "Your partner here is going to shoot you, and then he's going to jump off the bridge in remorse. The cop you had with you will never even know I was here."

Nobody moved a muscle. "I don't think so," I said.

"Oh, that's exactly what's going to happen," Barry said. He raised the gun while standing next to Duffy, just far enough away that Duffy couldn't reach him. He pointed it at me.

I'd like to say my whole life flashed before me, but basically I was just thinking about who my publisher would hire to finish the terrible Duffy Madison book on my hard drive. I hoped it was someone I liked.

"Wait," Duffy said. "Shoot me instead."

My eyes, which I had not noticed had closed, opened. And Barry looked almost as incredulous as I felt. He actually lowered the gun. "What?"

"Shoot me. Let Rachel shoot me. You'll be doing me a favor." Duffy looked at me. "I've never really known who I am.

This way I can just be over. I can stop wondering and just be at peace."

To say I was stunned would be like saying Raymond Chandler wrote a couple of okay books. My mouth opened, but I couldn't make a coherent sound. I think I actually held out my hands to Duffy, but I didn't move my feet to get closer to him. After all this, he was finally opening up about his pain, and it was too late. I wanted to give him a hug and tell him it was going to be okay, that we could work through this now.

But it wasn't going to be okay. Barry looked at Duffy, and his eyebrows met in the middle. "You heard the part about where you jump off the bridge, right?" he said.

"You don't have to hurt Rachel," Duffy told him, still oddly wary of the gun. "She doesn't have any evidence against you; only I do. You give her the gun and let her shoot me, and you'll be helping us both. I'll be free, and she'll be free of me."

"Duffy," I managed. I wanted to tell him he wasn't a burden, that I didn't want to lose him this way.

He shook his head. "No, it's true. I've done nothing but place you in dangerous situations since we met, and you haven't blamed me for it, but it was my fault. You don't need me, Rachel. Take the gun from Barry and shoot me, just once, right between the eyes. Like Hercule Poirot." He probably should have put a *spoiler alert* ahead of that, but it was in conversation. What can you do?

"I was going to shoot her myself and get your fingerprints on the gun," Barry said, attempting to regain control of the situation, not entirely understanding what was happening. "She doesn't have to shoot you. I can do it."

"No. It's symbolic. Rachel should be the one. She created me, and she can end me."

Now Barry was *really* in over his head. "She's your mom?" He asked with a surprised tone.

"Just give her the gun," Duffy said.

"No chance. She'll shoot me instead of you. I know how these things work."

Duffy walked toward me before Barry could react. "Do exactly as I say, Rachel," he said. "Take the gun and shoot me right between the eyes. Point-blank. There won't be any chance for you to shoot Barry because I'll be directly in front of you. It's what I want."

He reached a point so close to me that I thought he wanted us to tango. "Here," he said more loudly to Barry. "I'll be here. You can stand wherever you like. Let Rachel shoot me, and then let her go."

"Go?" I said incredulously. "How can I go? You want me to kill you and then go get dessert?"

"It's what I want," he repeated quietly. "Just fire once, that's all."

"*I don't want to shoot you!*"

"I want you to," Duffy said.

I should at least have been torn. I mean, Duffy had been nothing but a source of anxiety and tension in my life since I'd met the flesh-and-blood version. I'd wished I'd never met him. I should have been feeling some curiosity about what it would be like to have him gone.

But now, faced with that scenario, the last thing I wanted was to lose Duffy Madison. And to be the one to pull the trigger and make him die? I wanted to throw up.

"You two are both nuts," said Barry. He appeared on my right and dropped the cartridge of bullets out of the gun. "You only have the one in the chamber. You *can't* shoot me after you shoot him."

He handed me the gun and then hurried behind Duffy to a steel wastebasket only ten feet away and half-crouched down behind it, sticking out just enough that he could see the entertainment in front of him. Even if I'd wanted to shoot him, I wouldn't have been able to see him clearly.

"I can't do this," I whispered to Duffy.

"Yes, you can. Trust me. One shot right between the eyes." We were nose-to-nose; I actually would have to back up to aim the gun. "Trust me, Rachel."

Duffy was all about tactics and ways to keep me alive. I was feeling like a little girl at a scary movie. I didn't want to look, and I just wanted it to be over. "He's going to kill me after you're gone," I said. "He won't keep his word."

"Yes, he will."

"No talking!" Barry shouted. "Just shooting!"

"Do it," Duffy said. "Now."

"Did you used to be Damien Mosley?" I asked him. If I had to say good-bye . . . no! I wasn't going to do this!

"If you want to think so, certainly. Shoot me."

I took a step back and raised the gun just to buy time and show Barry he didn't have to intervene. "Duffy, what's the gag?" I said very quietly. Duffy always has a way out.

"Pull the trigger, Rachel. Help me. This is how to help me."

"Shoot him now, or I'll do it!" Barry said. "And then I'll reload and shoot you!" He actually took a few steps out toward Duffy.

The gun was pointed directly at Duffy's forehead. I figured I could aim above his head and maybe just singe his scalp a little. It might give us the time we needed to subdue a seated Barry. I aimed over Duffy's head.

"He'll see," he said. "Lower the gun. Right between the eyes. Now!"

Barry stood up. "That's enough," he said, taking a step forward.

"Please," Duffy murmured.

I closed my eyes but held the gun up. A tear fell from my left eye. But you must forgive me. I took a breath and pulled the trigger. Right between the eyes. Or where I thought that would be. I didn't want to look.

The gun clicked, and there was no loud report. I opened my eyes. I have never been so relieved to still be in danger in my whole life.

Duffy took the moment to twist and dive backward, landing flat on Barry and immobilizing him. Barry, shouting and struggling, was no match. The fight was over before it began.

"Come here, Rachel!" Duffy shouted. "Reach into his pocket and get your cell phone."

I ran to them, the gun at my side forgotten, and did as Duffy instructed even as Barry was complaining that he, Duffy, should be dead on the ground now so Barry could have picked me up and thrown me off the bridge. He had promised not to shoot me, after all.

"I don't understand," I said to Duffy. "How did you know the gun wouldn't be loaded?"

Duffy had positioned himself so that his knees were on Barry's legs and his hands were holding Barry's straining arms to the pavement. "I stumbled onto him coming out of the car," he said. "I couldn't grab the gun out of his pocket, but I could eject the bullet in the chamber. Once Barry took out the clip, it was even easier." He looked down. "Bad move, Barry."

Barry said something I won't repeat, but by then I was calling 9-1-1.

Chapter 31

"So let me get this straight." Ben Preston leaned on his crutches as I packed his bag for the ride home. I did not look at what I was packing since Ben had clearly not done so when he had left. Everything that was in the bag—since Ben hadn't unpacked when we'd gotten to the hotel room—was clean. Everything I was stuffing into it now was at the very least questionable. "Damien Mosley killed Michelle Testaverde."

Once the Poughkeepsie police, the ambulance (presumably for Barry Spader, who wasn't terribly hurt but did seem mightily embarrassed to be defeated so easily—he thought it had been *easy* to pull that trigger!), and the county cops showed up, allowing Duffy the opportunity to stand up and remove himself from Barry, I'd taken the opportunity to check my phone for missed messages. I'd been worried about Ben after he failed to show up and rescue me.

It turned out I had every reason to be concerned, but not for Ben's overall safety. No doubt while I was being driven to my supposed doom on the footbridge, Ben had texted: *Fell over park bench. Think I broke my foot. Cops there yet?* I'd turned the ringer off, so I hadn't heard anything the phone did while it was in Barry's pocket. My laughter at reading the text probably wouldn't have buoyed Ben's spirits anyway.

The other texts were all from Paula: *Spader spent time in rehab after leaving Poughkeepsie.* Then, *Spader not listed in Arlington, VA.* Then, *You might want to look @ Spader.* Finally, *Are you OK?* I texted back to her that everything was all right now and I'd talk to her in the morning.

"Yes," Duffy said now to Ben's question. He, of course, had nothing to pack—he hadn't even gotten to a clothing store tonight, what with being hit over the head and abducted—so he was free to watch me take care of Ben's stuff (and my own). His feet and hands were working, yet he did not seem moved to pitch in.

What with his having saved my life—*again*—it seemed impolite to bring all that up.

Technically, I wasn't sure Duffy had actually saved my life. Barry had been so inept about trying to kill us—handing me the gun, hiding behind the guy I was supposed to shoot—there was a decent chance he was going to mess it up no matter what Duffy had done. But the intent was certainly there, and the only action I'd taken was to raise a gun to Duffy's forehead and pull the trigger. I was still wrestling with that moment, and I would be for quite some time. Therapy would probably be required. That moment on the bridge was as awful as I've felt in my life.

"Apparently Damien was consumed with jealousy when he found out Michelle, who never married him, was involved with Barry Spader," Duffy continued. "He shot her in a rage, raided her closets, and made her appear to be a homeless woman, then left her body under a railroad pass where it was discovered without ID. Apparently, Michelle was not in touch with any family since she was never reported missing. Her friends all believed, as Damien told them, that she had married him after many proposals and then moved into the apartment. He hired a van to move her belongings and actually did bring them to West New York. He lived there very briefly."

Ben looked at me as I zipped up the bag he'd brought. He looked sheepish, at least, which was a start. "So from what you told me Barry said, he didn't believe Michelle had left him for Damien, and he tracked them to West New York, then forced Damien into admitting what he'd done."

I hefted the bag, which wasn't terribly heavy, and threw it at Duffy. "You take this one," I said. He looked a little startled as he caught it but didn't argue.

We were heading for the door (Ben hobbling along on the crutches) to begin the trip home when there was a knock. I looked at the two guys, who shrugged. I reached into my purse for my pepper spray, just in case, and opened the door.

Walt Kendig, head down and shoulders bobbing in some kind of expression of shyness, glanced at me and the two men. "I heard there was an arrest," he mumbled. "Wanted to make sure you were all right."

"We're fine, Walt," I assured him. "I was going to text you from the car. But I'm sure your sources in the police department have already given you most of the juiciest facts."

Walt looked up just for a moment, still subdued. I couldn't figure out why he was suddenly so worried about seeing us—or me. "I heard some," he said. "I was at the station getting back my car. Turns out Barry Spader stole it to use around town that night because he knew where I lived, and he didn't want to use his own car in case he was spotted. People would think it was me, right? Then he ditched it on a side street when he needed the bigger car to, you know, drive you guys around. Can I come in?"

"We're just leaving," Ben said, and we moved through the doorway into the hall in an attempt to make it to the elevators.

Walt followed along. I felt for the hotel key in my pocket, looked over the room one last time because I always feel like I'm going to leave something behind, and closed the door firmly behind us. Wouldn't want someone sneaking in and stealing one of the beds on my watch.

"I called a few people from our high school class and found Damien Mosley's mom, Dorothy," Walt said.

Everybody stopped walking. "What?" Ben rasped.

"Yeah. She's in an assisted living home in Jersey. Said she's going to have to sell the place in West New York to pay her fees there. Probably go on the market within a month."

We all looked at each other. "You're a big help, Walt," I said.

He blushed. "Really?"

"Really." We started walking again.

"How come you're leaving tonight?" Walt wanted to know as we shuffled down the hall, me dragging my wheeled bag, Duffy carrying Ben's. Duffy was watching Walt carefully, either suspecting him of something or merely storing his personality away for future consideration. Duffy collects people in his head.

"We want to get home," I told him because it was the truth. "I need to get some writing done." I wasn't sure the Duffy Madison adventure in my head could compare with the Duffy Madison adventure I'd just had, but I had to send my editor *something*, so it would be a thousand words after I got home no matter what the time. A regimen is a regimen.

Besides, I'm always terrified that if I take a day off, I'll never write again, and then I would have to get a real job. The very thought makes me break out in a cold sweat.

"Are you gonna write about this?" Walt asked. People always think you just take stuff from your life and put it into your writing, which indicates they think we have much more exciting lives than we do. Of course, lately I'd found that the opposite was true: I'd created something in my writing who insisted he was now standing in front of me, and my life had been considerably too exciting by half ever since. Maybe I was doing this whole author thing the wrong way.

"No, Walt. I'm making something up entirely. It's what I do." I probably sounded too weary to talk to a loyal reader. I always try to be nice and upbeat for them, but this had been one hell of a day.

"I get that," he said in a voice that indicated he didn't get it at all. "Um, can I ask you a question?" He seemed to be directing his words to Duffy, who stopped as we reached the elevator. I pushed the button. I'm a button pusher.

"You may," Duffy said.

Walt's eyes narrowed a little. "Did you . . . did you think . . . was I ever a suspect?" I got the impression he really hoped in his heart of hearts that Duffy had thought he was a murderous mastermind capable of incredible violence and brilliant subterfuge.

"No," Duffy said.

"Oh. Um . . . good. I'm glad to hear it." Walt wasn't the least bit glad to hear it coming from his favorite investigator, but Duffy doesn't lie. Especially to people he has deemed of little consequence.

"You didn't kill anybody, did you, Walt?" Ben asked as the doors opened. He got on the elevator first because he was going to take up the most room. For a guy with a broken foot, he seemed in better spirits than everybody else. He hadn't been on that bridge. I shivered thinking about it.

"No! Of course not!" Walt's taking the question seriously provided Ben with a sly smile. It was a little bit mean, but he was on painkillers.

We were all on the elevator, and the doors were closing when it occurred to me that someone should call poor Rod Wilkerson and tell him his client was going to be a little late. Like twenty years to life without parole.

"Well then, don't worry about it," Ben told him. Walt didn't smile, but he didn't apologize for anything he hadn't done, so I assumed that was progress. We dropped off our keys at the desk despite there being no need to do so. Duffy made us.

Walt seemed so woeful that I tried to assure him we were okay before the four of us made it to the car. "It was very nice meeting and working with you," I told him.

"Working with me?" For the first time since he'd arrived at the hotel room door, Walt made eye contact with me.

"Certainly." We walked out into the cool night air and toward my car in the parking lot. I was glad Duffy didn't have luggage. I wasn't sure it would fit. The Prius c gets amazing gas mileage at the price of having virtually no cargo space. Walt's vintage MG, battered though it was, probably would fit more stuff.

I opened the hatch and put my bag, the larger one, inside. Duffy dropped Ben's little overnight bag next to it, and voila, the space was filled. I closed up the hatch for fear that another car's trunk might come by and tease mine until it cried.

Duffy smiled and held out a hand to Walt. "We couldn't have done it without you." No doubt he was thinking that we couldn't have been captured and almost killed without Walt's invaluable service, but that would be unfair as well. In truth, Walt had steered us in some right directions.

If I had been writing this story, this would probably be the moment when Walt revealed himself to be the evil mastermind behind both murders and threaten us all, but he shook Duffy's hand and thanked him far too much. I kissed him on the cheek, which seemed to both delight and embarrass him, and we said our farewells. Just as I was about to straighten up again, he whispered, "I'm your biggest fan." Which seemed sort of obvious by now. I kissed him again, and we piled into the car, Ben in back so he could stretch out the bad leg.

As I was helping him into the back seat, he looked at me significantly and said very quietly, "I'm telling Petrosky that Duffy was wrongly accused," he said. "He'll be reinstated on the consultant list." Before I could answer, Duffy was in the passenger seat and within earshot. I got in and started up the car.

We were barely on the road for ten minutes before Ben started to snore.

Duffy and I were silent for some time. I don't know if we were simply tired or if we were both thinking over all that had happened the past few days. Personally, I was already making revisions in the story I'd been writing and considered changing the guy at the bottom of the ditch to a guy discovered on the top branch of a tree. It seemed like a way to change my luck, and there were possibilities for a really interesting cover.

Just about the time we reached the Tappan Zee Bridge and all its charming uncertainty, Duffy broke the silence by quietly saying, "I received a text from Nelson Sanders. Sgt. Dougherty has been arrested for accepting graft and altering evidence. There never were fingerprints on the gun, not even Barry's. He just altered a report from the forensics department to make it seem that way. The charges against me have been dropped."

"I can't say that's a huge surprise." There were not many cars on the bridge this time of night, but I felt a little tingle in my stomach. I hoped I wasn't developing a lifelong fear of bridges.

"Also, the North Bergen medical examiner has confirmed that the body they found in the ditch was that of Damien Mosley. But he had not been shot. Apparently, Barry fired at him and missed, hitting the tree as we saw in the photographs. But Damien must have jumped at the sound, fell, and landed hard on the rocks at the bottom."

"Poor Damien," I said. "Guy couldn't catch a break."

"How do you mean?"

"First, the woman he loved didn't love him back, and then his friend shoots at him and makes him fall to his death."

Duffy took a moment. "You left out the part where he got so angry at that woman that he deliberately shot and killed her."

"You have a point."

There was another long silence, although Duffy seemed to be working up his nerve about something; he cleared his throat twice and coughed once. It was either his way of gathering courage, or he had an infection I hoped was not airborne.

"I didn't mean it, you know."

No, I didn't know. "You didn't mean it? Mean what?"

"What I said on the footbridge, when I was trying to convince you to 'shoot' me." He mimed the quotes, which I could see only through peripheral vision. Driving at night doesn't worry me, but it does require a little more concentration. "About having no meaning in my life and just wanting it to be over. I didn't mean a word of that. I am quite content with the life I have."

That was the most introspective I'd ever heard him get about himself in one sitting, so I absorbed and processed it for a moment. "I'm glad to hear it," I said finally. Even *I* didn't know what I meant by that. Was I glad that Duffy had never been Damien Mosley? Did I secretly wish the mystery of his existence had been solved so I could go back to thinking only about the Duffy I'd made up on my own?

"You don't sound especially glad," he said without judgment in his tone. "Are you still being perplexed by my presence?"

How do you answer that? "I'm still puzzled by it," I tried. "How do you explain the fact that you're listed in the Poughkeepsie High School yearbook the same year as all the people we met up there? How can you reconcile the idea that you're a grown man in his thirties who thinks he's only been alive for five years?"

"I can't," Duffy answered slowly, explaining it to someone less intelligent than himself. "But I have made my peace with the fact that I can't." He paused for a moment. "Do you still want me to go away and never come back?" He sounded like a small boy asking a friend if she was still a friend.

"No. My problems writing are my problems. I know you're there. Even if you don't show up at my door, I'll have you in my head. Maybe I have to give you another name mentally so I can write Duffy Madison when I have to."

"Daniel Monahan," he suggested. He smiled, and so did I.

"Duffy," I said, "I want you to know I didn't really want to shoot you at all." I thought that had to be put out there.

He actually laughed. "I never thought so."

"I mean, that was about the worst moment I've ever had. I don't want you to . . ." I couldn't even say it.

"Neither do I, and I didn't on the bridge, either. Let's say no more about it."

Duffy really had accepted himself for what he believed he was. Maybe I had to do the same. I arrived at my house at two in the morning and read over what I'd written so far. To my amazement, it wasn't bad at all. I added the thousand words without any of the angst I'd been feeling lately and slept well and deeply until eleven the next morning.

It was a scheduled lunch-with-Brian day, so I showered and dressed and was about to head for the car when my phone buzzed. There was a text from Paula.

Susannah Hong called back. Then a smiley face emoji.

Acknowledgments

Rachel Goldman seems to have brought Duffy Madison to life quite by accident, but believe me, it's not that easy. I get a lot of help in bringing Duffy (and Rachel and the gang) to you, and you can trust me that each and every person who worked on this book is indispensable. Maybe even me.

Thanks to Josh Getzler and the astonishing team at HSG Agency for bringing my strange imaginations to the right people every single time and for caring and for being good friends and for exploding every negative stereotype assigned to agents. There wouldn't be an E. J. Copperman without them, I can tell you.

You wouldn't ever have seen this book or heard of Duffy without the wonderful people at Crooked Lane Books: Matt Martz, Sarah Poppe, Heather Boak, and Dana Kaye, especially. It's nice to work with people who see books as something other than numbers on a ledger report. Although making the occasional dollar isn't a bad thing, either.

Thanks to Louis Malcangi for the cover design of *Written Off*, along with Robert Crawford for the cover illustration and Jennifer Canzone for book design. I send impersonal computer files; they make it look like a book. Kudos, guys.

I must take a moment to acknowledge the wonderful work done by the staff at Audible for the audiobook versions of Duffy's adventures. Amanda Ronconi, who brings all the characters to life, does a mind-blowing job living and breathing for all the oddballs I create, and she makes *me* believe it when I listen. Which I do.

The crime fiction community has been remarkably open and welcoming to me for some years now. Authors are a strange bunch, but you can't find better company anywhere. I've made many friends, and that's better than anything. But the readers are the best of all—you all should be decorated with distinguished service medals and sent boxes of chocolates on your birthdays. Suffice it to say, this author is awfully grateful to anyone who reads these books.

See, it's a solitary life, writing. Except you get to deal with all these lovely people.

E. J. Copperman
Deepest New Jersey
October 2016